The Sweet Spot

The Homestand Series | Book 3

Michael Geraghty

Hold Fast Publishing

Chapter 1

The snow and sleet pelted against the window loudly enough to rouse Wes Martin from a deep sleep, or at least as deep as slumber came to him in the recent weeks. He rolled over to look at Kristin and peered through a half-opened eye, but all he saw were the propped-up pillows and rumpled down comforter on her side of the bed. Wes bolted upright, concerned about where Kristin might be. The clock showed it was just 5 AM, much too early for her to get out of bed, especially since he knew it was his turn to take the morning feeding if the baby got up early again.

Wes' feet hit the carpeting, and he immediately went over to the bathroom to see if Kristin was there, but the room was dark, and the door wide open. He paced quickly out of the bedroom and had to squint right away as he was hit with the glowing lights from the kitchen. There was also an unusual amount of noise in the kitchen for the crack of dawn.

Wes spied Kristin seated at the kitchen table, her slippered feet propped up on one of the other chairs as she held Molly, their weeks-old newborn. The local TV station blared on the TV across the room where Wes's daughter Izzy stood. Izzy had just poured boiling water into a mug before she turned to look at her father.

"Morning, Dad," Izzy chirped, way too chipper for this time of day.

"Kris, I'm so sorry," Wes told her as he moved to where Kristin sat. He gently ran the palm of his hand across the soft, downy blonde hair of Molly. "Why didn't you wake me up?" Wes asked her as he moved over to sit next to where his fiancée sat.

"I'm fine, Wes," Kristin answered. "I just couldn't get comfortable in bed anymore, and Molly was up and moving around too much. We were both getting restless." Kristin gently rubbed Molly's back as she smiled down at the baby.

"You're such the worry-wart, Dad," Izzy noted as she placed a cup of tea down in front of Kristin. "Were you like this when I was born?"

"Honestly, Izzy, I wasn't around the months right before or after you were born," Wes answered as he gave Kristin a kiss on top of her head. "I was in the minors playing right up until the day you were born and only had one day to see you after that before I was off again. I missed all of this. What are you doing up so early?"

Wes had moved over to the coffeemaker now to start brewing a pot since he was up. Kristin had long stopped caffeine after learning she was pregnant and hadn't started up again with coffee since Molly was born. While Izzy drank some occasionally, it was usually just Wes who helped himself at this point.

"I heard Kris down here and thought she might need some help," Izzy replied. Izzy had gone back to the stove and poured some hot water into another mug, mixing up the packet of hot chocolate she had emptied into the rest earlier. "Besides, I wanted to hear about the school closings."

"Really? They closed school today? Well, back when I was in Chandler High..." Izzy's groan interrupted Wes.

"Dad, if you tell me once more about how school never closed and Grandpa made sure you went even if you had to walk to get there, I'm going to scream."

"Well, we didn't have off from school very often for the weather, that's for sure," Wes responded.

"The snow is pretty bad out there today," Kristin said as she peered through the dark of the back doors toward the hill in the backyard. The wind howled a bit more, and snow and sleet rattled the windows once again.

"I guess that means it's going to be a day to lounge in pajamas," Izzy smiled.

"Hey, just because you're home doesn't mean you won't have stuff to do," We chided. "I'm sure you have homework or studying, and I'll probably need help shoveling a bit so we can clear space in case we need to go out."

"Where are we going to need to go?" Izzy said as she pointed to the back door.

"Suppose Kris needs something, or Molly needs to go to the doctor?"

"Wes, I'm feeling much better every day, really," Kristin added. "I just had an appointment two days ago, and everything was fine. And there's nothing wrong with Molly. She's happy and healthy. There's zero to worry about."

"At the very least, you can clean your room and finish your college applications. I saw the paperwork for Pitt still sitting on your desk the other day, and none of it was filled out," Wes told Izzy as he sipped his coffee.

"Dad, I will do it," Izzy eye-rolled. "Besides, what are you doing in my room? We had an agreement."

"I was bringing up the piles of books and clothes you keep leaving down here instead of putting them away, which was also part of our agreement. Now, if you want to argue about it..."

Kristin stood up from the table and went between Wes and Izzy.

"If you two are just going to argue all day long, I'm locking myself in the bedroom with Molly. At least her crying and complaining is legitimate," Kristin said. Kristin took Wes by the hand.

"Wes, come back to bed with Molly and me. Izzy, thanks for your help and company this morning," Kristin said as she led Wes away towards the bedroom. Wes glanced back at Izzy and could see a smug smile on her face before she stuck her tongue out playfully at her father.

Wes closed the bedroom door behind them and gently took Molly from Kristin's arms before he placed the baby in the white bassinet that sat next to the bed now. He then turned and helped Kristin get back into the bed. He fluffed the pillows behind her back so that she could be more comfortable.

"Do you need anything else?" Wes asked before he walked back to the bassinet to pick up the fidgeting Molly.

"Yes, I do," Kristin said as she placed her right hand gently on Wes' cheek. "Stop riding Izzy at every chance you get."

"What are you talking about? I don't do that," Wes replied before climbing onto the bed next to Kristin.

"Wes, you do it so much you don't even realize you're doing it anymore. She's almost eighteen, she's in her last year of high school. You must give her some space and not get on her about every little thing. At this time next year, she'll be away at college..."

"Not at the rate she is going with those applications she won't," Wes interrupted as he adjusted the blankets.

"See? There you go again! You have to let her do these things, Wes."

"Kris, those applications have deadlines. If she doesn't get them done on time, she won't even get consideration. Between that and spending every waking moment with Bradley and working less on the farm, she's shirking responsibilities. I'm just trying to make sure she stays on track."

"Trust me, it will all get done. Izzy knows what she is doing. We have talked plenty about all of this," Kristin reassured him.

"You guys talk about this stuff without me?" Wes said.

"Of course we do, Wes. It would be silly if we didn't. Izzy comes to me when she has questions about things, just like she comes to you."

"What does she come to you about?" Wes said as he sat up and took a more significant interest.

"I'm not going to go into specifics with you, Wes, especially when she tells me in confidence. If it were something you needed to know about, I would tell you."

"It's about sex, isn't it?" Wes thundered. "She better not be having sex with Bradley. I warned that guy..."

Kristin reached over and gently grabbed Wes's arm so he didn't startle the baby he held.

"Wes, relax. She's not having sex with Bradley. See, this is what I mean about you. You need to calm down. Come here," Kristin told him. She took Wes's right hand and interlaced it with her own before she laid her head on his shoulder. She placed a small kiss on Molly's head to calm her down and then kissed his cheek.

"See, you're getting the little one all upset too," Kristin scolded.

"Nah, she's just excited to hear her Dad's voice, isn't that right, buddy?" Wes added as he talked directly to Molly.

"Now, can we calm down a bit?" Kristin asked softly as she squeaked out a small yawn.

"Yes," Wes answered. "Go back to sleep, honey. I'll take care of her."

Wes stared down at Molly, who laid on his chest now, comforted by his breathing and closing her eyes. Wes watched his newborn girl as a thousand different thoughts ran through his head. There were so many things going on that it was getting difficult to keep track. Kristin and the baby were undoubtedly number one on the list. Molly had been born weeks before she was expected because of complications Kristin experienced. There was panic, a rush to the hospital, an emergency C-section, time for Molly in the PICU, and more. Kristin was still healing herself from the event and was slow to get around, and this caused Wes to switch into fourth gear as he took over everything he could.

Along with Molly and Kristin, there was everything going on, or not going with Izzy, and that mattered a great deal as well. There were concerns about baseball that still existed too. Wes had finished last season with the Washington Wild Things, an Independent team not far from Chandler. The season started slowly but ended well for Wes and the team. The team made the playoffs and worked their way past the first round before getting eliminated. Wes had a good year in terms of statistics, hitting thirty home runs and batting nearly .300. Still, he had been disappointed that no major league teams came calling. He had good numbers, and scouts had shown up a few times to watch him play, but no offers ever came out of it. Now that it was well into the off-season, his agent Randy had not received any interest yet. He thought the Wild Things would be happy to have him back, but Wes hadn't had a contract offer from them again either. He wasn't sure if he wanted to go through another year of independent ball without much hope or prospects.

So where did that leave him? He could go back to work on the farm with his father. There was always plenty to be done, taking care of the horses and running the business. He could also look forward to just staying at home with the new baby, something he had little chance to do when Izzy was growing up. He was financially secure and didn't need to work anymore if he didn't want to. The opportunity to be a Dad again appealed to him tremendously. Wes might get the chance to do things right, to be there for his new child and for Izzy as she went through college. Baseball didn't necessarily have to be part of what was to come next, but Wes wasn't sure if he was ready to give it up. He made the mistake of stopping playing too soon once already, and it nearly cost him Kristin. Wes was sure he wasn't going to go through all that again. He vowed that this time would be different.

Wes looked down to see that Molly was breathing peacefully, eyes now closed. He gingerly rose from the bed to place her back in her bed, covering her with a light pink blanket. Wes went back to the bed and then rolled to his left and saw Kristin snuggled into her pillow, softly sighing as she slept. A smile crept across his face as he watched her, and he reached over to brush a few stray strands of blond hair away from her eyes. Kristin's eyes fluttered and barely opened, and she peered at Wes. She smiled back at him as he watched her.

"What are you doing?" Kristin mumbled as she inched closer to Wes's touch.

"Sorry, I didn't mean to wake you. I was just watching you."

"Hmmm, that's sweet. You should go back to sleep."

"Do you need anything?" Wes asked softly.

"Nope, I've got everything I need right here," Kristin answered. Her eyes closed as she placed her right hand under her pillow and the fingers on her left hand intertwined with Wes'.

"You should go back to sleep," Kristin told Wes. "Molly's resting, and there's nothing that has to get done today. We can just relax, enjoy the day, and think about nothing for a change."

Wes' felt Kristin's fingers loosen in his own as she drifted back off.

If only it were that simple to think about nothing, Wes felt, his eyes still wide open.

Chapter 2

S now blanketed the region for more than a day, dumping over a foot during that time, enough to keep the schools closed for one extra day, to the delight of Izzy. All the precipitation also meant Kristin had to stay put for another day instead of going down to the library like she hoped. She had done no library work when Molly was born. With the recuperation she needed as she recovered and the care Molly required, there had been little, if any time, to do any work from home like she had planned. Her assistant at the library, Karen, had more responsibility to oversee operations, which was the plan once the baby was born, and Kristin was out on maternity leave. Everything leaped forward a few weeks earlier than expected, but all had gone well so far. Kristin could still help and do some work from home if she needed, but for the most part, Karen would handle everything that came along while she was out.

Once the snow event ended, and Wes and his father dutifully worked to clear the driveways and roads, Kristin decided she wanted to venture to the library and see how things were going. Wes was reluctant to let her tackle the task herself.

"Wes, I'll be fine," Kristin stated as she slipped into her snow boots to get better traction.

"I can drive you down, it's not a problem," Wes answered back as he grabbed his coat from the hall closet. "I just want to make sure you have no trouble on the roads. And what if the sidewalk by the library isn't cleared yet? Falling is not an option right now. Are you sure you're up for this? Did you clear this with Dr. Walker?"

Kristin pulled her own jacket out of the closet and struggled to put it on.

"Dr. Walker and I talked about it when I saw her, and she said as long as I am careful and don't overdo it, going out now is fine."

"You're going to wear that jacket? Why not wear the other one I got you?" Wes said as he pulled the coat off the hanger and held it up for Kristin to see.

"Wes, I'm not wearing that," Kristin protested.

"Why not? It looks nice." Wes held the coat higher as it rustled.

"Because it is so puffy, I look ridiculous in it, and I can barely get it on and off without help. I can't even move my arms high enough to steer the car when I have it on. The coat I am wearing is perfect."

"I can help you put it on, drive you to work, help you in, and then pick you up later when you are done."

"Wes, really, you don't have to do that. I can drive myself, and Tom Shepherd said he would use his snowblower on the sidewalks and put sand down to walk on."

"Tom Shepherd? Really? His glasses are so thick he can barely see where he is walking, never mind use a snowblower. It will be a mess. I'll take you."

"You need to stay here and watch Molly," Kristin told him.

"I can bring her along," Wes answered. "Let me get her ready." Wes went off to get everything Molly would need for an outing before Kristin could say anything to stop him.

Izzy galloped down the stairs as Kristin stood and waited by the door. Izzy tried to stealthily move past to grab her coat and slip out of the house unnoticed.

"Why don't you drive Izzy to school?" Kristin remarked as she saw Izzy slide by. "The ride to school is longer than my ride to work."

Wes came out of the bedroom with Molly in tow just in time to see Izzy grab her keys off the pegboard Wes had hung up, so keys were always in one place.

Izzy froze in her tracks.

"You don't need to do that, Dad," Izzy said. "Besides, I was going to pick up Bradley on my way in."

"All the more reason for me to drive you," Wes replied. He walked over and gave Kristin a kiss and then walked back toward Izzy to get his keys. "Meet me in the car," he told Izzy as he walked out the front door, carrying Molly in her seat.

Izzy stared as her father went outside and then looked to Kristin.

"What was that?" Izzy said with her hands on her hips.

"I'm sorry to throw you under the bus like that, Izzy, I really am," Kristin apologized. "But it was the only way I could get him to let me do things for myself today. I haven't been out of the house myself in almost six weeks, and I just wanted some time to go down to the library, see how things are going, and take a breath. He's stressed about everything – me, Molly, you, baseball. Hopefully, it will be over soon."

Izzy sighed as she tugged her wool hat on over her long red hair, stuffing some under the cap.

"Fine," Izzy offered. "I'll take one for the team, but you owe me. You know how he is with Bradley. Bradley always ends up afraid of him after they are together."

"Thanks, Izzy," Kristin said as the two walked out of the house together and towards the cars. Wes had already cleaned off his truck and warmed up Kristin's Jeep for her and was scraping the windows when they got outside. Izzy helped Kristin maneuver down the steps to the driveway and then over to her Jeep.

Kristin was off and down the driveway without any trouble before Izzy had even got into the passenger's seat of her Dad's truck. She typed a quick text to Bradley before Wes got into the cab of the truck so she could warn her boyfriend that her father and sister were tagging along for the morning ride.

Wes climbed in as the last of the melting ice trickled down the front of the windshield. His cheeks shone red from the cold as his gloved hands gripped the steering wheel.

"All set?" Wes asked his daughters. Izzy barely glanced up from her cell phone.

"I guess so," Izzy grumbled.

Wes worked his way down the slushy roads towards Chandler High School with hardly more than two words from Izzy. It wasn't until they were almost to Bradley's house, which was just a mile or so from the school, that Izzy remarked anything.

"Don't forget about Bradley, Dad," Izzy reminded.

"Not even if I tried to," Wes answered as he slowed down so he wouldn't speed past the driveway that led to Bradley's parents' home.

"What do you have against Bradley now?" Izzy asked, frustration in her voice. The truck idled at the top of the driveway as they waited for Bradley to come out.

"What more of a reason do I need than that he's dating my teenage daughter?"

"He's never been anything but nice and polite to you, no matter how much you try to intimidate him."

"It's the nice and polite ones you have to watch out for," Wes warned as he turned towards his daughter. "And intimidating him is half the fun of being a father."

Izzy rolled her eyes as she spied Bradley as he made his way down his driveway. Bradley stumbled briefly on a patch of ice before he regained his balance and reached the truck door.

"Please, Dad," Izzy begged, "just be nice to him."

Izzy switched open the rear doors of the truck so Bradley could climb in. Bradley beamed at Izzy adoringly as he got in and leaned forward to give her a quick kiss. It was then he noticed Wes glaring at him and pulled back before his lips could meet hers.

"Good... good morning, Mr. Martin," Bradley stuttered.

"Bradley," Wes stated with a nod before he turned his attention back to the road. Izzy looked back and forth between the two and shook her head when she realized no kiss was forthcoming.

"Bradley," Izzy began, "the Christmas dance is in ten days. Abby and Charlie want to know if we are riding over with them."

"Sure, I guess we can," Bradley answered. "I'll have to clean out my car a bit first, but that will be cool."

"A dance, huh?" Wes interrupted. "When is that?"

"It's on the 11th," Izzy replied. "Next Friday. I already checked with Kris, and we have nothing going on." Izzy was prepared to defend herself against whatever excuse her father could come up with to thwart her plans for the night.

"I didn't think we did, don't worry," Wes told her as he saw the lights for the school cutting through the light fog. "But you do have to pay attention. We have a lot going on right now, and we may need you for something. You might not be available."

"Don't worry, Mr. Martin," Bradley said as he leaned forward. "I can help Izzy with whatever you might need. It's not a problem."

"I didn't think it would be Bradley," Wes said as he stared into the rearview mirror, catching Bradley's gaze so that he sat back and took his hand off Izzy's shoulder.

Wes pulled up in front of the school, coming to an abrupt stop, so Bradley lurched forward against the seats. A sly grin crossed Wes' lips before he looked at Izzy, who fumed.

"Thanks for the ride, Mr. Martin," Bradley said quickly as he gathered his bag and jumped out of the truck.

"Any time Bradley," Wes said snidely.

"Yeah, thanks, Dad," Izzy said sarcastically. Bradley opened the door for Izzy to climb out and then shut the door behind her. Izzy turned and looked right at her father as she took Bradley's hand and then moved in and kissed him, making sure her father saw it all. Bradley reciprocated until he realized Wes watched on, and then he abruptly ended the kiss. Izzy looked back at her father and smirked before the two teens headed off towards the front doors of the school.

Wes stared for a moment, following his daughter and her boyfriend into the school with his gaze. It wasn't until a car behind him honked twice to get him to move along that he snapped back and drove away from the school.

"Your sister is going to be the death of me, Molly," Wes said aloud to the infant in her car seat.

As Wes pulled back into Martin Way, he stopped the truck in his parent's driveway. The driveway displayed nothing but black as Wes' father Wyatt already made sure his area was completely clear of any snow. Wes strode up the front wooden porch carefully as he carried Molly in her seat. The trip to the front door was just like he had done so many times over the years, stomping his boots on the welcome mat before entering the house. He made sure to slip out of his wet boots before getting beyond the front door, something that had always been a strict rule of his mother's.

The smell of freshly brewed coffee permeated the air, and Wes walked right to the kitchen to get a cup for himself. He turned the corner into the kitchen and spotted his mother sitting at the kitchen table, humming lightly to the music playing in the background from the radio on the counter. Jenny Martin sat, draped in her favorite green cardigan, as she sipped her coffee.

"Morning, Mom," Wes said to her as he bent down to kiss her cheek. He placed Molly, still in her seat, carefully on the table in front of his mother before he moved towards the coffeemaker.

"Oh, Wes," Jenny said with a start. "I didn't even hear you come in. I was in my own little world this morning, I guess. What are you doing up so early? And why did you drag poor Molly out in this weather? Although it's wonderful to see you, my beautiful granddaughter," Jenny added as she undid the safety harness on the seat and slid Molly out of her winter coat before pulling the infant closer to her. Molly cooed as she looked at her grandmother, laughing and smiling at her.

"I was going to drive Kris down to the library this morning. I didn't want her to trek down on her own, but she talked me out of it. I drove Izzy and Bradley to school instead and figured we would stop by on the way home for a visit."

Wes poured coffee into a white porcelain mug before he joined his mother at the table.

"I'm sure Izzy was thrilled with that," Jenny said sarcastically.

"No, she sure wasn't, and I don't think Bradley was either," Wes laughed.

"Wesley, did you give that boy a hard time again? You really should be nicer," his mother scolded.

"Oh, he knows I don't mean anything by it."

"No, I don't think he does," Jenny told him. "He's scared to death of you."

"There's nothing wrong with a little fear," Wes said proudly. "it keeps him on his toes, so he knows I am watching how he is with my daughter."

Jenny gave Wes a sideways glare as she took another sip of her coffee.

"Where's Dad?" Wes asked as he reached over to the loaf of banana bread on a platter and cut himself a slice.

"Oh, he went down to plow out around the stables and the lower road. You know how he is. He could let one of the workers do it, but he has to do it himself. He should be back in a few minutes."

Jenny broke off into a steady, throaty cough that shook her body. Molly's body jostled next to Jenny's as she coughed. Wes moved over to his mother, put his hand on her shoulder, and offered to take the baby from her.

"Are you okay? Do you need your oxygen? And why aren't you wearing your oxygen?" Wes asked with concern. Jenny waved him off and shifted Molly to her other shoulder.

"I'm fine," Jenny reassured. "And I hate wearing that thing all the time. It's a nuisance and dries me out. I don't need it constantly."

"Well, the doctors disagree with you," Wes told her. "If it helps and makes you more comfortable, you should just wear it. I'll go get it."

Wes went to move toward his parent's bedroom before Jenny reached over and grabbed Wes's arm.

"Wesley, sit down," Jenny commanded. "I said I'll be fine, and I will. I cough... a lot... you need to deal with it."

"What if Dad comes in and sees you without your oxygen?"

"Your father won't say a word. He and I have an understanding. If I don't want to use the oxygen, I'm not going to, and no one is going to force me to... not you, your father, the doctors, or anyone else. I'm a grown woman. I can make my own decisions. Now, sit down, eat your banana bread, and be pleasant company."

Wes sat back across from his mother. He picked up his slice of banana bread and took a bite, chewing it slowly and savoring the rich banana flavor and the bits of walnut his mother always put in her recipe.

"What is it with the women in my life?" Wes asked, picking up his coffee.

"You have wonderful women in your life, Wes... beautiful, strong, intelligent, willful women. Isn't that right, Molly?" Jenny told the baby as she lifted her up. "Be grateful for that," Jenny said proudly. "And wipe the crumbs off your shirt."

***

Kristin's Jeep pulled to her usual spot in the library parking lot without any trouble. Chandler was used to dealing with snowstorms large and small and had no problem making sure all its roads, sidewalks, and parking areas stayed passable and clean. The long-time residents of the town were evident by how well their paths were kept, with not even the slightest traces of precipitation remaining visible as soon as they were able to get out and start shoveling, snow-blowing, or sweeping.

Kristin gingerly moved from her vehicle towards the library doors, even though everything looked good to her. The last thing she wanted to do was take a fall right now, and being overly cautious was undoubtedly prudent. She had her bag slung over her right shoulder as she moved along the sidewalk, and Kristin felt the rock salt crunch beneath her boots as she walked.

Kristin arrived at the front door and tugged it open. She wedged her right foot against the door to hold it open so that she could slide in while she maneuvered the foyer. She huffed a bit as she walked into the library and spotted Karen sitting behind the counter, unzipping her sheepskin boots.

"Hey, what are you doing here so early, or even at all?" Karen asked. "You didn't have to come down with the weather like this. And where's little Miss Molly?"

"I was going stir crazy in the house, Karen. I needed to get out and do something different. Wes has Molly this morning."

Kristin walked to her office and took her hat off, shaking the stray snowflakes that had fallen out before she hung it on the coat rack. She unzipped her jacket but had difficulty getting her left arm out of the sleeve. She still felt twinges of pain now and then from the surgery. Kristin struggled for a bit before Karen came over to assist her and pulled one sleeve so Kristin could get the jacket off. Karen hung up the coat as Kristin moved over to her desk and sat down, pushing herself a bit away from her desk so she could adjust the chair and sit comfortably.

"I can't imagine there is going to be much going on down here today," Karen told her. "Even with the streets clean, you know how it is right after a snowstorm. Everyone stays home for a bit before getting back to normal. Add in that people are going to be Christmas shopping, I expect a quiet day."

"I'm okay with a quiet day," Kristin admitted. "I just want to feel like I am out doing something. It will help take my mind off things for a bit."

"Everything going okay? You're feeling alright?" Karen sat down across from Kristin.

"I feel fine," Kristin told her. "And everything is going great, but I think Wes... well, he's a bit anxious about the whole thing. I know he never got to experience much of it when Izzy was born, but his anxiety and his hovering and asking questions, well..."

"It makes you want to punch him?" Karen said with a smile.

"It does!" Kristin admitted. "I love him dearly, but he's making me nuts. It's sweet, and I know he's just trying to help, but it's too much lately. I just needed a little break today, even if I don't really do much of anything here."

"No problem, Kris," Karen told her as she stood up. "Do whatever you feel up to today. Stay in here and kick back or sit out at the counter. Either way is fine with me. Just let me know if you need anything."

Kristin spent most of the morning working on tying up some loose ends with vendors, suppliers, and others so that they knew they could get in touch with Karen or herself over the next few weeks if they needed anything before Kristin returned to the office. Kristin also checked in with a few of the part-timers to ensure that they paid attention to schedules, so all the hours were covered, and Karen had help when she needed it.

As she sent off the messages, Kristin considered more about work and what would happen in the coming weeks. Before Molly was born, she hadn't thought much about the prospect of not returning to work. Kristin loved the library and her job, but the weeks home with Molly made her understand why many women changed their minds and stayed away longer. Wes had told her many times that she did not need to return to work if she didn't want to. They were financially secure, no matter what her decision would be. The thought made Kristin nervous about the future. Her plate would be fuller than ever before, with the baby, work, planning the wedding for the fall, Izzy finishing her last year of school, Wes and baseball, and who knows what else might come along. The last few months had allowed Wes, Izzy, and Kristin to slip into a routine, making sure everyone's needs got met along the way. Once Molly arrived, they realized there was no planning for everything, and finding time was not always so easy. Would there even be enough hours in the day to do everything?

Kristin lapsed into a daydream about it all and snapped out only when there was a loud knock on her office door. She sat up quickly in her chair, trying to make herself as comfortable as she could before yelling out, "come in!"

The office door creaked open and there stood Wes with a grin on his face.

"Hey there," Kristin said with a smile.

Wes entered the office and closed the door behind him. He carried two tote bags with him. It was then Kristin realized he didn't have the baby with him.

"Where's Molly?" she said with more panic than she knew she should feel.

"I left her with my Mom and Dad," Wes assured her. "They offered and wanted some time with her, so I took them up on it so I could come down and see you."

"I brought you some lunch," Wes said as he sat. "I didn't think you had grabbed anything before you left, and I wasn't sure what you might feel like having so I got a little of everything – wonton soup, a burger from the diner, spaghetti and meatballs, warm chicken salad, and fruit salad and some yogurt."

"You're too much," Kristin told him. She reached across her desk to take Wes' hand.

"Well, you need to eat, and I didn't want you to have to go out and get anything."

"Hmmm, no salad for me. Lately, it gives me heartburn. I'll take the fruit and yogurt... and did you get fries with the burger?" Kristin said, hopefully.

"And onion rings," Wes said proudly, pulling the covered foil pan out of the bag.

"Ooh, I will take those," Kristin said as she grabbed the pan and pulled the top off, digging into a crispy onion ring.

Wes passed the fruit salad bowl and yogurt across the table. He handed some plastic utensils to Kristin, along with a cold bottle of water. Kristin took the plastic off the fruit bowl and popped a grape into her mouth. She watched as Wes went into the other tote bag and pulled out a small, round glass vase with some red and white roses arranged in it.

"Wes, that's so sweet, thank you," Kristin cooed. She held the vase under her nose and took in the aroma of the flowers. "What did I do to deserve this?"

"What didn't you do," Wes told her. "You don't need to do anything but be you, yet you still do more each day, including taking care of our family and putting up with me. I know I've been a bit much the last few weeks, but I'm just excited about us, the baby, and the future, and I want to make sure that you have everything you need."

"Wes, I've never felt more like I have everything I need than I do now, and I'm excited about the future too. Thank you for taking care of me."

Wes rose from his chair and moved over to where Kristin sat. He bent down and kissed her, lightly at first, then with more passion and feeling. They broke their kiss, and Kristin sighed and smiled.

"Hmmm," she hummed lightly.

Kristin swiveled her chair so she sat facing Wes and put her hands on his waist to hold him as they kissed more.

"I've missed that," Kristin sighed.

"What?" Wes asked. "I kiss you all the time."

"Not like that, you don't. At least not lately. Sometimes I think you're afraid you're going to break me," Kristin said with a smile.

"I just didn't know what you felt up to is all," Wes answered as he took Kristin's hands and helped her out of her chair. He slipped his hands around her and pulled her close, kissing her with more fervor.

"I'm stronger than you think, Mr. Martin," Kristin replied. "And Dr. Walker said sex is okay since it's been more than six weeks since the C-section," she whispered in his ear.

A glint shone in Wes's eyes that Kristin hadn't seen in a while.

Wes slowly trailed his hands up Kristin's sides and closer to her breasts before Kristin reached up and pushed his hands back down.

"I didn't mean right now," Kristin scolded playfully.

"Hmm, that's too bad," Wes told her. "But you could come home with me now, while Izzy is at school and Molly is with my parents. We have a couple of hours to ourselves."

Kristin raced over to her coat rack and grabbed her jacket while Wes tossed the food back into the bags. Kristin grabbed Wes's hand and tugged him out the door.

"I'm done for today, Karen," Kristin said as she pulled Wes toward the library door.

"Okay," Karen answered. "If I need anything, I'll call."

"Or you can just use your best judgment. I trust you," Kristin yelled, hoping to avoid any interruptions.

"Race you home," she told Wes as she got to her car door, keys in hand.

Chapter 3

The accumulated snow turned to gray ice after a few days, only to become a pristine white again thanks to a fresh coat of a few inches that fell just a week later. While the snow morphed on the roadways and in front of the Martin house, the hills in the back glowed with the untouched snow in the moonlight. Just a look out at it made Wes long for the days when he was younger, and he and his friends would take their sleds out to the top of the hill where his indoor batting cage stood now. The trip down the "mountain" as they called it back then, on a sled, made it like an Olympic bobsled run. If the kids hit the curves just right, the sleds became airborne for several feet before slamming back into the ice and snow.

Wes stood at the back door and looked at the hill as the moonlight lit it with a magical aura perfect for the holiday season. He sipped on a vodka martini on the rocks he had made for himself, a special treat for the evening. Slow footsteps made thuds coming down the main staircase, and it wasn't long before Kristin appeared in the doorway to the kitchen, beaming at Wes.

"She's all ready," Kristin uttered. "Make sure you let her know how beautiful she looks."

"I always do," Wes stated in self-defense.

"I know you do, but each event at school this year is the last time Izzy gets to do something like this, so it means more to her. She wants to look her best for the dance tonight."

Soft moves down the staircase could be heard, and Kristin walked to Wes and grabbed his left hand so she could tug him out of the kitchen and out toward the living room. As he passed the bedroom door, he took a nervous peek into the bedroom and heard nothing but a soft, small snore from Molly. Wes made sure to grab the baby monitor before leaving the kitchen so he would notice any noise. The lights in the living room were off, except for the colored lights of the Christmas tree. The room was illuminated as colored rainbows glistened off glass ornaments and tinsel. All this created an effect on the small silver snowflakes that adorned the dress Izzy wore. The dress was light blue and sleeveless with a modest scoop neck and a pleated skirt, and it suited the winter theme of the school dance perfectly. She gave a casual spin after descending the staircase, letting the skirt flare out a bit for effect.

"Well?" Izzy asked. Kristin gave a light nudge with her elbow into Wes' stomach.

"You look beautiful honey," Wes admitted. Izzy smiled even more full than before.

"Thanks, Dad."

"Let me get a picture of the two of you in front of the tree," Kristin offered as she went off to grab her smartphone.

Izzy and Wes strode over and stood in front of the tree, both looking at the various ornaments on the tree as they waited. Izzy reached over and took hold of a paper Christmas tree that stood out among the many crystal ornaments on the tree.

"Dad, you really put this one on there?" Izzy complained.

"Why not? It's one of my favorites," Wes replied, taking the ornament from her. The tree was imperfectly cut and colored green with crayons and then dotted with different colors to create lights. At the top of the tree was a small photo of Izzy from when she was about six, with front teeth missing as she grinned in her green and red plaid Christmas dress.

"I look horrible in this picture with my teeth like that," Izzy bemoaned.

"I think you look beautiful, and it's special to me because you made it for me for Christmas."

"Yeah, Mom made me wear that dress too. I never liked that one, but she insisted on it," Izzy stated. "I think that was the last Christmas before she left," she noted quietly.

Wes flipped the ornament over to check the date on it, and sure enough, it was marked with that final Christmas date. Rachel left Wes and Izzy the following spring without much fanfare to take up life in New York with her hedge fund billionaire boyfriend no one knew about.

Wes hung the ornament back on the tree and then put an arm around Izzy.

"I think we've done pretty well since then," Wes told her. "And you've grown up to be an amazing young woman that I am so proud of."

"Dad don't make me cry and mess up my make up," Izzy told him as she choked up.

Kristin reappeared in the living room with her phone, and she had Wes and Izzy pose several times in front of the tree so she could get the best shots. Wes then insisted on taking pictures of Kristin and Izzy together in the same spot before a ring of the doorbell interrupted them.

"That's Bradley," Izzy said excitedly, and she raced to the door.

"Oh goody," Wes mumbled before he looked over and saw Kristin scowl at him. He snapped off a picture of her before she could say anything, laughing at the shot he got of her.

Bradley entered the house wearing a dark suit and tie. Izzy, who was tall all on her own, towered over her boyfriend now with the heels that she wore.

"You look very nice, Bradley," Kristin offered.

"Thank you, Ms. Arthur," Bradley replied as he straightened his tie. He smiled at Izzy and offered her the corsage he carried in a plastic case. Ever since Wes had bought a corsage for Bradley to provide for his daughter on their first official date to a school dance, Bradley had undertaken the routine and always had one for her, even if none of the other kids seemed to follow this tradition anymore.

Bradley removed the delicate white corsage from the case and stood before Izzy, who stared at it and smiled. Bradley reached over to attempt to pin the corsage to Izzy's dress until he heard Wes loudly clear his throat as Wes watched the teenager bring his hands up near Izzy's chest. Bradley quickly pulled his hands back down and turned to Kristin.

"Maybe... maybe you can do this, Ms. Arthur," he uttered nervously as he handed the corsage over. Wes nodded and smiled as Izzy twisted her face in embarrassment. Kristin walked over to Izzy to pin on the corsage and then directed the teens over in front of the tree so she could snap a few pictures of them together.

The two stood inches apart for the first few pictures before Izzy insisted they get closer, and Bradley put his arm around her waist. He did so dutifully but kept a close eye on Wes to see what his reaction would be. Wes peered at him the entire time until the pictures were done, and then walked over to the teenagers before they could escape quickly out the door.

"Have a nice time, honey," Wes said gently as he kissed his daughter in the cheek.

"Thanks, Dad," Izzy told him, giving him a hug.

Wes then turned his attention to Bradley.

"Home by 11, right, Bradley?" Wes commanded.

"11?" Izzy yelled. "Dad, it's already almost 8:30. Come on, can't we make it at least 12 tonight?"

"I think 11 is plenty fair, Izzy. Don't you, Bradley?"

Bradley just nodded frantically, not wanting to get on the wrong side of Wes.

"Wes..." Kristin chimed in.

"Now Kris, I think I am being very reasonable about this," Wes retorted as he stared at Bradley.

"Wes!" Kristin yelled emphatically. Her yell had urgency and was quickly followed by a groan as Wes looked over and saw Kristin tumble to the floor.

Wes turned to see Kristin down, holding herself. He rushed to her side. "Everything okay?" Wes said with concern.

"I don't know. I moved towards you and felt this sharp pain, and then my legs gave out," she said through gritted teeth.

"Izzy, you need to stay here with Molly. I have to get Kris to the emergency room." Wes said with urgency. Wes deftly bent down and scooped Kristin into his arms and moved toward the door. Bradley sprinted over and opened the door, so Wes jumped right out and down the steps towards his truck.

Izzy followed the couple outside and looked at Kristin as Wes placed her gently into the passenger seat of the truck. She looked at Kristin and could see a mixture of fear and pain on her face. Kristin tried to reassure Izzy she was okay, but she didn't know for sure that she was. Kristin began the breathing techniques she had learned while pregnant, hoping it would help her ease the pain she felt now and keep her calm.

Wes ran around to the driver's side and opened his door before turning to his daughter.

"Izzy, you need to get back inside and watch your sister. Call your grandparents and let them know what's going on," Wes told her.

"Okay, Dad, I will. Call me as soon as you know something," Izzy answered.

"I will, I promise. Make sure to leave your phone on and pay attention to it," Wes said firmly.

"Dad now is not the time," Izzy said with frustration.

Wes got in the truck, started the engine, and tore down the driveway. He left the two teenagers standing in the driveway and saw them in the rearview mirror as they both walked towards the house. The truck was out onto Route 5 in no time, speeding towards the hospital.

Wes glanced over at Kristin and saw the worried look she had on her face, making Wes drive faster.

"You doing okay?" Wes said with concern as he darted into the left lane to move past a slow-driving Buick LeSabre.

"I don't know. I'm scared, Wes," Kristin said with a wince as she gripped her sides.

Wes drove rapidly and tried not to be reckless as the truck swerved in and out of traffic before reaching the hospital. Wes stopped the truck in front of the emergency room entrance, threw it into park, and jumped out. He pulled Kristin out like a rag doll and took her into his arms as he moved through the sliding glass doors of the hospital and up to the emergency room counter.

"We need help here!" Wes yelled as 2 nurses jumped up and wheeled a gurney over that Wes placed Kristin on. The nurses whisked Kristin into the emergency room while Wes followed closely behind.

Everything has to be okay, Wes told himself as he looked up at the ceiling and found himself with clasped hands and saying a private prayer while nurses and a doctor quickly tended to his fiancée.

Chapter 4

Izzy crept in her stockinged feet into her Dad's bedroom to peek in on Molly as she slept. The infant breathed softly, nestled under her blanket, as peaceful as could be. Izzy smiled down at her sister and tiptoed back out of the bedroom, closing the door but leaving it ajar slightly. She went back into the kitchen and picked up the baby monitor and placed it on the table where she and Bradley had been sitting. Bradley watched her as she sat down across from him at the table.

"How's Molly?" Bradley asked

"She's sound asleep. She might sleep for a while now. You know, you don't have to stay if you don't want to," Izzy told him. "I don't know how long they will be gone or when I'll hear from my Dad. If you want to go on to the dance, it's fine."

Bradley reached his hand across the table and mingled his fingers with Izzy's.

"No, I can stay here with you. The dance wouldn't be much fun without you," Bradley told her.

The two stared at each other for a moment in the silence.

"Maybe we can watch a movie," Izzy suggested.

"Can we go down to your Dad's man cave to watch it?" Bradley asked excitedly. "I've never had the chance to hang out down there. All the guys will be so jealous."

"Sure, I guess so," Izzy said, grabbing the baby monitor as she rose.

Bradley followed Izzy over to the doorway and then down the stairs to Wes' room, as all in the house called it. She flipped the light switch, and the room illuminated quickly, bringing life to the place and a look of awe on Bradley's face.

"This space is phenomenal," Bradley gushed as he walked over to the pool table. His left hand glided across the green felt of the table before he turned his eyes to the large projection screen on the wall.

Izzy walked over to the couch nearest to the front of the screen and picked up the remote sitting there. In a flash, the screen came to life, listing a choice of channels.

"What do you want to watch?" Izzy asked as she looked at the movie choices on the screen.

"Hey, let's watch Live PD," Bradley exclaimed with excitement as he saw the choice scroll by.

Izzy turned and gave him an incredulous look.

"Seriously? A cop show? I thought you wanted to watch a movie."

"Come on," Bradley whined as he plopped on the sofa. "This show is awesome. It will be fun."

Izzy sighed and sat down next to Bradley, positioning the baby monitor on the coffee table in front of them. Bradley draped his right arm over Izzy's shoulder as he pulled her close. Bradley got caught up in the action of the show every time something looked like it might happen while Izzy just stared at the screen.

"Does anything ever happen on this show? All I see are traffic stops," Izzy remarked as she bent down to grab the remote.

"Don't change the channel!" Bradley yelled. "You never know when one of these traffic stops might turn into a car chase or something."

Izzy released the remote, and Bradley snatched it up right away, guarding it like a dog hovering over a bone or favorite toy. Finally, when a commercial break came around, Bradley sat back.

"You know what might make this better for you?" Bradley remarked.

"A lobotomy?" Izzy cracked.

"Not quite." Bradley rose from the couch and made his way over to the bar that ran the length of the far wall. He swept behind the bar and looked at all the different bottles of liquor Wes had available. Bradley reached up to the top shelf and grabbed an unopened bottle of Macallan's 12-year-old Scotch without really knowing what it was. He held the bottle up to Izzy and smiled.

"Forget it, Bradley," Izzy warned. "My Dad would kill us both if he knew we were drinking down here. Even before you died, he would revive you just so he could kill you again. Do you really need another reason for him not to like you?"

"Come on, Izzy. You mean you aren't even tempted a little to try something with all this stuff down here? It would be a shame for this opportunity to go to waste."

Izzy walked over to where Bradley stood, took the bottle from his hand, and examined it. She turned the bottle in her palm a moment before smiling at Bradley. She then slid past him and placed it back on the shelf, bent down to the refrigerator behind the bar, and grabbed two bottles of Coke instead, handing one to her boyfriend, who now looked crestfallen.

"Wow, that's a buzzkill, Izzy," Bradley told her. She planted a kiss on his lips as she walked by him and laughed.

The two teens sat on the couch some more, watching the mindless police action on the screen until another commercial break came about. Instead of looking at the TV ad, Bradley turned to Izzy and pulled her to him, kissing her. Izzy always got lost in Bradley's kisses, and she closed her eyes as she got caught up in the moment. The two kissed passionately before Izzy began to feel Bradley's left hand gliding up her stockinged right leg.

"Bradley, stop," Izzy whispered into breaks of their lips.

"Come on, Izzy," Bradley groaned lightly, kissing her neck. He kept trying to move his hand forward, and for a moment, it seemed like his passionate pleas and motions might work. That was when Izzy took his left hand in her right and held it in place just beyond the hem of her dress.

"Don't, Bradley," she said emphatically.

"Why not? No one is home and might not be all night. Molly is sleeping. We're both going to be eighteen soon. All the stars are aligning." Bradley went back to kissing Izzy's neck before she twisted away from him and sat up, placing Bradley's hands in his own lap.

"You know why not," Izzy scolded. "I told you I wasn't ready, and I'm not. And we don't know when anyone is coming home. And lastly, because I said no."

Izzy moved away from Bradley on the couch, picked up the remote and changed the channel so that it switched to a Law and Order rerun.

"All right, I'm sorry," Bradley moped, trying to get close to Izzy again. "Geez, I just thought since we couldn't go to the dance that maybe we would do something fun tonight. I didn't know you were going to be..."

"Think about what you're going to say next, Bradley," Izzy interrupted. "If you really thought that we were just going to come down here, get drunk and have sex, then you really don't know me as well as I thought you did."

The two sat in silence for a few minutes, blankly staring at the TV screen as detectives investigated a murder scene.

"Maybe you should just go to the dance," Izzy stated without looking at Bradley.

"Maybe I should," Bradley said, standing up and straightening his rumpled shirt. "See you later."

Bradley marched up the stairs, and Izzy heard the front door slam loudly behind him, shocking her and bringing a rousing cry over the baby monitor. She walked up the steps to Wes and Kristin's bedroom, where the crib was right now and picked up her startled and sobbing baby sister.

"It's okay," Izzy said, trying to soothe Molly just as much as she tried to feel better herself. Soon enough, they were both crying.

***

Wes sat in the uncomfortable chair positioned next to the bed Kristin lay on in the emergency room. He kept close watch over her, looking at all the monitors they had hooked her to as they beeped incessantly. About an hour ago, they had whisked Kristin off to have x-rays and an MRI done, but since her return, they had not seen a nurse or a doctor come in. Kristin was now on an IV of some kind, something for the pain she was having, but Wes hadn't focused enough when the nurse explained it to him just what it was. All he knew for sure is that Kristin was fidgeting just as much in the bed as he was in the chair.

Wes heard a light groan escape Kristin's lips, and he jumped out of the chair to be at her side.

Kristin peered at Wes through her barely open eyes.

"Wes, I'm terrified. I don't know what's wrong."

That was all Wes needed to hear to reach his breaking point.

"I'll be right back," he stated as he flung the curtain that ringed Kristin's bed open just as a doctor and nurse were about to walk through it, startling both.

"Mr. Martin?" the young man in blue scrubs asked as he stared up at Wes. "I'm Doctor Young."

You certainly are, Wes thought to himself as he looked at the man who seemed to be barely out of high school.

"What's going on, doctor? We've been waiting, and they have done all kinds of tests, but no one is telling us anything."

Dr. Young nodded to the nurse, who then pulled the curtain back around Kristin's bed. Kristin lay on her side, knees pulled up towards her chest because it was the only position she could be in where she didn't feel intense pain.

"Mr. Martin, I've looked at Kristin's MRI and ultrasound, and they indicate that she has a strangulated hernia. Part of the intestine is caught behind the hernia, and its blood supply is cut off. It's most likely the result of the C-section from the birth. It's rare, but it does happen. Whatever the cause, it needs to be addressed right away. We're prepping a room for surgery now and should be able to take her up shortly, but we need to get her ready now."

The doctor was very abrupt in what he said and just stared up at Wes, looking for a response.

Wes just had images flash through his head, and none of them were happy or pleasant.

"Mr. Martin?" Wes heard through the fog he was in as the doctor tried to get his attention.

Wes felt a hand reach out and grab him, and he blinked back to reality. He looked down to see Kristin holding his hand with tears in her eyes.

"Wes?" she pled. He immediately knelt, so his face was next to hers.

"You need surgery, honey, but everything is going to be okay. They'll take the best care of you, and I'll be right here the whole time waiting for you when you get out."

Wes reached over and gave Kristin a kiss on her forehead. He lingered there for a moment and whispered softly to Kristin.

"I love you."

Kristin smiled weakly at him and sighed.

"I know you do."

The nurse came over to Wes and placed a hand on his shoulder.

"Mr. Martin, I can take you over to the surgical waiting area. You can stay there, and the doctor will come in after the surgery to let you know how everything went and what room she will be in afterward."

Wes nodded at the nurse and followed her. He turned back to see a team of other nurses and doctors come in to start getting Kristin ready to move to the operating room.

Chapter 5

As soon as Wes got to the waiting room, he made a call to his parents to let them know what was going on. He then called Izzy's phone to inform her that he would be at the hospital late, perhaps even all night, and was she okay with Molly.

"I'll be fine, Dad," Izzy whispered. "She just went back to sleep. I fed her and changed her, and rocked in the rocking chair for a bit. It was some good sisterly bonding time."

"Great, thanks so much for holding down the fort, Izzy."

Wes paused for a moment.

"Bradley isn't still there, is he?" he questioned.

Wes heard Izzy take a deep breath before answering.

"No, Dad. He left a long time ago. Did you really think I would let him stay here all night with all this going on?"

"I don't know," Wes said honestly. "I would hope not, but... I was just checking is all."

"Go take care of Kris," Izzy told him. "I can handle everything. Give her a hug for me."

"Okay, I'll see you in the morning. Bye."

Wes scanned the waiting room and saw he was the only person in there now. Not surprising since it was after 11 PM, but he also noticed that the coffee maker was turned off and the cabinet that clearly had the coffee in it was locked tight. Wes remembered he had passed some vending machines on his way to the room and worked his way down the maze of hallways to get back to where he could get something. He picked out a can of soda, a bottle of iced tea, and some water, and since he didn't know how long he might be here, Wes tried to find a snack that wasn't filled with salt or sugar that he could eat. When nothing seemed to fit the bill, he selected a bag of Swedish fish and headed back to the waiting room.

Even with no one in the room, the giant TV screen was on CNN displaying the news. There were lots of stories about how the economy was doing right before Christmas, the latest political battles going on in Washington, and what everyone could expect as the NFL season got closer to the end. Wes pulled a couple of chairs close together so he could put his feet up, popped open the bottle of mango tea he had, and tore into the Swedish fish. He savored that first bite of a candy he hadn't eaten since he was a teenager.

After a few minutes and a few more red fish, Wes grew bored with CNN and found the remote so he could change the channel. He flipped away, hoping to come across anything that might be remotely interesting before settling on ESPN. Sports news was something he could relate to, so he left it on, not really paying much attention to what was being said beyond a big-name free agent first baseman that signed a new 5-year contract for $100 million.

Wes shook his head, remembering when he was that big name, or when he would even get offers for a contract. The last thing he wanted to do at the moment was get caught up in self-pity, especially with Kristin struggling with everything right now. How long would the surgery take? What was involved? What were the risks? He suddenly thought of all these questions that he should have asked the doctor when he was standing in front of him.

Wes noticed there was another smaller TV screen on the far wall that listed all the current surgeries in progress. Only one showed on the board, and since it had started not that long ago, Wes assumed that was Kristin, even if he couldn't decipher the code that it all was in. No names were used other than the doctors involved.

The last sip of iced tea drained from the bottle, and Wes looked up at the ceiling tiles and began mindlessly counting them, and then looked at shapes forming in the speckles, dots, and water stains on the panels. Patterns reminded him of the Pittsburgh Pirates' stadium, the overhead shape, and the form of it. Another looked just like the freckles that dotted Izzy's face when she had been out in the sun during the summer. There was even one that matched the design that his parents had when he was a child for the linoleum of the kitchen floor.

Wes tried everything he could to keep busy as the clock ticked further and further along. No changes occurred on the surgical update screen, no one came in to let him know how things were going, and he didn't know where to go even if he wanted more information. He considered closing his eyes and trying to nap, but every time he did, all he saw was Kristin falling to the floor or laying on the gurney in pain, and him standing there helpless, unable to do anything for her. Worst-case scenarios darted through his imagery again, and he did his best to shake them from his head.

A tap on his shoulder came from behind him and startled Wes. He hadn't heard anyone come into the room. When he spun around, he saw his father standing there, wearing his typical brown Stetson and sheepskin coat that he wore around the stables all the time.

"Jesus, Dad, you scared me. I didn't hear anyone come in the room."

"That's because you were asleep, Wes," his father replied. Wyatt Martin sat in the chair next to his son and tapped Wes on the knee.

"What time is it?" Wes asked. He didn't realize he had fallen asleep and wondered how much of what he thought about really happened.

"2 AM," Wyatt told him as he stretched out his legs.

"What? Fuck, Kris is still in surgery? Why hasn't anyone updated me on anything?" Wes remarked with panic. He shot up out of his chair and went over to the small screen. The screen was blank now, with everything cleared off.

"She's not up here," Wes said, walking over to the phone. "I don't even know who to call to find out what's going on," he said as he slammed the phone down in disgust.

"Calm down, Wes," Wyatt reassured. "Let's go get some answers."

Wyatt put his arm around his son and led him out of the waiting room. Wes suddenly felt like a teenager again, his father comforting him after a rough day at school or bad practice or game.

"Dad, how are we going to find out anything? This place is a friggin' maze, and no one is around."

"Trust me, Wes. I've spent enough time here with your mother over the last few years to know where to go and what to do," Wyatt told him as they walked through one set of doors after another.

Wyatt navigated the hospital labyrinth until they reached a desk that had a couple of nurses sitting at it.

"Wyatt? What are you doing here? Jenny isn't here, is she?" an older brunette said to Wes' father. She rose from her chair and came out from behind the desk to give Wyatt a hug.

"No, no, Rosalie, Jenny is fine. She's home. I'll tell her I saw you. I'm here with my son. His fiancée had some emergency surgery tonight, and we just want to know where we can find her. They left him stranded in the waiting room."

"I'll find out for you, Wyatt, no problem. What's her name, hon?" Rosalie asked as she turned to Wes.

"Kristin... Kristin Arthur," Wes answered.

Rosalie quickly typed information into her computer. The other nurse, a younger woman in her mid-twenties with brown hair and eyes, stood looking at Wes.

"You're Wes Martin, aren't you?" she asked softly.

"Yes," Wes answered. He tried to sound as polite as he could and hoped this was not the time for an autograph request or picture.

"Tanya, why don't you go and check on Mrs. Quinlan in 8B? It's time to check her vitals," Rosalie ordered. She had recognized the situation and quickly diffused it.

Tanya nodded and walked off in the direction of the appropriate room.

"Thanks," Wes offered.

"I'm sorry about that," Rosalie said sincerely to Wes. "She's new and probably got a bit starstruck."

Rosalie glanced back down at her computer and then picked up her phone. She punched in a few numbers and waited for someone to pick up.

"Maura, hi, it's Rosalie. I've got a couple of wanderers up here, and I think they belong down by you. Do you have a Kristin Artur down there?"

Wes watched as Rosalie waited and then nodded a few times before she thanked Maura and hung up.

"Okay," Rosalie said with a big exhale. "She's down on the third floor, in a room. 12A."

"How is she? Is she alright?" Wes said urgently.

"I don't know any of the details, but I'm sure if you go down there, you can find everything out. Maura said she's only been there for about 30 minutes or so. She might be sleeping or pretty groggy, at least."

"Thanks, Rosalie," Wyatt told her with his country smile.

"Oh, anything for you, darlin', you know that," Rosalie told him. "You give Jenny my best and tell her I am glad I haven't seen her lately."

"You bet I will."

Wyatt gave Rosalie a casual wave and led Wes over towards the elevator so they could go three floors down. Once they were on the elevator and moving, Wyatt saw the angry look on Wes' face.

"Why wouldn't they call me and let me know, or send someone to get me? I would still be sitting up there waiting if you hadn't come along," Wes said with disgust.

"Maybe they did call, and you were asleep," Wyatt rationalized. "And if she just came out of surgery, they might not have had anyone free to come up and check on you. It is two in the morning, after all."

The elevator arrived on the third floor, and Wes dashed out of the door over to the nearby desk.

"I'm looking for Kristin Arthur's room," Wes told the nurse anxiously. He looked at the tag hanging on the lanyard around her neck to see it was Maura.

"Are you family?" she asked politely.

"Yes, I mean... she's the mother of our child and my fiancée, that's enough, right?" Wes said excitedly and with little patience.

"Easy, son," Wyatt said to him, putting his steady hand on Wes' shoulder.

"I'm... I'm sorry," Wes told the nurse as she looked on. "it's been a long, stressful night."

"it's okay," Maura told him with a comforting smile. "She's in 12A. She's probably resting, and maybe still a bit out of it from the anesthesia. I think Dr. Morales is still here. I'll buzz him and see if he can come down."

"Thank you," Wyatt told Maura as Wes was already off looking for the correct room.

Wes marched down the hall as quietly as he could until he reached Kristin's room. He pushed the door open gently and saw Kristin in the bed closest to the door, eyes closed. Machines were beeping all around her, and she was on oxygen, which made Wes worry. He peeked around the curtain, separating the room and saw there was no one else in the room with Kristin. Wes pulled over one of the cushioned wood chairs in the room so he could sit next to Kristin. He took her right hand in his, being careful not to jostle her or where she was hooked to an IV.

Kristin barely stirred when Wes held her hand, but she did grip his hand, recognizing his touch. Wes brought their mingled hands up to his lips and kissed her hand. He sat watching Kristin for a few minutes, holding her, and saw that her breathing and heart rate relaxed and became steady and calm.

"Wes," Wyatt whispered from the doorway. Wes turned to see his father partially lit from the hall light.

"The doctor is out here to meet with you."

Wes placed Kristin's hand down on the bed and rose from his chair. He moved quickly and quietly, trying to avoid squeaking his sneakers on the floor. He closed the door, just leaving it open a crack, and walked back over to the nurses' station where he saw his father standing with another man.

Dr. Raul Morales was engaged with Wyatt, talking about horses, when Wes came up. Wes stood a full six inches taller than the doctor. Dr. Morales was in his forties, his dark hair tightly and neatly cut. He gave a firm handshake to Wes as the two men introduced themselves to each other.

"How is she?" were the anxious words that shot from Wes' mouth.

"She came through the surgery well considering how complicated it was," Dr. Morales said. He looked down at his notes and information on the tablet he held before him.

"A section of her intestines had moved behind the hernia and was losing blood supply. Luckily, we caught it when we did so we could repair it. The surgery was more detailed than we thought it might be. We had to do open surgery instead of laparoscopic, and there was untangling to do to straighten everything out and then deal with the hernia, but we took care of it all. She's going to be sore for a while, sorer than she was from the c-section. It might lay her up for another 4 or 6 weeks while she recovers, and she certainly shouldn't be lifting anything heavy, including the baby, for a bit. We're going to want to keep her here for a few days just to watch her and make sure she's doing alright, and we'll get her up and walking so she can move around a little."

Wes processed the information, all while peering at the door to Kristin's room. No matter what the doctor said, he still harbored concerns about how she would be right now and in the coming days. She looked weak in the hospital bed, nothing like the strong woman Wes loved and saw every day.

"Do you have any questions, Mr. Martin?" Dr. Morales offered. The doctor's question broke the trance Wes fell into.

"No... no, I think that's it for now," Wes replied as he turned to face Dr. Morales. "Thank you for everything."

"I'll be back later in the day to check in on her, but the doctor on duty starting at seven will probably come in and check on her this morning. I know that's only a few hours away, but maybe you want to go home and get a bit of rest before you come back."

"Is it alright if I just stay here with her?" Wes didn't want to leave Kristin's side, not with her in the state she was in.

"Well, we don't normally let people spend the night in the rooms like that," Dr. Morales told him.

"Please, I don't want her to wake up and be alone like that. I'll be glad to pay to move her to a private room if that's what is needed. Or I can just stay in one of the chairs in the room."

Dr. Morales knew by the look on Wes' face that he wasn't going to take no for an answer.

"I'd prefer not to move her around right now. Since there isn't anyone else in the room at the moment, I don't think it will be a problem. I'll let the nurses know you will be here."

"Thank you," Wes said gratefully as he turned to walk back to Kristin's room to be at her side.

Dr. Morales quietly excused himself, shaking Wyatt's hand as he left.

Wyatt placed his hand on Wes' shoulder.

"I'm going to head back home unless you want me to stay with you," Wyatt told him.

"No, go home and get some rest, Dad," Wes answered quietly. "Thanks for coming down and helping out."

"No big deal. Do you need me to bring anything over for you or Kris?"

"No, I'll wait on that for now until we see how long she is going to be here. Can you go check on Izzy and Molly? I don't want Izzy to worry too much."

"I already took care of it. Before I came here, I brought the girls down to our house to stay with your mother. It gave Izzy an extra set of hands with Molly and gives me someone to watch out for your Mom," Wyatt told his son.

"Always a step ahead, Dad," Wes remarked.

"I try to be. Get some rest if you can, Wes. I'll call you later and see how things are going."

Wyatt placed his Stetson back on his head and ambled down the hallway, leaving Wes alone to be with Kristin. All Wes heard was the beeping of the machines and Kristin's soft breaths when he reentered the room.

Maura walked in just as Wes sat, carrying a blanket and pillow and stopped to face Wes.

"These might help you feel a bit more comfortable," she whispered. "I know that the chair isn't much, and it's not great for getting any rest."

Wes took the blue blanket and pillow and smiled at the nurse.

"Thanks so much," Wes told her as he put the pillow behind his head, so he didn't have to lean against the wall.

"No trouble at all. We'll be in to check on her periodically, and I'm here until 7 AM if you need anything else. Don't worry, Mr. Martin. She's in good hands, and she's doing great."

Maura left the room, closing the door, but leaving it just ajar so a small slit of light came through.

Wes glanced at Kristin as she slept, then turned his eyes up towards the ceiling as his head pushed back into the pillow.

"Thank You," he said softly as he gazed up before closing his eyes. As much as Wes wanted to get some rest, he knew it wasn't likely to come.

Chapter 6

Kristin's eyes fluttered open, and she spied a nurse changing one of the IV bags that hung from the pole next to her bed. She felt like she had been asleep for a week, and the temptation was great just to close her eyes again and doze off, but Kristin fought it as she tried to clear her head a bit and figure out what was going on.

"Hey there," the female nurse said to her with a big smile. "How are you feeling?"

"Like I got hit by a car," Kristin rasped, her throat feeling parched.

"You had a long surgery, but everything looks good so far. The doctor will be in soon to check on you and talk to you. How's your pain on a scale of one to ten?"

Kristin didn't need to think too long about it. The moment she had tried to sit up, she felt a stabbing pain in her side where what she assumed the incision was from the surgery.

"When I do that, about a seven," she winced.

"I just switched your pain meds, so you should get some relief in a bit. I know it sounds harsh, but you may not want to move around too much just yet, though at some point today, we are going to get you out of bed and try to walk you around a bit."

Kristin let out a small cough and felt the searing pain in her side again. Tears formed in the corners of her eyes.

"Coughing and laughing will hurt, too," the nurse told her, "until things start to heal a bit more. Let me get you some water and see if the doctor will be here. Maybe we can get you something for breakfast too."

The nurse scurried out of the room. Kristin watched the woman leave, and then her gaze fell on Wes. Wes was contorted in the small chair beside the bed. The pillow wedged between his head and the wall while his feet stretched out far in front of him.

"Wes," Kristin croaked. She tried her best to clear her throat without bringing on another cough that might cause pain.

Wes stirred and awakened. He stretched his arms high above his head, yawned, and moved his neck from side to side, so it cracked the kinks out. When he spied Kristin looking at him, he bolted upright and then got out of his chair.

"Kris!" he exclaimed as he took her head and bent down to kiss her. He gave a gentle kiss on her lips, and both could feel the cracked, chapped skin that had formed.

Wes ran his hand through her blonde hair as he watched her crack a smile.

"How are you feeling? Do you need anything?"

"The nurse just went to get me some water," Kristin said. Her voice continued to crackle. "I'm pretty sore. Exactly what happened?"

"The surgery was more challenging than originally thought," a woman in her lab coat remarked as she entered the room. The nurse followed right behind her, holding a small pink container of ice water.

"I'm Dr. Kingery," the woman stated, "the doctor on duty this morning. Dr. Morales, who performed the surgery, will be by later today to check on you, but for now, I just want to see how you are doing."

Dr. Kingery slid over to the left side of the hospital bed, nudging Wes away so she could get closer to Kristin and where the surgical incision was made on Kristin's body. Dr. Kingery pulled down the blanket covering Kristin and lifted the thin hospital gown to reveal the area covered in bandages.

"They tried to go in where your C-section scar was, but they may have extended it just a bit," Dr. Kingery said as she examined the area. Wes peeked over the doctor's shoulder and could see the elongated scar that resided on Kristin's red and tender flesh.

"It looks clean, but we'll change the dressing on it now. I'm sure it's still sensitive to you, so you'll need to be careful. Rest up this morning, and Dr. Morales will check it this afternoon. Maybe then we can get you out of bed and try walking around a bit."

"Walking already?" Kristin said. Her voice felt better after taking a long sip of cold water.

"Yep, we need to make sure you can move around, and we don't want any blood clots or issues, so we get you going right away. The faster you can do things, the faster we can get you home," Dr. Kingery told her as she pulled Kristin's gown back into place.

The doctor left after making a few notes, leaving Wes and Kristin alone in the room.

"How's Molly?" were the first words from Kristin upon everyone else leaving.

"She's fine," Wes reassured her. "Izzy had her last night, and then my Dad brought the two of them down to my parents' house, so Mom was there to help out if they needed it. I'll give Izzy a call and make sure everything is okay, but I'm sure they are fine."

"Are you sure your Mom can handle it? She's got enough of her own stuff to do. And what about Izzy and school? You'll have to be home with the baby..."

"Kris, relax," Wes told her. He pulled his chair across the linoleum floor so he could sit closer to Kristin.

"It's Saturday. Izzy doesn't have school until Monday, and I'm sure we can work everything out, so we have coverage. Besides, it sounds like the doctor is going to try to have you out of here by Monday anyway. You need to concentrate on feeling better. I can take care of Molly, Izzy, the house, and whatever else needs to get done. Trust me; there's nothing to worry about."

Kristin leaned back into her pillow and then pressed her finger on the control for the bed so she could sit up more. As she sat up straight, she felt a tug around the incision for the surgery.

"How the hell did I get a hernia?" she wondered aloud. "I've felt fine since Molly's birth. I didn't notice any bulges or anything. It was just all of a sudden, and I was down on the floor."

"I know," Wes consoled. "It was scary. From what the doctors have said, hernias aren't uncommon after a C-section, and you don't always have symptoms right away. Yours was just more complicated. It's a good thing they caught it when they did so they could repair it. Now you'll just be laid up for a while."

"How long did they say to you?" Kristin asked worriedly.

Wes sat back in the chair and saw the concern on Kristin's face.

"Dr. Morales said it could be six weeks, maybe more. It depends on how it heals."

"Six weeks?" Kristin exclaimed. "Wes, I can't go six weeks without picking up Molly. I'll go crazy."

"Kris, you don't really have much of a choice. You don't want to rupture anything and make it worse and end up with bigger problems. This was scary enough. We'll do whatever we need to so we can be sure you're healthy and safe."

Kristin rubbed her temples as she contemplated what the immediate future might hold. She had just started to get into a comfort zone of motherhood and its routines. She was even doing a little bit of work for the library as well, and now it all was thrown into a tumult.

The morning nurse appeared holding a tray and came over to Kristin.

"Dr. Kingery said you could have some breakfast, so I brought you a choice of things," the young lady said. "I know it's not much, but there's some yogurt, some scrambled eggs, juice, and I can get you tea if you want. Soft foods for breakfast, so we can see how you do."

"Thank you..." Kristin offered, pulling the tray closer to her and then glancing at the dry erase board so she could see that the nurse's name was Gloria.

"Thanks, Gloria," she said, suddenly feeling hungry and popping open the yogurt.

"If you're hungry, Mr. Martin, the cafeteria is open," Gloria mentioned as she checked all the readings on the equipment.

"No, I'm fine," Wes insisted.

"You should get something to eat, Wes," Kristin said to him in between spoonfuls of blueberry yogurt. "Besides, you've been crunched in that chair all night. Stretching your legs might not be a bad idea."

Wes nodded and rose from the chair, feeling a familiar ache in his left knee.

"Okay, I won't be long," Wes told Kristin. "I'll grab something and give Izzy a call to see how they are doing."

Wes bent down and gave Kristin a light kiss on the lips, tasting the last of the yogurt Kristin had polished off. Wes reached into his pocket and pulled out Kristin's cellphone and left it with her.

"If you need anything or want me, just call. I'll be right back."

Wes walked out of the room, leaving Kristin alone with Gloria.

"If you don't mind me saying so, you've got a good man there," Gloria said with a smile. "There aren't many guys that would have stayed up for hours and then slept like a pretzel to be with their partners."

"He is a good man," Kristin announced proudly as she picked up the spork to use for her eggs.

"And he's easy on the eyes, too," Gloria said with a chuckle.

"That he is, Gloria. That he is," Kristin answered with a stifled laugh.

***

Wes took the elevator down to the first floor and followed the directions for the cafeteria. Hunger wasn't foremost on his mind, and after looking at what was offered for breakfast, he left right away and walked over to the kiosk down the hall and instead got a cup of coffee. He sat at one of the empty high-top tables nearby, pulled out his cell phone, and pressed the number for Izzy's phone.

The phone rang several times before Izzy answered with a sleepy hello.

"It's me," Wes told her. "Were you sleeping? It's 9 AM. Who's got Molly?"

"Take it easy, Dad," Izzy yawned. "I was up with her at 6 and fed her and changed her and played with her. She went back down to sleep about an hour ago, so Grandma said I could leave her out in the living room in the bassinet there. She's fine. I was exhausted. How's Kris?"

"She's doing alright," Wes said, feeling disarmed. "She has some pain, obviously, but the doctor said she is doing okay. They are hoping she'll be out in a day or two."

"That's good to hear. Can we come up to visit her?"

"I don't think they'll let you bring Molly onto the floor, but you can come up if you like. I'm sure she would appreciate it. Check and see if Grandpa is planning to come back and come with him. Just let me know when to expect you."

"Got it," Izzy replied. "I'll send you a text when we are leaving. Is it okay if I go back to sleep for a bit? It's been a long couple of days."

"Sure, honey," Wes said to her. "You okay?"

"I'm good," Izzy fibbed. "Go take care of Kris. Give her a hug and kiss for me."

"Will do," Wes told his daughter. "See you later."

No sooner had Wes hung up when he saw that his phone was ringing again. He expected it to be his father checking in, but he was surprised when he saw that it was Tom Killian, the President and General Manager of the Washington Wild Things, the independent baseball team Wes had played for last season. Wes stared down at the phone ringing, hesitant to answer it. He hadn't expected the team to call him with any information about a potential contract until after the new year. A call now indicated something was up, and bad vibes shot through Wes' mind over it. Finally, after four or five rings, Wes sighed and pressed the answer button.

"Hello," he said as professionally as he could.

"Wes? Hi, it's Tom Killian from the Wild Things. How are you?"

"I'm okay, Tom. How are you doing?"

"Oh, you know, trying to get things organized for next season. There is never a dull moment, I guess, even around the holidays. We're ramping up for Christmas and trying to sell some ticket packages, you know, the usual stuff."

Wes sensed Tom was evasive with what he wanted to say, and Wes had little patience for any of it right now. He would rather find out bluntly if the team didn't want him back next year so he could make his plans one way or the other.

"Tom, I don't mean to be rude, but I'm here at the hospital with Kristin. She had some surgery last night, and I need to get back to her, so..."

"Oh, geez, Wes, I'm sorry I had no idea. I hope she's okay. Let me get right to the point. I'm sure you saw the news that the Frontier League and the Can-Am League have merged, so we have five more teams that we will play against for the coming season. It should be exciting, with new audiences opening up the potential for the league and all, and we're thrilled to be a part of it..."

"Tom!" Wes said emphatically. "Please, just get to the point. If you guys don't want me back next year, I understand. I know you took a chance on me, and I appreciate it. I had fun and put up some good numbers, so I'm sure I can latch on somewhere else if I want to."

Tom was silent for a moment.

"Wes, it's not that we don't want you back. You were great for us last year. You played well, brought crowds to the game, and did everything we asked and more. That being said, we have made some changes that I wanted you to be aware of."

Here it comes, Wes thought. He had heard this conversation when he was cut from the Pirates.

"John Clines, our manager last year, just took a job in the Cardinals organization as one of their low minors managers. As you can guess, that leaves us in kind of a bind as we are planning out the roster for next year. I'm trying to get a manager in place as quickly as I can, and that's when I thought of you."

"Thought of me for what? I probably know a few guys that I can recommend to you if you want someone new for the job. Let me call you after I get home..."

Tom interrupted Wes right away.

"No, Wes, you misunderstand me. I don't want recommendations. I want to know if you want the job."

Now it was Wes' turn to be silent.

"Wes? You still there?" Tom asked, feeling like the cell signal might have been lost.

"I'm still here, Tom. You want me to manage? I don't have any experience like that. Why would you want me? I... I think of myself still as a player."

"Well, we can certainly talk more about that. Maybe we can work something out where you could be our player/manager. Yeah, the fans would love that! It's got a lot of possibilities, Wes. The players respect you greatly. We're working to have a lot of the same guys back from last season, and some new additions to boost up our weak areas, so I think we'll have a good core for you to work with. So, what do you think?"

Wes's mind churned with all kinds of ideas. In a perfect world, he would be back in the majors playing for someone, but the chances of that got slimmer and slimmer with each passing day. Staying home and just being a husband and father had great appeal to him as well, and even though he had never considered managing in the past, it created new opportunities for him. It might also open a different path to get back into the majors.

"Can I think about it a bit, Tom?" Wes answered. "My plate is kind of full right now with Kristin and the baby and all."

"I get that Wes, I really do," Tom replied. "The problem I have is that I need you to decide soon if you can. If you aren't interested, I need to get some candidates in here fast so I can do interviews and such. Word is already out that John is gone. The Cardinals had a press release this morning."

"I promise I will get back to you within the next day or two. I just need to think about it, talk to Kristin, and see what is going on with her."

"Fair enough," Tom told him. "I'll give you a call on Monday or Tuesday to see where we are at. Give my best to Kristin. I hope everything is okay."

"Thanks, Tom. I'll talk to you soon," Wes told him before hanging up.

Wes stood frozen for a moment, looking at his phone. The call was completely unexpected, at least in the manner it had played out. Being a player/manager might give Wes a chance to do something not done very often in baseball anymore, and it could give him greater visibility. It also meant more responsibility that could keep him away from home, something he wasn't sure he wanted to do again. He had already missed so much of Izzy's life growing up; it didn't seem fair to do the same thing to Molly.

Wes knew one thing for sure – he had to talk to Kristin about all of this and hash it out. The problems he had caused last year when he was looking to play again were enough of a strain on their relationship, and he had no desire to put her through that once more.

While he stared at his phone, two text messages blinked in. The first was from Izzy to let him know that she was on her way to the hospital with Wyatt. The second was from Kristin.

You coming back? That must be some breakfast. They want to try and get me out of bed for a little walking, and I thought you could help me.

Wes walked to the elevators and pressed the up button. The doors swooshed open, and a small crowd filed out while others crammed in with Wes to go up to the various floors. Wes pressed "3" and waited as the room slowly glided up, buying him a few more seconds to figure out what he would say to Kristin.

Chapter 7

Kristin sat on the edge of the bed and waited for Wes to get back to the room. Gloria had assisted her, first with the removal of the catheter that was in place (something Kristin didn't relish experiencing again after going through it when Molly was born), and then with sitting up and getting to the edge of the bed. Gloria tightened the ties on the back of Kristin's gown and waited with her.

"Feeling okay?" Gloria asked. "Getting this far is a good first step."

Kristin looked as her feet dangled off the side of the bed. She wiggled her toes in the blue hospital socks with the rubber grips on them. She always hated these socks and couldn't wait to get out of them and back into her own clothes and be in her house.

"I'm okay," Kristin answered anxiously.

"I'm here," Wes stated as he came through the door and spied Kristin sitting up.

"Boy, you really are ready to get moving," Wes told her as he moved to where she sat on the bed.

"The faster I move, the faster I go home," Kristin stated as she flashed a smile to Gloria.

"Okay, let's do this," Gloria said. She and Wes stood on opposite sides of Kristin and helped her off the bed until her feet were on the floor. Kristin wobbled a bit at first, and Wes gripped her elbow to hold her tightly.

"Nice start, Kristin," Gloria glowed. "You got your feet under you? You let me know when you are ready to move."

Kristin turned to the nurse and nodded and shuffled forward a bit. It had only been about twelve hours or so since she had been off her feet, so her muscles were there, but she still felt weak and scared. Kristin also noticed the tightness in her side where the surgical scar started, and it made moving more challenging.

Slow, deliberate steps led Kristin and her keepers towards the door of the room and then out into the hallway. Each move gave her more confidence, and before she knew it, Gloria had let go of her right side, leaving just Wes right next to her.

"Try to do a couple of laps around the nurses' station," Gloria told Kristin as Kristin walked away. "Then, head back to your bed, and we can do some more later."

"Hey, you're doing great," Wes told her. "You feel okay?"

They had reached the first turn in the hallway, and Kristin kept moving, holding onto the IV pole with her right hand as Wes stayed next to her on the left.

"I feel fine," she told him. "But it's a little drafty in the back of my gown."

Wes glanced down and saw the bottom ties of the gown had loosened.

"Hold on a second," Wes told Kristin as he moved behind her. He retied the gown so that it covered her previously exposed bottom.

"As cute as it looked, I can see why you would want that closed," Wes smiled.

Kristin blushed at the thought of flashing anyone that had been behind her, but she also giggled at Wes.

"I'm glad you still like it," Kristin remarked as she moved again.

"Of course, I still like it," Wes told her. "Why wouldn't I? You're beautiful."

"I sure don't feel that way right now," Kristin lamented. "I still have twenty pounds of baby weight, scars, and I feel a mess right now, not to mention I'm barely clothed. It's not much to look at."

"It's all I want to look at," Wes told her as he took her hand in his. The two continued walking down the hall, back towards her room.

The couple returned to Kristin's hospital room, and Wes helped maneuver Kristin back to where she could get into bed on her own.

"I'd say that went pretty well," Wes told her as he leaned in to give her a kiss.

Kristin smiled and felt invigorated and accomplished.

"Now, what do I do with the rest of the day?" Kristin asked. "Sitting around in this bed all day is not going to cut it."

"Well, Izzy and my dad are on their way here so they can see you," Wes started.

"Are they bringing Molly?" Kristin asked, hopefully.

"Honey, they won't allow her in the rooms. She's too young, and there are too many risks involved."

Disappointment engulfed Kristin's face.

"I think this is the longest I have gone without seeing her," she told Wes, "and I don't like it."

"You know, you're going to have to resign yourself to not picking her up or anything up for a while," Wes told her. "You don't want to cause problems."

"I know, I know," Kristin answered. "It's a good thing it happened when it did, I guess. At least you'll be home to take care of us both."

Kristin noticed a change in Wes's expression before he sat at the foot of the bed.

"I have to tell you something," Wes said seriously.

"What is it?" Kristin prepared herself, sitting up straight in the bed.

"Tom Killian called me while I was downstairs getting coffee."

"Tom from the Wild Things? Is it about a contract for next season? You know, it's okay with me either way if you do or don't play next season. It still gives us a few months before training starts, right?"

"It was about next year, sort of," Wes told her. "You remember John Clines, the manager?"

Kristin nodded as she listened.

"Well, John got a job with the St. Louis Cardinals organization, so he's gone. Tom's looking for a new manager, and he asked me if I wanted the job."

Kristin considered the statement for a moment and then beamed.

"That's wonderful, Wes! It will be great for you. It's a new career opportunity, and even though you will be traveling some, you'll be around us more often. Did you give him an answer?"

"I didn't, not yet," Wes answered. "Kris, there's more to it than you might realize. The league has expanded, so there are more teams now, including New York, New Jersey, and Canada. And as the manager, I would have to spend more time doing things with the team. There are more responsibilities. I would have to start doing work right away."

"Oh," Kristin said softly.

"The timing of it all sucks," Wes said as he rose from the bed and paced the floor. "I'm going to have to tell Tom I can't do it, not now."

"If you turn the job down, will they still want you as a player next season?" Kristin asked.

"I got the impression from Tom that it was this or nothing else."

Kristin and Wes just stared at each other without saying a word.

"Wes, if this is the best opportunity for you, and you want to do it, then you should. You know we can make it work. We did it last year."

"I know, but last year we didn't have a newborn to take care of, you weren't recovering from anything like this, Izzy wasn't graduating from high school, we weren't planning a wedding – there are a lot of things going on right now that I should be here for."

"Even though it may not look like it at this moment, I'm a lot stronger than you think, Wes. Sure, this is going to slow me down for a bit, but I'll be back on my feet and taking care of things. Maybe I can give up my job and..."

"No," Wes said emphatically. "You love your job just as much as I love mine, and I would never ask or expect you to do that, not again. It's not fair to you. The easiest solution is for me to just move on."

"Move on from what?"

Wes and Kristin both turned quickly towards the door. Izzy and Wyatt both stood there, Izzy holding a small duffle bag and Wyatt with some flowers.

Izzy moved over to Kristin and gave her a hug, making sure not to squeeze her too tightly.

"I brought you a few things from home that I thought you might want – toiletries, some crosswords, a hairbrush, and some clothes. It's just sweats and t-shirts, and a nightshirt and some underwear," Izzy told her, handing Kristin the bag.

"I never thought I would be so happy to have underwear," Kristin told Izzy.

"So, what do you have to move on from, Dad?" Izzy asked as she turned to her father.

"Yeah," Wyatt reiterated as he kissed Kristin's cheek and put the flowers on the small nightstand next to her bed.

"Okay, I guess we're going to get into this now," Wes stated. "The Wild Things offered me their manager's job this morning, but I don't know that it's the right time to take it and be away from home so much. So, it might be time for me to move on from baseball."

"Haven't we been down this road before?" Izzy said.

"Hey, don't be smart," Wes admonished.

"All I'm saying is that you thought you were ready to be done once, and you weren't, and you were miserable and made us miserable. I just want you to be sure you are ready to be done, Dad. Besides, why is now any different than before?"

"Why? Because we have Molly, Kris is recovering, we're planning a wedding, you're trying to decide about college, or at least that's what I'm told..."

"Do we have to get into this argument again, right now, Dad?" Izzy said, steadily raising her voice.

"Enough, you two," Wyatt interjected. "Can we look at this rationally, like a family should talk about things? Wes, are you interested in the job, yes or no?"

"Yes, I am, but..." Wes said before Wyatt cut him off.

"No buts," Wyatt told him. Wyatt turned to face Kristin.

"Kris, are you okay with Wes taking the job? Be honest."

Kristin considered it all for a second and then turned to Wes and smiled.

"Yes, I am okay with it."

"Even if it means I'm not around to help with..." Wes tried to add before Wyatt cut him off again.

"No one asked you anything yet, Wes. Izzy, how do you feel about it? Are you okay with it, even if it means picking up some extra slack at home during senior year?

"I'm okay with it, Grandpa," Izzy responded. "Kris and Dad know I am always willing to help..."

Wes guffawed when he heard this. "Always willing? What about..."

Wyatt hit Wes's shoulder with his Stetson.

"Boy, I'm not too old to wrestle you to the ground. We all know Izzy means well and does her best, better than most teenagers do. We're trying to work this out. Okay, so we're all on the same page here. Wes, you should take the job. I know for me personally, I think it's a great stepping stone for you. It keeps you in the game and who knows what it will bring. You know your mother and I will do all we can to support you and help. That's what family does."

"Okay, I get it," Wes conceded. "But what do we do about Molly? Kris isn't going to be able to lift and carry her for weeks. Izzy has school, you have the farm and Mom to take care of, and I won't be home most of the day. I don't know how this will work."

All four contemplated the dilemma before Wyatt spoke up.

"Have you considered hiring a nanny?"

Wes and Kristin looked at each other before Wes replied.

"No, we never even talked about it, but I guess it is something we should have considered at some point."

"Well, even if you were playing, you would be going back to work for training in April. Kris would have been back at work by then, so you were going to need a solution, even if it was daycare. Getting a nanny now might be the most practical step. She can come in and help out right away, and you will have someone that Molly gets familiar with as she gets older."

Wyatt sat down in the extra chair in the room and smiled.

"What do you think, Kris? It might be the best solution."

Kristin considered the proposition carefully. She did plan to go back to work at some point, even though she felt unsure about leaving Molly. A nanny would be ideal, especially now when her abilities were limited.

"I think it's the best decision. We were going to have to do something eventually, and as much as I want to, I know I won't be able to do everything I need to for Molly right now. I think we should do it."

"Okay, so it's settled. Wes will call the team and accept the job, and then we can set to work on finding someone for you. Marcy Andrews runs the job staffing service in Chandler. She's helped me find people to work on the farm. I'm sure she can give us some leads or tell us where to go to look at candidates and set up interviews. I'll give her a call right now," Wyatt said as he pulled out his cell phone and stepped out of the room.

"I guess I should call Tom back," Wes spoke. "Are you sure about this, Kris?"

"I am Wes. It will be best for all of us, and it will be a lot stressful. I can't believe I didn't think of it before."

"I know," Wes said. "Now I'll have to listen to my father gloat about how right he is all the time. I'll go call Tom."

Wes left the room, leaving Izzy alone with Kristin.

"Wow, that all happened fast," Izzy said. "it will be good to have someone there with you during the day while you get better, and then to be with Molly while you are working. It seems like everything is working out for everyone."

Izzy fiddled with the package of toothpaste she had brought for Kristin, unscrewing the top and then putting it back on over and over.

"What's going on, Izzy?" Kristin said as she laid back into the pillow that was propping her up.

"What are you talking about?"

"You may as well be nervously twirling your hair with what you're doing with that toothpaste. Something's bugging you."

"Okay, but you can't say anything to Dad," Izzy said as she came closer.

"You know what is between you and me stays that way."

"Bradley and I had a fight last night, and he ended up storming out of the house last night and went to the dance without me. I tried to text him this morning, but he never answered me. I think he's mad."

"What was the fight about?" Kristin asked.

Izzy turned her eyes up to Kristin and hesitated.

"Well, while Molly was sleeping, we went downstairs to watch some TV. Bradley was in awe of Dad's room. First, he wanted to have something from the bar, which I said no to."

"Good decision," Kristin added.

"Then... well, we started kissing, and you know... Bradley wanted to go further..."

Kristin tried to control herself so she could remain calm.

"And?"

"And I said no," Izzy told her. "I told him I wasn't ready. That kind of ticked him off too, and after a few more minutes, he left and said he was going to the dance without me."

"I know you're bothered that he hasn't gotten back to you, Izzy, but he probably just needs time to cool off. You did the right thing and made the best decisions for you. Bradley should respect that if he cares about you."

"He's the only real boyfriend I've ever had, Kris. I don't want to mess it up."

"I get it, Izzy. You aren't thinking about the long-term, but what was going to happen when you both go to college in the fall? Things were bound to change then."

Izzy stayed quiet for a minute.

"Bradley is planning to go to Columbia. I thought about applying there too."

"Izzy, don't go to a school just because Bradley is going there. Choose a school that is best for you and what you want. What's wrong with Pittsburgh?"

"You sound like Dad now, Kris," Izzy chimed in. "He just wants me to stay close to home so he can keep his vision of me as a little girl that needs Daddy for everything. He doesn't see me as my own person that can make mature decisions."

"Look, I'm not trying to be like your Dad," Kristin explained. "I know you're just about eighteen, and you are at a point where you should make more of your own decisions. Just make sure you make them for the right reasons."

Wes re-entered the room, with Wyatt trailing right behind him.

"I talked to Tom and took the job. They are going to have a press conference this week, but I asked him if we could hold off on starting the job until after the new year. This way, I can help out at home and it gives us a chance to find a nanny."

"On that note," Wyatt said, "I talked to Marcy Andrews. She told me she can have a list of candidates set up on Monday and will send the information over to you so you can choose who you want to interview for the job. Hopefully, you find someone that fits what you need."

"Wow, we sure got a lot accomplished today," Kristin said.

"I'll say," Wyatt added, "and all before lunch."

"Well, maybe you two gentlemen can go take a walk or figure out what you want to do for lunch," Kristin said happily.

"Why do we need to leave?" Wes asked.

"I was hoping Izzy could help me get to the restroom, and she can wash my hair and assist me in getting dressed, at least into a nightshirt, and some underwear if you really have to know," Kristin remarked.

"I didn't need to know," Wyatt said with a flustered look. "Come on, Wes. Let's allow the ladies their time. You can buy me some lunch."

"Why do I have to buy you lunch?" Wes asked.

"Because I raised you right, and because I only have a hundred-dollar bill in my wallet."

"You've been using that excuse for twenty years," Wes said as they walked toward the door. "That must be the oldest hundred-dollar bill still in circulation."

Chapter 8

Kristin returned home on Monday and walked from the car to the bedroom without any difficulty. No sooner was she inside and in the bed when she asked for Molly to be brought to her. Izzy obliged, bringing her sister in from her feeding in the kitchen and placing her in between Kristin's legs as she stretched out on the bed.

"Hello, my sweet!" Kristin cooed. Molly gurgled back at the recognition of her mother's voice, and Kristin let Molly grip her pinky and hold it. Kristin tried to bend down to give her child a kiss, but she winced when she tried to move that way and found it too difficult to do in the position she was in. Izzy recognized the dilemma and scooped up Molly and brought her up to Kristin's face so she could kiss Molly and rub the baby's cheek against her own.

The next few days were challenging as Kristin tried to do what she could around the house without lifting anything more than just a couple of pounds. She had plenty of visitors, with Wyatt and Jenny both stopping by frequently to check on her, get meals when needed, or help with Molly. Karen stopped by as well to see her friend, let her know what was going on at the library, and just provide support.

Wes had started going out to the team offices on Tuesday, first for the press conference and then to begin planning, talking about roster make up, and the like, even if it was just for a couple of hours each day. He would go in the mornings while Molly was usually napping and when Jenny or Wyatt could come up and help Kristin until he got back home. Kristin and Wes also spent time going over resumes of potential candidates for the nanny position, turning aside several because they did not fit what they were hoping for, before settling on a group of four to interview. They sent the names back to Marcy Andrews, and she arranged for interviewees to come out to the Martin house in the days just before Christmas.

Kristin had spent a lot of time going over the CVs of the nannies, looking closely at previous jobs, background, and experience. She made a list of questions she intended to ask during the interview and was thoroughly prepared.

If they were going to have someone for this position, Kristin needed it to be a perfect fit.

The first three candidates interviewed failed to meet Kristin's standards. After each left the interview, she gave Wes her reasons why she did not want to hire them for the job. Wes did ask questions during the process as well, but he found himself deferring to Kristin more. In the fourth interview, a woman named Martha Stuart arrived right on time. Wes and Kristin had laughed often about the name and waited with anticipation to see who would show up on the day of the interview.

Martha was a woman in her forties, her shoulder-length brown hair speckled with flecks of gray. The gray identically matched the color of her eyes, and she flashed an inviting smile from the time Wes opened the front door.

Wes led Martha into the kitchen, where Kristin sat in one of the chairs with arms to make it easier for her to get up and down. Molly lay in the bassinet next to Kristin, wide awake and enjoying the cloth mobile that was clipped to the side. Martha greeted Kristin with the smile she gave to Wes and sat down across from Kristin, while Wes offered coffee or tea.

Wes brought over the coffee percolator and mugs and began to pour coffee.

"I have to say, you must get a lot of jokes about your name," Wes said with a laugh.

"Jokes?" Martha asked as she poured some half-and-half into her coffee. "I'm not sure what you mean."

Wes looked at Martha, unsure if she was pulling his leg or not, as he sat down. "You know, Martha Stuart? Like the other Martha Stewart, the one on TV?"

"Oh, I don't watch much television," Martha said as she sipped her coffee.

"Well, she's written a bunch of books too," Wes added.

"I'm not familiar with them," Martha said with all seriousness.

"But she was in the news..." Wes started before Kristin put up her hand to stop him.

"Let's just move on with the interview, shall we?" Kristin said politely. Kristin proceeded to ask the litany of questions she had asked the other candidates, presenting them with situations and how they would react, asking about previous employers, talking about transportation, possibilities of working late, other tasks they might be willing to help with and so on. Martha took each question in stride, answering them in just the manner Kristin was looking for. When she was done with her queries, she sat back, feeling confident that they may have found their nanny.

Kristin asked Martha to come over and pick up Molly so she could see how they interacted. Martha was charming, doing her best to communicate with Molly, but Molly did not want any part of it. She fidgeted and fussed, made noise, and eventually started crying lightly. After a moment or two of trying, Wes stepped in and took Molly in efforts to calm her down.

"She might be getting a little hungry," Kristin excused.

"Do you breastfeed her?" Martha asked bluntly.

"I did before my surgery. Now I just pump, and we give her the bottles since I can't lift and hold her yet," Kristin answered.

"I see," Martha replied. Kristin thought she heard a tinge of condescension in Martha's tone.

"I do have a couple of questions if you don't mind," Martha said as she sat back down.

"Of course," Wes said. "Fire away."

"Is this going to be a live-in position?" Martha asked.

Wes and Kristin looked at each other.

"We hadn't really considered it up to this point," Wes told her. "We do have the extra rooms upstairs, so I suppose it could be if you needed it. You would certainly be able to stay if the weather was bad, or it was a late night."

Martha nodded at Wes' answer.

"Do you have a salary in mind?" Martha asked.

"We do have a number that we think is fair."

"And what is it?" Martha chirped.

"Oh, well, we thought twenty dollars an hour was fair since the hours needed might vary each day," Wes told her.

"Hmmph," Martha grunted.

"Is something wrong?" Kristin stepped in.

"Well, there are a few things that would have to change before I would take the job," Martha said as she got up from the chair.

"First, I would only do nanny work, no other chores. If you need help like that, you should also hire a housekeeper. You clearly can afford it."

"I beg your pardon?" Kristin said. She felt her temperature starting to rise.

"Secondly, I would need a higher salary. I think the minimum I would take is forty dollars an hour. Fifty would be more acceptable. Again, it looks like that shouldn't be a problem for you."

"Excuse me, but just because my husband has made a good salary does not mean that we are willing to pay any price for something. Our lifestyle and livelihood are not part of the equation here." Kristin now rose from her chair.

"Ms. Arthur," Martha interjected, "Mr. Martin is not your husband. I don't see a wedding ring on your hand. That's another reason why I could not live-in here. If you two are living together out of wedlock and have a child together, well…"

"Okay, that's enough!" Kristin shouted. "The interview is over. Thank you for your time, Ms. Stuart. We'll consider your input and your candidacy. Have a nice day."

"Let me show you out," Wes said to her.

"Don't bother," Martha shot back. "I'll find my own way out. Best of luck to you."

Martha grabbed her handbag and stormed out of the house, slamming the door behind her.

"Can you believe that witch?" Kristin yelled, still worked up. "The nerve of her to look down on me, and on us."

Wes put Molly back in her bassinet and came over to comfort Kristin.

"It's fine, Kris. Let her go. She wasn't right for the job anyway. Molly knew before we did. Besides, what kind of woman with the name Martha Stuart doesn't know about THE Martha Stewart? That's just wrong."

Kristin let out a laugh and began to feel better.

"Seriously, Wes," Kristin said as she slowly sat back down. "What are we going to do? None of the candidates have been good so far. It's almost Christmas, and then the new year, and you have to start working more, and we aren't any closer to having someone."

"We have one more interview, right? Maybe she will be our Mary Poppins."

"I don't want Mary Poppins," Kristin told him. "I always thought she was kind of curt and creepy."

"What?" Wes said in surprise. "Julie Andrews? Flying with an umbrella, songs, dances, dancing penguins? Come on."

"Read the books, Wes. She's not quite the same," Kristin said as she stirred her coffee mindlessly.

"Okay, so she doesn't have to be Mary Poppins. She just must be not Martha Stuart. I have faith the next person will be great. Who is it?"

Kristin picked up the folder from the table and flipped it open.

"Melissa Palmer," Kristin said as she looked over the resume. "She's only twenty-two, but she has nanny experience from all through college, got her degree nursing, and is CPR, and First Aid certified."

"See, she seems good," Wes said as he cleaned up the coffee mugs.

"We thought Martha Stuart was going to be the one, too. How do we know that Melissa isn't a Satan worshipper or wants $100,000 a year to work for us?"

Wes walked towards Kristin and gently tugged her out of the chair. He gave her a deep kiss, the kind that always made Kristin stand on her tiptoes and lose her breath.

"Trust me, this will all work out. Have faith," Wes said softly. "What time is she coming today?"

"Two o'clock," Kristin sighed, reaching up for another kiss.

"Let's get some pastries from the bakery delivered here before she comes," Wes said. "We'll put out this great spread, dazzle her, make sure Molly loves her, and she will be begging for this job. And if all that doesn't work, I can take my shirt off and start swinging the bat a bit or go outside and chop some wood while she watches."

Kristin stepped back and laughed heartily.

"Really? Shirtless wood chopping is going to win her over?"

"It always works in romance novels, doesn't it?"

"How many romance novels have you read, Mr. Martin?" Kristin asked.

"Well, none," Wes replied. "But I did flip through a copy of Fifty Shades that someone left on a plane once, so I get the gist of them," he said proudly.

"Not really the same thing," Kristin said as she hugged Wes. "We'll go with the pastries, but you can keep your shirt on while she is here."

"Okay, but don't blame me if she doesn't want the job," Wes cracked.

Wes started looking up a food delivery service to bring pastries, but Kristin stopped him.

"Thank you," Kristin said to him.

"For what?" Wes asked, putting his arms around her again.

"For this. For everything. For all you do for me, and for us, as a family. You're an amazing man."

Kristin went in for another kiss, and her hands began to unbutton Wes' shirt.

"Wow, and I didn't even have to chop any wood," Wes said as Kristin finished unbuttoning his shirt and ran her palms over his chest.

Wes tried to return the favor and began to unbutton Kristin's blouse, but as soon as he had two buttons undone and there was just a hint of Kristin's lacy bra showing, Molly began to fuss.

"Looks like you're on duty, Mr. Martin," Kristin whispered.

Wes smiled and began to button up his shirt.

"You order the pastries, and I'll take care of Little Miss Interrupter," Wes said as he swooped Molly out of the bassinet.

***

Wes made sure to have everything ready for two o'clock, setting out the food, making coffee and tea, making sure Molly was changed, and straightening up anything that might need it. The doorbell rang right at two, and Kristin and Wes both stared at each other before Wes got up and moved to the door.

Wes opened the door, and before him was Melissa Palmer. Melissa had long brown hair with brown eyes to match. She wore a brown leather jacket with fringe that reminded Wes of the kind Davy Crockett wore in all those Disney movies of long ago. She wiped her black boots on the welcome mat before extending her hand to Wes.

"Mr. Martin. I'm Melissa Palmer. It is a real privilege to meet you. My father and I watch Pirates games all the time, and you were always one of my favorites."

Wes shook Melissa's hand and invited her into the house. She slowly walked around, taking note of the Christmas tree that decorated the living room.

"Your tree is beautiful," Melissa said as she unzipped her jacket to reveal a black Foo Fighters t-shirt underneath.

"A Foo Fighters fan, I see," Wes said, pointing at her shirt.

"I love them," she said, looking down at her shirt. "I've seen them in concert about a dozen times, and they get better all the time. Do you like them?"

"I do, but I've never seen them in concert," Wes said. "My Hero was my walk-up song for a few years."

"That's right!" Melissa squealed. "I forgot all about that."

Wes led Melissa into the kitchen, where Kristin sat sipping some tea.

"Kris, this is Melissa Palmer. Melissa, this is Kristin Arthur," Wes said, giving the introductions.

Kristin extended her hand, but instead, Melissa leaned in and gave her a hug.

"Oh, okay," Kristin said as she hugged Melissa back.

"it's so nice to meet you, Ms. Arthur. I've been down to the library a bunch of times. You have done amazing things with the place since you got to Chandler."

"Thank you, Melissa," Kristin said as she broke the hug. "You can call me Kristin."

"Thank you, Kristin," she said with a smile.

"Can I get you coffee or tea, Melissa?" Wes offered.

"I'll have some tea, please," Melissa said, "but let me get it. Kristin, do you want some?"

"That would be wonderful, thank you," Kristin said as she and Wes watched Melissa go over to the stove and pour hot water into two mugs.

"I hope you don't mind, but I carry my own teabags," Melissa said, reaching into her bag and pulling out a Ziploc bag holding a variety of teas.

"I order it right from a plantation in India. It's a bit more expensive, but there is nothing like the flavor. Chamomile, okay?"

"Yes, that's perfect," Kristin said as Melissa brought over the mugs.

"Oh, and this must be Miss Molly," Melissa said as she saw the baby in the bassinet. Before Wes or Kristin could even say anything, Melissa had picked Molly up and was holding her. Molly sat quietly in Melissa's arms before she sat down in the chair across from Kristin and Wes.

"So, what do you want to ask me?" Melissa said with a smile. She lightly hummed as she looked down at Molly, and she sat peacefully looking up at the young woman.

"Well," Kristin said as she tried to compose herself after being caught off guard, "I see you have lots of experience as a nanny."

"Yes, I worked with two families over the four years I went to the University of Pittsburgh to get my nursing degree. The first family, the Millers, I worked with for only a year before they moved from the area. I helped them with their two young children. I then worked as a live-in with the Olivers for three years. They had four children, including a newborn, when I started, right up to a teenager. I got my bachelor's in nursing with a specialty in pediatrics, but then my father got sick, and I came back to Chandler to take care of him."

"Is your dad Derrick Palmer of Palmer's Plumbing?" Wes asked.

"That's right," Melissa answered.

"They've done the plumbing at the farm for years," Wes told Kristin.

"We have," Melissa answered proudly. "I used to work at the office, answering the phones when I was in high school."

"I didn't realize your father had gotten ill," Wes said seriously.

"Well, he did about two years ago. He had a lot of headaches, and then they found a tumor, and well, he couldn't work anymore and needed regular care, so I came home. My brother Tommy took over the business."

"How's your Dad doing?" Kristin asked solemnly.

"Oh, he passed six months ago, peacefully and at home, the way he wanted it."

"I'm so sorry," Kristin responded.

"Thank you," Melissa said, reaching out and taking Kristin's hand. "We were prepared for it. It's taken a while to clean up his stuff, clear out the house and put it on the market, but it's finally done. Tommy has his own place with his wife and family, and that old house was too big and lonely for just me. So here I am."

"How come you don't just go back to nursing?" Wes asked.

"I suppose I could, but I'm not quite ready to yet. I wasn't sure what I would do, but I always had fun working as a nanny, and Ms. Andrews down at the staffing services office already had my name in case any nursing jobs came up. When she told me about this one, it sounded like the perfect fit, isn't that right, Miss Molly?" Melissa smiled into Molly's face and gave her a kiss.

"It feels like she needs a change," Melissa said as she felt Molly's diaper. "Do you want me to do it?"

"Um, sure, if you'd like," Wes said. "Let me show you where the changing table is. I think we are out of lotion in there, though. Let me run upstairs and get another bottle."

"Oh, don't bother," Melissa answered. "I have an ointment in my bag that is gentle, hypoallergenic, and is calming. I can use that if it's okay?"

"You bet," Wes answered. "Follow me."

Wes directed Melissa into the master bedroom where the changing table was. After Melissa walked in ahead of him, Wes turned to Kristin and mouthed, "Mary Poppins."

Kristin tried to stifle her laugh as Wes's phone rang.

"I have to take this," Wes said. "It's Tom Killian."

"Go downstairs, I'm fine," Kristin told him. Wes nodded and went down the stairs closing the door behind him.

Kristin sat and sipped her tea until she heard Melissa gently singing in the bedroom. Kristin got up from her chair and walked over to the bedroom door. She peered in and saw Melissa changing Molly. Melissa turned to see Kristin there and smiled at her and waved her to come over.

"What were you singing?" Kristin asked. "It sounded so familiar."

"Ha," Melissa said as she closed the fresh diaper around the baby. "It's a little embarrassing. It was "Just the Way You Are" by Bruno Mars. I find that babies don't really care so much about what you're singing if it's in a voice and melody they like. There, all clean, Miss Molly."

Melissa snapped the buttons on Molly's onesie and picked her up, holding her. She turned and could see Kristin's face.

"I know Miss Andrews said you had some surgery, and that's why you needed help now. I'm sure it's not easy for you. Have you held her since you've been home?"

Kristin shook her head no and felt tears welling in her eyes.

"Let's fix that," Melissa said softly.

She took Kristin by the hand and led her over to the bed.

"You sit," Melissa said as she guided Kristin down.

"I'm not supposed to..." Kristin tried to say.

"It's going to be okay," Melissa reassured her. She placed Molly gently into Kristin's arms and then came around on the bed and sat behind Kristin. Melissa put her legs on either side of Kristin and pulled her close so that she put her arms underneath Kristin's to support the weight of the baby.

"Hello, sweetheart," Kristin said as she cradled Molly, and Molly cooed back at her. Melissa used her arms to lift Molly closer so that Kristin could kiss her and rub her cheek on hers. Tears flowed from Kristin's eyes as she sat, and Kristin and Melissa both hummed Bruno Mars.

Wes came back upstairs and into the bedroom and saw the two women there.

"Is everything okay?" he said as he rushed around to the side of the bed so he could face Kristin. He saw her crying and smiling.

"Everything's fine," she said with a laugh. "Give her whatever she wants, but do not let her leave this house without hiring her."

Chapter 9

Comfort and routine quickly settled in at the Martin household. With Melissa there to assist Kristin while she healed, the stress melted away, and everyone was content. Christmas was joyful since it was Molly's first holiday, and even though she was too young to really grasp what was going on, Wes made sure to lavish her with all kinds of toys and stuffed animals. In contrast, Kristin made sure to get a few practical items along the way. Wes also outfitted Izzy with everything she could want or need for college, including a couple of University of Pittsburgh hoodies that he hoped might sway her decision.

A quiet New Years' celebration with just the family took place, and immediately following that day, Wes took up full work mode as the new manager of the Wild Things. There was a lot to do, going through potential roster players so that Tom Killian could make contract offers and bring in some new blood that might put them over the top for the coming season. Long days at the team offices, combined with Wes's training and practice he would do at the batting cage facility he had at home, meant he didn't see much of anyone during the day or even at night. More than once he arrived home past nine or ten at night when Molly was sound asleep, Kristin would be in bed and Izzy was up in her room.

Once February rolled around, things shifted gears once again. Kristin had recovered and received clearance from her doctors to go back to work. She still had to use caution with lifting, but she had more freedom now than existed in the months since Molly was born. Melissa's hours with the family grew as she arrived by six in the morning and often stayed until eight or nine so that she could give Molly the attention she required and help with household chores. Melissa made sure to bring Molly down to Kristin at the library for the occasional lunch visit, or she swung by Wes's parents so that they could get time with their grandchild. Melissa also helped with Jenny, checking in on her, and seeing if she needed any assistance.

February 11th marked Izzy's birthday. She woke up in the morning with high expectations now that she was eighteen. Texts filled her phone with wishes and pictures from her friends, and Izzy looked forward to the day at school and what was to come on Friday, which was February 14th – Valentine's Day. Even though her relationship with Bradley had been strained since Kristin went into the hospital, they remained together, and Izzy was excited about the Valentine's Day plans that Bradley had made for them.

Izzy chose one of the new outfits that she had been holding onto since she got them on Christmas. Naturally, Kristin had picked them out for her, and even though it was February in Chandler and snow was on the ground, that did not deter Izzy from putting on the short-flared skirt and matching blouse to wear. She bounded down the stairs and was greeted by the smiling faces of Kristin and Melissa in the kitchen, along with a bouquet of balloons and flowers.

"Happy Birthday!" they shouted and even cued Molly to raise her hands and squeal and smile.

Izzy dashed over to give her little sister a kiss, blowing on her cheek to make her giggle even more. She hugged Kristin and Melissa and then went over to pour coffee into her travel mug to bring to school with her.

"That outfit is cute," Melissa said to her as she wiped oatmeal off Molly's chin.

"It seemed perfect to wear for my birthday today," Izzy stated proudly as she twirled.

Wes walked in and went straight over to Izzy and kissed her on the cheek.

"Happy Birthday, Izzy," he said to her.

"Thanks, Dad."

"I'm sorry I have to run. We have early meetings at the office today. We are all still on for dinner tonight, right? Seven o'clock at Angelo's?" Wes said as he put on his leather jacket.

"We'll be there," Kristin told him, looking over at Izzy to make sure she nodded in agreement. "I made the reservations for the five of us."

"Are you sure?" Melissa asked. "I can watch Molly here if the three of you want to just go."

"Oh no, it's the whole family tonight," Kristin insisted.

As Wes gave Kristin a kiss goodbye, and then kissed Molly, he glanced over at Izzy to see her sipping her coffee and looking at her phone.

"Is that what you're wearing to school?" Wes asked.

"Yes... why? What's wrong now?" Izzy did her best to hold her tongue.

"Wes, not now, just let her be," Kristin whispered.

"It's just that it's February and cold out and that skirt... well, it's a bit short for school, don't you think?"

"Dad, please stop. It's not short, I'm wearing tights underneath it, and I like it. It's fine."

Izzy went to the hall closet and grabbed her coat, putting it on quickly.

"I'm leaving before he starts complaining about my makeup, too," Izzy gruffed.

She was out the door before anyone could get another word out. Melissa took the cue and sensed that Kristin and Wes were going to talk. She grabbed Molly out of her highchair.

"Come on, Miss Molly," Melissa said. "Let's go play in the living room."

"Wes," Kristin started, as she zipped up her handbag, "Why did you have to say that? What she was wearing was fine. I showed it to you when I bought it for her for Christmas, and you had no problem with it then."

"That was before I saw her wearing it," Wes replied. "It just seemed a little revealing for school is all."

"You have to stop goading her into arguments to make your points. She's eighteen now, and she wants to be her own person and express herself. You fighting her on every little thing isn't going to help."

"Okay, point made," Wes answered. "I'll work on it and apologize tonight at dinner. I'll see you later."

Wes gave Kristin an extended kiss before heading towards the door.

Kristin followed shortly, stopping in the living room to see Melissa sitting on the floor with Molly while Molly lay on the blanket, reaching up for the toys hanging over her.

"Goodbye, my sweet," Kristin singsonged to Molly before kissing her on the head.

"Do you need anything today?" Melissa asked. "We can come down for lunch if you want."

"I think I'm good today, thanks. It's probably better not to come down for lunch today and let her sleep this afternoon if you can. This way, she won't be too cranky at dinner. I'll be home around four if you need to go home and get anything before we go to dinner."

"I'm good," Melissa told her. "I brought clothes to change into from home."

"You know, if you wanted to leave some things here for convenience, there are extra rooms upstairs you can put stuff in. I'm sure Wes would be fine with it as well."

"That would be helpful, thanks," Melissa replied. "I think we have a buyer for my Dad's house, so I'm going to need to start to get my things out of there anyway. If I could leave some stuff here, it would be great."

"Do you have a place to go to yet?" Kristin asked.

"Sort of. I have a friend who has an apartment in Chandler, and she said I could stay with her and split the rent, but she hasn't been very committed to the whole thing. I can always crash at my brother's house for a bit until I find something. I'll work it out."

Kristin nodded without saying anything, but she already knew what she wanted to approach Wes about.

"Okay, I'll see you two later," Kristin smiled as she headed out the door to her car. The cold wind of the day hit her immediately, and she ducked her head a bit as she pushed out to her car and got inside. She turned the vehicle on and got the heat going, and then took out her phone to send a quick text to Wes.

I have an idea I want to run past you. Call me when you get to the stadium. Love you.

***

Izzy put her father's complaints behind her as soon as she pulled into the senior parking lot at school. Her friends greeted her at her locker with hugs and kisses and a few small presents. She was a bit surprised and disappointed that Bradley hadn't met her at her locker before classes started.

The school day trudged on for Izzy without any sign of Bradley anywhere. Even when it came to lunch, where they usually sat together, he was nowhere to be found. Izzy sat with her regular lunch group and kept standing or craning her neck to see if she saw him anyplace.

"Izzy," her friend Amber said as she pulled Izzy back down into her seat, "you look like a giraffe every time you do that. What are you looking at?"

"I was looking for Bradley," Izzy answered as she picked at the tater tots on her cafeteria tray. "Has anyone seen him today?"

Her friends all looked at each other without saying anything. Amber and Allison both shook their heads no, while Brianna just looked down at her food and gave Izzy a quick glance.

"Bri? Have you seen him? I always know when you're holding something back," Izzy stated.

"Well..." Brianna began.

"Bri, we all promised, not today," Allison chided her friend to hush her.

"Promised what? What the heck is going on with you guys today?"

"Izzy, it's your birthday," Amber said. "Let's celebrate. What are you planning to do tonight?"

"Don't change the subject," Izzy told Amber forcefully. "What do you guys know that you're not telling me?"

"He's over in the other cafeteria sitting with Eden Watson," Brianna blurted out.

"Bri!" Amber yelled.

"I'm sorry, but she deserves to know," Brianna retorted. "That's where he is, Izzy. I saw them walk in together when I was coming to lunch."

Izzy stared at her friends, but none of them wanted to look at her. Izzy dropped the half-eaten tater tot in her hand back onto the tray, picked up her purse, and left the table, heading for the other cafeteria. Amber got up to try to stop her.

"Izzy, wait!"

"Just let me go, Amber. I have to see him," Izzy told her friend as she pulled away from Amber's hands.

Izzy marched to the other, larger room and scanned the tables that were there. She finally spotted Bradley, sitting shoulder to shoulder, with Eden. As Izzy neared the table, it was evident that the two of them were also holding hands. The gnawing in her stomach grew more robust with each approaching step she took. When she was finally right in front of the group at the table, they all looked up, with Bradley turning last.

"Hey, Izzy," Eden said with a smirk.

Bradley let go of Eden's hand and stood up to face Izzy.

"Izzy... let me explain... let's go out in the hall," he said as he reached for Izzy's hand.

Izzy jerked her hand away.

"You have nothing to explain, Bradley. It's clear what's going on. Why are you doing this?"

Bradley fumbled for words but didn't come up with any. Instead, Eden got up and stood next to him.

"It's probably because I'm nicer to him and not quite the prude you are," Eden said spitefully. "At least that's what he told me at the dance in December."

Audible gasps from other teens at the table filled the air, and the loud din of the room seemed to quiet so more people could hear what was going on.

"Is that it, Bradley?" Izzy asked, her face getting hot. "Has it been going on for two months?"

"Eden, you're not helping," Bradley said sharply. "Izzy, please, let's just go..."

"Forget it," Izzy said as she stepped back. "Thanks for the birthday present."

"Izzy, wait!" Bradley yelled as she turned to go.

"Fuck off, Bradley!" Izzy yelled, eliciting all kinds of loud "Whoa!" shouts from the people around.

Amber had reached Izzy by the time she was working her way back towards her original seat. Izzy was too angry even to let herself cry.

"Izzy, I'm sorry," Amber said to her as she tried to keep up with Izzy marching toward the door. "We didn't know what to tell you..."

Izzy stopped after she had cleared the cafeteria and was in the hallway.

"You guys knew this was going on for two months and never said anything to me," Izzy raged. "If Aaron was doing that to you and I found out, I would tell you right away. That's what friends do, Amber."

"It's not as easy as that, Izzy," Amber said as she tried to come up with something to help her friend.

"Yeah, it really is," Izzy shot back. She spun around and marched down the hall towards the entrance to the school.

"Izzy, where are you going?" Amber yelled.

"Away from here," Izzy said as she pushed her way towards the front of the school. She reached the security desk, where one of the guards was busy talking to one of the school vice-principals.

"Ms. Martin, where are you going?" the balding gentleman in a wrinkled tan suit asked in as official a manner as he could.

"Out," Izzy said as she strode past him and into the parking lot before he could even respond.

Izzy got into her car, exhausted and out of breath. She sat for a moment and contemplated what to do. She thought about going right to the library to see Kristin, but she didn't know how much help it would be at this point. She considered just driving, driving as far away as she could get, to be alone. She started the Jeep up and got moving, and it was almost like the car had a mind of its own, and she found herself on the pathway to get home.

She sped along the roads and made a sharp turn to get onto Martin Way, flying by her grandparents' house and up to the top of the hill where her home was. There were no cars in front of the house, letting her know that not even Melissa was there with Molly, making it ideal for Izzy to be by herself.

She raced up the short steps and unlocked the front door, remembering to turn the alarm off before the police were notified, and both Kristin and her father found out the alarm was sounding. She tossed her bags onto the couch, stood in the living room, and shouted at the top of her lungs to let some of the anger go.

When the shouting ended, Izzy panted for a few seconds. Instead of just going up to her room, locking the door and putting on her music as loud as she could, she headed downstairs. She flipped on the lights and illuminated the room and the bar. Izzy grabbed her phone, used the Bluetooth to connect to the speakers throughout the room, and put her music on loudly. She heard the constant interruptions of her music with the notifications of text messages coming in from Amber, Allison, Brianna, Bradley, and other friends, all wondering where she was and what she was doing.

She ignored each one that came and made the music louder. As she danced around and shed some of the pent-up aggression she felt, she came to a stop as the song ended and found herself staring at the bar.

"No time like the present," Izzy said out loud as she shrugged. She hopped behind the bar and grabbed the first bottle she got her hands on. Izzy examined the Jameson's Irish whiskey label, but the reality was she cared little about what its contents were. She twisted the cap open, put the bottle to her lips, and took a long swig. The alcohol burned right away as it made its way past her lips and down her throat. She coughed and choked and wondered why anyone would drink something like this in the first place, but that did not stop her from having more. And more. And more.

Izzy was unsure how much she had drunk, but her head swam, and she forgot all about Bradley, school, her birthday, and everything else. She slumped onto the couch, clutching the half-empty bottle in one hand. After a moment, her slump progressed further, and she was on her side on the sofa with the bottle dangling in her hand. Izzy looked around the room and tried to focus her vision on something, anything, that might help keep the room from spinning so much. It was then she noticed the bookcase on the far wall.

Izzy pushed herself off the couch and found her way to the bookcase with a few staggering steps. The shelf with photo albums on it was at eye level, and she pulled one off and started to flip through it. Pictures of her childhood filled the book. She saw photos of when she was five or six, many with her grandparents and some with her Dad, even a few of him in his baseball uniform at the stadium. Izzy also came upon several pictures of her and her mother. One thing was prominent in many of the photos with her Mom – her mother never seemed to smile.

Izzy kept flipping page after page and then brought the album over to the bar so she could sit on one of the bar chairs without having to try to balance the whiskey bottle and photo album. It was then that in the back of her mind, Izzy thought she heard the door open.

"Izzy? Are you down here?"

Izzy turned her head towards the staircase and saw Melissa descend the stairs with Molly propped on her arm.

"Hey, Mel!" Izzy yelled over the music. She waved hurriedly and got up out of the chair. She wobbled over to Melissa and Molly.

"How's my little sister?" Izzy slurred as she kissed Molly's cheek.

"Why are you home?" Melissa asked. "And how much have you had to drink?"

"Oh, not that much," Izzy giggled as she grabbed the bottle off the bar and shook it in front of Melissa's face.

"I see," Melissa said with concern. "Let me go put Molly in the playpen, and I'll be right back down, okay?"

"You bet!" Izzy shouted. "We can share a drink."

"Uh-huh," Melissa said as she spied Izzy sitting back down at the bar.

Melissa jogged up the stairs and placed Molly in her playpen in the living room. She made sure to grab the baby monitor and a few towels that she thought she might need to have with her.

By the time Melissa got back downstairs, Izzy had already helped herself to some more whiskey. Melissa reached over and grabbed the bottle.

"I think you've probably had enough for now," Melissa said, taking the bottle and looking for the top. Unable to find it, she placed the whiskey out of Izzy's reach for now.

"Come on, don't you want any?" Izzy asked her.

"No, I'm good, thanks," Melissa said to her. "I don't think you should have had any to start with."

"Of course not," Izzy slurred, slamming her hand down on the bar and startling Melissa. "That's what everyone expects from me. I'm a good girl who always does the right thing. Nothing but a prude, right? Maybe I'm really more like her than my Dad than people think." Izzy pointed at one of the pictures in the photo album of her and her mother sitting out on the back patio.

"Who is that?" Melissa said as she looked at the picture. "Is that your Mom?"

"Sure is," Izzy said before she quickly slammed the photo album closed. "She wasn't a good girl, not by a long shot. Screwing around on my Dad for a long time before taking off and leaving me behind basically by myself. And now here I am, alone again."

"You're not alone, Izzy. You have your Dad, Kristin, your grandparents, Molly, and me. You have all your friends, you have Bradley..."

Izzy held up her index finger shakily.

"That's where you can stop Mel," Izzy said to her. "Seems I didn't have Bradley at all for the last few months and my friends, either."

"Oh," Melissa said as she got closer to Izzy. "Is that what this is all about?"

Izzy nodded when she heard Prince come on her playlist over the speakers.

"I love this song!" she shouted. She spun out of the bar chair and grabbed Melissa's hands.

"Let's dance!" Izzy yelled.

"Maybe that's not such a good idea right now," Melissa cautioned.

Izzy twirled in circles a few times before landing in Melissa's arms. Melissa did all she could to prevent Izzy from falling over.

"You okay?" Melissa asked.

"I think so," Izzy laughed. Izzy paused for a moment. "Nope, I'm not okay. I'm gonna puke."

Melissa rushed Izzy over to the bathroom on the far side of the room. No sooner had she gotten the door open, and Izzy vomited all over herself and the bathroom floor. Melissa steered the two of them closer to the toilet, lifted the lid, and let Izzy continue as she hugged the bowl.

Melissa reached over and pulled Izzy's long red hair back and away from her face. Strands of hair already clung to Izzy's cheeks as she wretched more.

When it looked like there was a pause in the action, Melissa went over to the towel rack and grabbed the towel that was there, laying it on the floor so that it soaked up the vomit on it. She placed the hand towel in the sink and ran cold water on it. She used that towel to wipe down Izzy's face and neck.

"How are you doing?" Melissa asked.

"This is awful," Izzy bemoaned. "Why do people do this?"

Melissa tried not to laugh.

"Good question," Melissa told her. "Most people don't try to drink half a bottle their first time out, and if they do, they end up just like this. Do you think you're done?"

"Can't I just stay here?" Izzy lamented. "The bowl feels nice and cool on my head."

"I know, but it's better if we get you upstairs to your room, I think. I can't leave Molly by herself, and this needs cleaning up before your Dad gets home. You need to sleep a bit before dinner tonight."

"Ugh, I can't even think about food," Izzy said as another small stream of vomit went from her mouth to the toilet.

"Okay," Melissa conceded. "you stay here for a few minutes while I straighten up and check on Molly. Just yell if you need me."

Izzy nodded and rested her head against the toilet and closed her eyes. Vibrant colors streamed across her closed eyelids, and she shut them tighter, hoping to block them out, so it didn't make her stomach churn again. Izzy was unsure just how much time passed, but it seemed like Melissa was back in an instant.

"How are we doing, Izzy?" Melissa asked.

Izzy lifted her head and peered at Melissa through barely opened eyes. She could see that Melissa had towels and a mop and must have just finished cleaning.

"Do you think you're ready to move now?"

"Do I have to?" Izzy whined.

"Yeah, you do. You need to be in bed and rest. Come on, I'll help you."

Melissa tossed the towels in the sink and put the mop down before she moved toward Izzy to assist her in rising from the floor.

Izzy stood and took small steps forward and out the bathroom door, trying not to slip on the damp spot on the floor that Melissa had just cleaned. Izzy struggled to focus on any one thing, but she saw that Melissa had straightened downstairs, putting everything back in its proper place.

"You're going to have to go up the stairs yourself," Melissa told her. "There isn't enough room for me to stand next to you. Don't worry, I'll be right behind you."

Izzy moved carefully, one step at a time, clutching the handrail before she made it to the top. Melissa then was next to her again to help maneuver through the living room to the flight of stairs leading up toward her room. Izzy glanced as they went past Molly's playpen, where Molly lay comfortably asleep now.

"More stairs?" Izzy complained. "Can't I just stay down here on the couch. It looks so comfy."

"It might not be the best way for your father to discover you. It's not that far. We can do it."

Melissa kept Izzy moving, pausing on each step so that they reached the top without incident. Melissa then guided Izzy toward her bedroom, where Izzy did all she could to get through the door and flop onto her bed.

Melissa disappeared for a moment before coming back into Izzy's room.

"Izzy?" Melissa asked loudly.

"Hmmm," Izzy replied as she buried her face into her pillow to stall the pounding in her head.

Melissa sat on the bed next to Izzy and pulled her hair back before tying it into a ponytail with a hairband she had on her wrist.

"There's a bottle of water on your nightstand for you," Melissa told her. "Hydrate, and you might feel better. I put a couple of ibuprofens there too that might help with the headache you are going to have. I brought your phone up and plugged it in. You have a ton of messages on there. I think everything is picked up as well, so get some rest."

"You're the best, Melissa. I love you," Izzy garbled through her pillow.

"I love you, too," Melissa smiled. "You may not think I'm the best, though. Your Dad and Kristin will be home shortly, and they are bound to ask about you. You know I have to tell them the truth. I can try to soften it for you as best as I can, but I can't lie about it. You understand that, right?"

"I know. It's gonna be bad."

"Maybe, and I'm sorry for that," Melissa told her. "Get some rest, and we'll see what happens. Do you want a blanket on?"

"No, I feel like I'm in a volcano right now," Izzy replied. She kicked what blankets were underneath her off the bed.

"If you change your mind, I put one next to you on the bed."

Melissa switched off the light and turned Izzy's ceiling fan on low to blow some more cooling air on her. Even though it was February, it felt like July to Izzy.

Izzy rolled onto her side and could see the glowing light of her cell phone and heard the beeps of messages coming in. The temptation was there to pick up the phone and see the texts, see the excuses from her friends and from Bradley, but she wanted no part of it. She grabbed her phone and turned it off, putting it back on her nightstand so that her room was dark again.

Melissa hurried downstairs to the bottom floor to finish what cleaning was left. She scooped up the dirty towels, trying not to hold them too close to her face, and rushed to the washing machine so she could toss the towels in and get them out of the way. She liberally sprayed disinfectant in the bathroom to cover any residual smells, rinsed out the mop, and brought it back upstairs with her.

No sooner had she completed all her tasks when Molly roused from her nap. She picked her up and smiled at her before taking her to the changing table for a quick diaper change. While in there, Melissa heard the front door open and close, with voices trailing into the house.

"You let me do the talking, Miss Molly," Melissa whispered as she picked the smiling baby up.

Melissa entered the kitchen just ahead of Wes and Kristin.

"Hey there," Melissa said to both.

"Where is she?" Wes said sternly.

"Who? Izzy?" Melissa asked.

"Wes, calm down," Kristin pled.

"Yes, Izzy," Wes stated. "I got a call from school while I was working. I didn't listen to the message until just before I left the office. Apparently, she walked out of school right past an official and security. She better have a good reason for it."

"Mr. Martin," Melissa said calmly, "She's upstairs in her room, but there's something you need to know. Something happened with her and Bradley at school that upset her a lot. She was home when I got back after shopping with Molly."

Melissa took a deep breath before continuing.

"She was downstairs, and well... she was drinking, and then she got sick. I helped her and got her cleaned up and brought her upstairs, but..."

Wes fumed with each passing second before he turned and moved towards the stairs.

Kristin followed quickly behind Wes but could not keep up with his pace. Wes took two steps at a time and was at Izzy's door before Kristin even hit the first step.

Wes threw the door open and switched the overhead lights on.

"Isabelle!" Wes roared.

Izzy lifted her head, blinded by the brightness of the light suddenly in the room. She blinked several times to clear her vision when she saw her father standing in the doorway.

"This is how you decided to celebrate turning eighteen? By leaving school early to come home and get drunk? What were you thinking? I can guarantee you will be grounded until your next birthday. You can forget about going out with friends or on dates with Bradley for a long time."

The lump in Izzy's throat finally let loose, and she started crying.

"That's fine," she said through her sobs. "It's not like I have any friends or a boyfriend left anyway."

Wes saw the smeared makeup around Izzy's eyes as her tears fell rapidly.

Wes softened his tone a bit and sat down on the bed next to his daughter.

"What's going on, Izzy? This isn't like you at all. You are always so responsible and..."

"And what?" Izzy said with frustration. "always reliable and the good girl? Good old Izzy – you can count on her to do anything and everything for you, but when she needs someone, there is no one there."

"Hey, that's not fair," Wes answered. "You know Kristin and I are always here for you if you need something. It sounds like Melissa went above and beyond to help you today too. I'm sorry if something happened with your friends and Bradley. I know it sucks when things fall apart like that. But that's no excuse for doing what you did. Leaving school, I can forgive. But coming home and drinking like that could have been dangerous for you, and Melissa and Molly when they got back. You know better."

Izzy rubbed her temples to make the pain in her head go away while her father kept talking. She picked up bits and pieces of what he was saying, and Izzy knew he had good intentions, but it was turning more and more into a lecture she didn't have the patience for. She also knew to provoke him would do no good, so she nodded in agreement when she thought it was appropriate.

"I think, given the circumstances and how you look like you feel, going out to dinner tonight might not be the best idea," Wes told her.

"I agree," Izzy said, stifling a burp that felt like it might bring something else up.

"We are going to talk more about this, right?"

"Yes, Dad," Izzy said as she flipped her pillow over, hoping the cool side of it would make her feel better.

Wes rose from the bed and walked out of the room, passing Kristin, who was now standing in the doorway watching. Kristin walked over to the side of the bed and sat down. She placed her hand on Izzy's back and gently rubbed.

"You okay?" Kristin asked quietly.

"Not really," Izzy sniffed.

"Oh honey, I don't know what happened, and I know it's breaking your heart right now, but it will get better. That much I can promise you."

"It sure doesn't seem like it right now, Kris."

Izzy rolled onto her back so she could look at Kristin.

Kristin grabbed a tissue off the nightstand and wiped the running mascara off Izzy's face.

"Do you want to put on something different? Maybe getting the smell away from you might help you feel better," Kristin offered with a small smile.

"That seems like a lot of effort," Izzy moaned.

Kristin walked over to Izzy's dresser and pulled out a blue t-shirt and a pair of shorts.

"Want help?"

Izzy's head flopped into a nod, and she lifted her hands like a toddler. Kristin helped her to change, taking the blouse and skirt, along with a few other items she saw on the floor that needed washing.

"It feels good to have that stuff off," Izzy said as she cuddled back into bed.

"Drink some water before you go back to sleep," Kristin advised, handing Izzy the water bottle on her nightstand.

Izzy took a long draw on the bottle, and the water tasted better than water ever had before as it soothed her parched throat.

"Thanks, Kris," Izzy told her before laying back down.

"Sure, Izzy," Kristin told her before giving her a kiss on the forehead. "Get some rest."

Kristin turned the lights off, and Izzy got underneath one of the blankets on her bed. She wanted nothing more than to just go to sleep and forget about everything that happened.

***

Kristin got downstairs and went right down to the laundry room to put the rank clothing she held in her hands into the wash. Melissa had already set the towels she had used to clean up into the dryer. When Kristin arrived in the kitchen, Wes was there, still brooding a bit, with a beer bottle in his hand. Melissa busily prepared Molly's small dinner of cereal, vegetables, and fruit.

"How is she?" Melissa asked as she mixed the cereal together.

"Hurting, physically, and mentally. I wish I knew what happened," Kristin said as she down next to Molly's highchair.

"It makes me want to go over to Bradley's house and..." Wes said as he bent the bottle cap from his beer bottle.

"And what?" Kristin said. "Threaten a kid, so you get arrested? That's not the answer either. It will all work itself out, Wes."

Melissa approached the kitchen table and offered the plate she had to Kristin.

"Do you want to feed her?" she asked Kristin.

"Thanks," Kristin said with a smile. She began offering small spoonfuls of the mix of vegetables and cereal to a smiling Molly.

"Since we aren't going out tonight," Melissa stated, "if you don't need me for anything else, do you mind if I go? I have a lot of packing and stuff I need to do at Dad's house."

"Of course, Melissa," Kristin insisted, "Thank you so much for all you did today. That goes above and beyond."

"Oh, it's no trouble. I remember what it was like for me. It hasn't been that long ago that I was in the same boat."

Melissa retrieved her coat from the closet and put her bag together to head out. Kristin reached over and gave Wes a kick to get his attention, and then mouthed 'Ask her' to him as he grabbed his sore shin.

"Melissa, wait," Wes said as he stood up. "Can you have a seat for a minute before you go?"

"Sure," she answered, grasping her bag. "Is everything okay? I am sorry about everything with Izzy. I probably should have called one of you right away when I saw her, but I thought I could..."

"No, no," Wes responded. "You did more than you needed to do, really. Kristin and I just wanted to talk to you about our arrangement."

"Did I do something wrong?"

"Not at all," Kristin interrupted. "We're thrilled to have you here, and Molly loves you."

"Kris told me about selling your father's house and needing somewhere to go," Wes began. "We have plenty of room here and would be happy to have you stay with us as a live-in if you are comfortable with it. We can work out your schedule, so you have time for yourself when you want or need it. You can have full use of the house, downstairs, the pool, and anything else, and you are more than welcome to join us for meals, outings, vacations, or whatever you want to be a part of."

Melissa sat for a moment without saying anything.

"So, what do you think?" Kristin asked anxiously. "You can have your pick of the empty room upstairs, whichever you want."

"That's an amazing offer," Melissa replied. "Are you sure you both are okay with that? I don't want to get in the way around here."

Kristin scooted her chair closer to Melissa's.

"Melissa, you are part of our family, and this is our way of showing how important you are to all of us. Wes and I had decided to ask you even before all this happened today, but the way you helped Izzy just convinces us even more. We want you here if you want to be here."

Melissa looked from Kristin to Wes to Molly, who was smiling at Melissa with cereal smeared over her face.

"Well, how can I say no to that?" Melissa said with a laugh. "Thank you both so much. I guess I better get home and start packing stuff up."

"We can talk about specifics tomorrow," Wes told her as he walked Melissa to the door. "We're happy to hire movers to come and get your things for you and help."

"Thank you, Mr. Martin," Melissa told him as they stood by the door.

"Melissa, you can call us Wes and Kristin, you know," he said with a laugh.

"Okay... Wes," she smiled. "I'll see you tomorrow morning.

Melissa headed out to her car as Wes returned to the kitchen, where Kristin had moved on to giving Molly some pureed plums.

"She's a wonderful girl," Kristin said as Wes sat down at the table.

"Yes, she is. I think it will be best for all of us, but especially for Izzy. She might need some extra supervision right now, and having someone close to her age could be good."

"You might be jumping to conclusions, Wes," Kristin told him. "This is probably just an isolated incident brought on by a lot of stress. You were eighteen once, too, all those years ago." Kristin smiled at him.

"It wasn't that long ago," Wes said. "I didn't go to school with George Washington or anything you know. I'm just hoping for a little calm around here for a change."

"You're going to be living in a house with four females," Kristin chided. "There will always be plenty going on."

Wes rolled his eyes and took a long sip of his beer.

***

The double ding from Izzy's cell phone rang louder than she thought it should. It was more from the first hangover she had ever had than anything else. Izzy made out the numbers on her alarm clock and saw that it was just after three in the morning. She had slept soundly for almost eleven hours now and felt like she could sleep at least ten more.

The cottonmouth she experienced made her mouth arid. Izzy picked up the water bottle and drained what was left in it into her body. She sat up in bed, looking down at the t-shirt and shorts she wore, not remembering how she got them on. She also was less than thrilled with the smell that seemed all around her, including in her hair, on her face, and on her hands. Izzy turned her bedside light on, putting it on the lowest setting as her eyes adjusted to the brightness, and picked up her phone.

There were countless messages on her phone, with a combination of birthday wishes and concerns about her. Still, the two that had just come in that woke her up are what caught her attention the most.

The first was just a simple text message from an unknown phone number: *Happy Birthday.*

It was odd that it was from an unknown number, but what struck Izzy as stranger was the next notification. It was an announcement of a deposit into her PayPal account, the account her father had set up for her, so she always had access to cash if she needed it. This deposit didn't come from her father or anyone she knew. It was from an email address she didn't recognize, pluckaduck@gmail.com. The sender was unknown, and the amount just stared Izzy in the face - $10,000.

Chapter 10

I zzy spent the next few days caught in a whirlwind. She had no desire to even go to school on the 12th. She did all she could to avoid it, pleading with her father that she felt lousy and didn't want to face her friends, Bradley, and any other witnesses. Unfortunately for Izzy, Wes did not view the situation the same way. He insisted she go and that she would have to face it at some point, and the hangover effects she experienced in the morning were adequate punishment for her behavior the day before. Wes did, however, restrict Izzy on what she could do after school, insisting she come right home to do homework and help Melissa as she transitioned to live-in status.

"Melissa is moving in?" Izzy asked with some surprise.

"Yes, Kris and I discussed it, and we asked her last night after you were... well, you were upstairs. We thought it would be best for Molly and for Melissa since she needed a place to go. It might be beneficial to you too, Izzy."

"How is it beneficial to me?"

"Having someone around close to your age and experiences. It might give you someone to talk to if Kris and I aren't around. You like Melissa, don't you?" Wes inquired as he poured coffee into his travel mug.

Izzy hesitated for a moment.

"Yeah, of course, I do," she told her father. "I just didn't realize she would be living here."

"And Melissa has agreed to pick you up from school each day," Wes added matter-of-factly.

"Wait... what? Why do I need to be picked up? I have my car."

"Not while you're grounded, you don't. No vehicle until I am convinced otherwise. Sorry, Izzy, but it's your own fault. You come home right after classes are done."

"But Dad," Izzy insisted, "What about the musical? I have rehearsals for Beauty and the Beast, and I'm playing Belle. I have to be there!"

Wes considered this for a moment as he sipped his coffee.

"Come on, I'll drive you to school, and we can talk about it."

Izzy begrudgingly picked up her bag and followed her father. Wes blew a kiss as they passed the bedroom door, where Kristin was nursing Molly. Kristin was going in late today so that Melissa could take time to finalize the sale of her father's house and be there for movers to pick up her things.

Izzy gave a slight wave to Kristin as she went by the door, letting Kristin know that she was dreading the rides to school in the morning.

The first few minutes of the ride were done in complete silence, with only the crackle of the news station Wes had on the radio spurting through to talk about the warm spell in the weather that was expected for Valentine's Day this year. Izzy put her Air Pods in and tried to lose herself in her music so that the ride would end quickly without many conversations.

"You do understand why I have to be strict about this, right?" Wes asked before he realized Izzy was listening to music and had her eyes closed. He tapped Izzy on the leg to get her attention, so she took one of the earpieces out and listened again.

"I do, Dad," Izzy replied. "I know I made mistakes – dumb ones. But you also know I am not like that. There were extenuating circumstances."

"The problem is that can't be the response every time something happens that you don't like or know how to deal with. You're eighteen now, Izzy. You want me to treat you like a young adult, then you need to act the part. I'm willing to make exceptions for the musical because I know how important it is for you, but I need to see the schedule, the times, and you will still get picked up by whoever is available until I feel I can trust you with your car again. I think that's being more than fair to you."

Izzy realized that this was the best sentence she was going to get for her crimes and nodded her head.

Wes had instinctively started to slow down when they reached Bradley's driveway, thinking they needed to pick him up until Izzy glared at him.

"Dad, what are you doing? You can't pick him up."

"Good enough for me," Wes answered, pulling away from the driveway just as he saw Bradley's silhouette crossing in front of the driveway lights as he tried to catch up to them.

"I don't know how I'm going to do this today," Izzy whispered.

Wes got Chandler High School and got his car in line to reach the front door.

"You'll be okay, Izzy," Wes said, as he tried to reassure his daughter but wasn't clear on just what to say. "Do you... you need anything?"

"Yeah, a ride back home... or a time machine to go back and erase yesterday," Izzy told him.

"Well, I can't provide you with either of those," Wes chuckled. "How about lunch money?" Wes began to reach into his coat for his wallet.

It was then Izzy thought more about the weird, enormous deposit into her PayPal account. She had not investigated it seriously because she thought it was some kind of joke or phishing scam. Still, she also didn't mention it to anyone else.

"No... I'm good, Dad. Thanks." Izzy hopped out of the car and took a quick look around, making sure she didn't see any friends so she could get to her locker and to class before others, especially Bradley, tried to cut her off. She made a beeline to her locker, exchanged books, grabbed what she needed, and closed up.

Izzy walked past Bradley's locker to get to her history class, and there she spied Eden standing and waiting for Bradley. Eden was wearing what Izzy thought was an obscenely short skirt, and Eden flashed Izzy a wicked smile and waved her long, pointed fingers at her. Izzy turned as fast as she could do get down the hall.

Izzy was able to get through her first two classes without any of her friends there. However, she knew there was whispering going on behind her about "the girl who lost it" in school yesterday in the cafeteria.

Even when she got to her math class and saw Amber, she did her best to put off talking to her and said they could hash things out lunch. Lunch arrived later, and as Izzy walked into the cafeteria, she was greeted by Mr. Larsen, the balding vice principal who she shot past when she left the school.

"I trust we'll have no incidents today, Ms. Martin?" Mr. Larsen said snootily.

Izzy painted the fakest smile she had on her face and walked by without saying a word so she could get to her customary lunch table. She tossed her bag on the table, slouched into a chair, and picked up her cell phone.

Her first move was to block Bradley from sending her any more messages. He hadn't stopped, though they had tapered off since yesterday, and Izzy was tired of hearing the beeps. She then opened her PayPal again to look at the transactions. The $10,000 was still there, staring at her. She saw the email it was from again and could not figure out who it was. Even the name attached to the account was as anonymous as possible – J. Smith LLC.

Amber walked behind Izzy, carrying her day's lunch tray, and saw the numbers on Izzy's screen.

"Whoa? Your Dad gave you ten grand? I have to start cutting out of school too," she said too loudly for Izzy's liking.

"Amber, shush," Izzy scolded. "It's not from Dad. I don't know who it's from. I don't even think it's real."

"Think what's real?" Allison said as she and Brianna slowly sat down in their chairs.

"Someone gave Izzy $10,000," Amber said excitedly.

"No way!" Allison shouted before coming over to the other side of the table where Izzy sat so she could see the phone. "Forget musical rehearsals, Izzy. Let's rent a limo and go over to Pittsburgh and shop!"

"We're not doing anything," Izzy said pragmatically. "It has to be a scam of some kind. Even the email and name on the account seem made up."

Brianna asked if she could see the phone and look at it, and Izzy obliged.

"You could always call PayPal and ask them about it," Brianna said. "Or try sending an email to the email account and see if you get a response."

"What if they want you to do that?" Allison told her. "then they set up a meeting or something, and you end up getting kidnapped by some creepy guy and sold to some sheik in Saudi Arabia."

"Stop watching those movies, Ally," Amber told her.

"I'm not going to do anything with it," Izzy said, putting her phone down. "I've got enough to deal with right now. Who knows what it's all about."

Izzy then walked up to get her lunch, opting for just yogurt and some fruit today. As she was walking away from the cashier, she had a tug on her arm pull her back. She spun around, and it was Bradley.

"Izzy, please talk to me," Bradley pled.

"Not a chance, Bradley. Go sit with Eden and have fun talking about me." Izzy tried to keep walking, but Bradley stepped in front of her again.

"Izzy, we let all of this get out of control," Bradley stated.

"What's out of control, Bradley?" Izzy said as she got louder. "That you cheated on me with Eden, or that you got caught trying to date two girls at once. I'd love to know. And what is the "we" part? I didn't do anything to you. I thought I was in love with you."

Izzy pushed past Bradley once again before he caught up again.

"You... you didn't give me any choice!" Bradley shouted, not knowing what else to say.

"What?" Izzy yelled, putting her tray down on the nearest table so she could put her hands on her hips and decipher Bradley's excuse.

"We went out for over a year, Izzy and... and, well, nothing ever happened, at all. Kissing, and that was it. I got... frustrated, I guess."

"That's the excuse you're taking into battle with you?" Izzy replied. "You know what, Bradley? You did me a favor. You're not nearly as nice or as smart as I thought you were. If the only reason you broke up with... oh, wait, you didn't break up with me. You just cheated. If the only reason you cheated on me was that I didn't have sex with you, then you're a shallow prick. Go back to Eden and have a good time."

Izzy reached over, picked up her tray, and then grabbed a milk carton from the guy sitting at the table.

"Can I borrow this?" she asked as he just nodded at her.

She opened the carton and proceeded to pour it all over the front of Bradley's pants. Kids turned and looked, laughed, and clapped as she emptied the milk onto her stunned ex-boyfriend.

As Izzy turned to go, Mr. Larsen walked up to her and the commotion.

"Is there a problem, Ms. Martin?" He asked.

"Not at all, Mr. Larsen," she said, batting her eyelashes. "But I think Bradley had some kind of accident. You may want to take him down to the nurse."

Izzy spun on her heels and walked back to her friends triumphantly.

***

Kristin had placed Molly down in her crib, an item that still resided in Wes' and Kristin's bedroom for the time being. Now that Melissa was moving in and had chosen one of the rooms upstairs, Kristin began to make plans to decorate one of the other rooms so that it could be Molly's. However, she needed to add this to the ever-growing list of tasks she was undertaking.

Many days appeared lately where it seemed like maybe Kristin had more than she could handle alone. Work was busy as usual, with more library programs to arrange than ever before. The library had become more popular than ever in recent months as families looked for things to do together in their small town, and Kristin did her best to keep everyone educated, informed, and entertained. She was continually booking new programs for adults and children alike. She had recently made sure to line up programs for the spring when the weather would be more beautiful so she could keep the crowds that came in the cold winter months coming back to the library.

On top of work, there was the turmoil going on at home with Izzy. Kristin tried to let Wes handle things by himself at times, but Kristin had also made a concerted effort to act more like a de facto parent and less like a friend to Izzy. Even though she and Wes weren't married yet, Kristin knew the importance of acting like a parent for Izzy with all that was going on. She did her best to step in when she thought it was appropriate. It also made her feel good that Wes consulted with and included her on decisions regarding Izzy, even if Izzy wasn't that much younger than her.

Having Melissa in the house would help Kristin and the family in more ways than just with Molly. Kristin knew that Melissa could become the sister and confidante that Izzy might need right now, a role that Kristin found herself in when she and Wes were just getting their footing together. Melissa's presence might make it easier for Kristin to transition into more of a parental role.

And then there was the wedding. There never seemed to be enough time for Kristin to plan things out the way she wanted to. While they knew all along that they wanted to have the wedding outdoors on the farm in September, it was February, and Kristin had done little so far in the way of booking anything for the date. Many evenings came along where she would open the journal where she wrote down plans and ideas for the wedding and kept contact information. Still, with work hours, Molly, recovery from the surgery, and everything else, she rarely had the energy to do anything.

Today was different, and with Molly asleep and Kristin home from work so that Melissa could get moved in, she had time to do things. Kristin had a stack of bride magazines, pages pinned on Pinterest, and ideas she had in her head that she had jotted down to go through about everything from table decorations to music, food, and more. Kristin had begun to jot down a list of names of who she wanted to invite before she realized there weren't many from her side of the family. Outside of her sister and her parents, she had little in the way of relatives that she knew even slightly, let alone well enough to invite to her wedding. Friends were also just a few outside of Karen here in Chandler. Kristin had some girlfriends in college, but she had not kept in touch with them much since getting out of school and moving to Pennsylvania.

When Kristin considered her side of the wedding, it looked minuscule compared to what she assumed Wes would have. Wes also had a small family, but he was royalty in Chandler and knew everyone in the area. He also had met so many people from his baseball career that Kristin had no idea who he might want to invite. She suddenly had visions of row upon row of guests on Wes' side of the aisle while she had ten people. The thought made her a little anxious.

On top of that anxiety was picking a gown. Kristin had ideas of the type of dress she wanted to wear, but she had yet to see it on any website or magazine. To make matters worse, she wasn't feeling at her best to look for a gown. Kristin still had twinges of pain from the surgery that lingered, and those made her fearful of doing too much exercise to help tone her body the way she wanted it. No matter how many times Wes told her how beautiful she was, in the back of her mind, she didn't feel it. Between the surgery and post-baby weight, her confidence was not where it usually was.

Kristin heard the lock on the front door turn and left the kitchen to peek who it was. She made sure to close the bedroom door, so Molly might sleep, and saw Melissa coming through with a few suitcases in tow.

"Welcome home," Kristin said with a smile.

"Thanks," Melissa told her, placing her suitcases down away from the door. "I thought we would stop here first to drop off the things I want before bringing the rest over to the storage unit I rented."

"Sure," Kristin added as two burly movers walked through the door behind Melissa.

"Wow," the younger of the two movers said as he walked in and looked around the large house. "Is this really Wes Martin's house?"

The older of the movers, tall and robust with a well-trimmed beard, elbowed his co-worker.

"My apologies, ladies," the man said politely as he wiped his feet on the mat inside the door. "Where are we bringing the items?"

"Upstairs, second door down the hall on the left," Melissa said as she pointed up the staircase.

The younger mover looked with trepidation as he realized they would have to carry the bed, dresser, and other items up the long flight of stairs.

"Not a problem," the older mover, who's name on his coveralls read Jerome, stated confidently. "Let's go, Keith," he ordered his partner as they moved back out to the truck.

"How's everything going?" Kristin asked Melissa.

"Good," she sighed. "I signed the papers on the sale of the house last night, so that's all done. We had all kinds of trucks out to the house to take some of Dad's old stuff that we donated away, things that were going to storage, stuff my brother was taking, and then what was coming here. I'm sure the neighbors thought it was an invasion, but the new owners were going to move in tomorrow, so I needed to get it all done. I can't thank you and Wes enough for all this."

"Please, Melissa, you don't have to thank us," Kristin insisted. "I should be thanking you for being willing to do all that you do for us. Want some tea?"

"That would be great," Melissa said as the movers came in with her oak dresser and began to lug it carefully up the stairs.

Melissa followed Kristin into the kitchen and sat as Kristin put the tea kettle on the stove. Melissa flipped through the stack of bridal magazines she saw on the table.

"Wedding plans today?" Melissa asked as she slowly leafed through the pages.

"Yes, at least that's what I am trying to do while Molly sleeps," Kristin said with exasperation. "It's not coming along too well, though."

"What's wrong?" Melissa asked.

"I don't know," Kristin admitted. "It's been challenging to get into the swing of it. I've thought about this time since I was little, but now that it's here, I can't seem to decide on anything or find just what I want. It's been frustrating, and we only have six months until the wedding day."

"I can see what you mean," Melissa said as she lifted one of the magazines. "This thing weighs ten pounds and has a thousand pages. It would take a week just to look through it."

"And that's just one magazine," Kristin bemoaned as she brought over the hot cups of tea and sat across from Melissa. "There are a million more suggestions online to look at, too. Every time I think I see something I might want, my eyes catch something else, and I second-guess."

"I don't know how much help I would be, but I'd give you a hand with whatever you need," Melissa responded as she sipped her tea.

"Let's get you settled in first before worrying about all this stuff," Kristin added as she tossed the magazines to the other side of the table. "I'm sure we can come up with a way to pull it all together." Kristin rolled her neck back and forth to ease some of the kinks she had.

"You know what might help you get rid of some that stress?" Melissa said.

"Chocolate chip cookies?" Kristin asked with a smile.

"For sure!" Melissa exclaimed. "But I was thinking more about yoga."

"I don't know," Kristin hesitated. "I don't know if I could go to a yoga studio. I feel out of shape as it is. That might make me more self-conscious."

"We don't have to go to a studio," Melissa told her. "I do it every other day from home. There are some great websites and videos we can follow to do it. It will be fun, and you will feel so much better. We can try some tonight if you want once everything is done. I know I could use it."

Kristin considered the question for a minute before approving.

"Okay, I'll give it a try."

"Fantastic!" Melissa said. "Now, let's make those chocolate chip cookies before Miss Molly wakes up."

***

Wes spent a large part of the day in Tom Killian's office as the two of them continued to fine-tune the roster for the Wild Thing's upcoming season. They had decided to bring back the core of players that they could, though a few had moved on to minor league teams that might give them a better path to get to the majors. There were still lists of recent college graduates, players from past minor league or independent teams, and even a few major league players that might be looking for one last shot just as Wes was.

Wes stood up from his chair and stretched before he paced the office a bit, looking at stats of potential pitchers to sign.

"I don't know how much more I can look at on these pages, Tom," Wes admitted. "All the numbers are starting to blur together."

"We just have to go over a few more names," Tom insisted. "If I can get a list of about twenty to approach, we can be finished with potential roster candidates."

"What do we do after that?" Wes asked, still working his way into this new part of baseball for him.

"I make some calls, set up meetings, and try to get players to come in and talk to us," Tom said. "Sometimes, we need to go on the road to meet guys to convince them. I hope you're up for that, too. I thought it might be good for us to travel up to see some of the stadiums of the newer clubs anyway. It might give you the layout, so you know what to expect."

"Is that necessary?" Wes responded. "I used to go to new ballparks all the time and just go in cold. I don't need to see what the places look like three months before we play a game there."

"Okay, it's not entirely necessary," Tom admitted. "I thought it would be good publicity for us and the league for other places to see that you are the manager. It might help to sell tickets for the road teams and bring us some press. It's all part of the job, Wes. I never did with John Clines because he wasn't a well-known player like you were... I mean are," as Tom tried to correct himself.

The slip did not go unnoticed by Wes.

"It's okay to say were, Tom," Wes said resignedly. "I've been thinking a lot about what you said about the player-manager thing, and I don't know how well it will work. I'd feel weird writing my name on a lineup card. Maybe it's best if we just give me the manager title, and that's it."

"Come on, Wes," Tom chided. "Selling it as a player-manager is a big deal. It hasn't been done in the majors since Pete Rose, and I think people will be intrigued about it. Think about you coming off the bench in the last inning to hit the winning home run..."

"Or to strike out to end the game," Wes interrupted. "And then I can see everyone second-guess me why I didn't have a younger guy come up instead. Every time I bat, people will think it's just an ego thing."

"Wes, don't decide on anything now, okay?" Tom pled. "We have three months until our first game, so you haven't plenty of time to make that call. For now, let's just leave it the way it is and see how it plays out. Just the idea of it has already helped us sell more season tickets this year. I think we can expect good crowds all the time."

"I get it, Tom," Wes conceded. "We can leave it for now, but I'm not making any promises about it."

"Fair enough," Tom smiled. "Now I just have one more question about the pitcher, Joe Johnson. I think he might be an excellent addition to the team. He's a Pittsburgh kid, he had good stats in high school, and for the one year he did in junior college. I'd like to go and talk to him. He lives locally, so we don't even have to travel far to go see him."

Wes scanned the statistics for Joe Johnson to see what he was all about. Tom was correct in saying the kid had potential. His stats in high school were out of this world good, good enough where Wes was surprised he didn't get a scholarship to a Division I school. Instead, Johnson went to Washington County Center, the community college in Washington. He pitched lights out for them last season, leaving Wes wondering why he would even want to leave school to play independent baseball.

"How is this kid even available?" Wes said with surprise. "He looks like he has the talent to be pitching Division I, or even in the minors somewhere else. I don't get it."

"I'm not sure," Tom told Wes. "All I know is that Johnson has turned down other offers, and he didn't even enroll for the fall semester at CCAC. He's at least worth talking to so we can find out if he's interested."

"Okay, set it up," Wes agreed. "Are we done for the day, Tom? I'm beat, and I need to get home. We've got a lot going on today."

"Just a couple of more things," Tom said before Wes could grab the jacket off the back of Tom's office door.

Wes let out an elongated sigh.

"First, you need to find a pitching coach," Tom said. "Will Penny, John's coach, followed him to his new job. Now, I don't have a huge budget for the coaching job, but if you can find someone interested in the job that you know and like, great. Otherwise, I can start lining up interviews of candidates."

"Let me think about it a bit, and I'll let you know," Wes said, firmly grasping his jacket this time.

"Okay," Tom said, looking at his calendar. "How's Friday for the meeting?"

"Tom, I'm not doing it on Friday," Wes answered emphatically.

"Why not?"

"Friday is Valentine's Day," Wes spoke. "I want to spend time with Kris. We haven't had a lot of time together lately. Don't you want to be home with your wife?"

"With Tricia?" Tom seemed surprised by the question. "Well, sure, but she understands how it is with running the team and all."

"Let's agree to take Friday to spend with our loved ones and not each other, and I promise I'll stay player-manager for at least the first week of the season," Wes bargained.

"Deal!" Tom said as he shot out of his chair to shake Wes' hand. "I'll see you in the morning."

Wes got out of the office as fast as he could, walking past the office of Dean Kramer, the new public relations person, and the other few office employees the team had, so he could get out to his truck and start for home.

As Wes began his journey home, he spoke to the Bluetooth in his vehicle so he could call Kristin.

"Hey there," Kristin answered pleasantly.

"Hey," Wes replied. "I'm on my way home. Traffic doesn't look like it will be too bad. Is Izzy home?"

"She's at rehearsals, Wes," Kristin told him. "They don't end until six. Your Dad agreed to pick her up tonight so that I could take care of Molly. Melissa is still getting everything moved in and settled."

"I'm just checking," Wes replied. "I want to make sure she knows we're serious about everything."

"I think she gets that. You can't be like the warden in prison doing bed checks. She'll be home in time for dinner. Don't worry."

"I'm not worried," Wes asserted. "I KNOW she'll be there. I think I'm entitled to act a little bit like a warden right now, don't you?"

"The more you press this and pressure her, the worse it's going to be for all of us, Wes," Kristin explained. "She knows she screwed up and has to pay the consequences. Let's just see where it goes from here. Forget about all that stuff for a minute. Molly's been babbling more today. I think she is almost ready to say, Mama, isn't that right sweet thing?" Kristin had her high-pitched sing-song voice on that she used when talking to Molly.

Wes heard Molly in the background babbling.

"Sounds more like 'Da Da' to me," Wes said proudly.

"We'll see about that," Kristin challenged.

"Is Melissa all moved in?" Wes inquired as he drove.

"All the moving in is complete," Kristin stated. "The movers weren't thrilled with bringing everything upstairs, but it's finished. I made sure to give them a good tip. Melissa is unpacking and getting settled. She'll be back to work tomorrow, so I can get back to work tomorrow. I have stuff piling up on my desk."

"Don't forget about Friday," Wes reminded.

"What about Friday?"

"It's Valentine's Day," Wes emphasized.

"So? I still have to go to work, you know."

"Come on, Kris," Wes stated. "I have planned out the whole day for us. With Melissa and Izzy there all night, we can do what we want."

"And just what is it that you want to do, Mr. Martin?" Kristin asked coyly.

"If I have to spell it out for you, then it has been too long since we've done it."

Kristin broke out in a teasing laugh.

"I am taking a half-day Friday," she explained. "Some of our part-timers are coming in so Karen and I can both leave early. I do love getting you all riled up, though," she said playfully.

"You think this is riled up," Wes said, "just wait until Friday."

Wes changed lanes to take the exit to get closer to home.

"I'm not far from home now," Wes told Kristin. "It should only be a few more minutes. What are you wearing?" Wes added a slight growl to his voice.

"What am I wearing?" Kristin said flabbergasted. "Wes, we've had movers in the house all day, Melissa is here, and I've been taking care of Molly. What do you think I'm wearing? One of your Pirates t-shirts and a pair of sweats."

"Oh," Wes said with disappointment. "I guess that makes sense."

"But," Kristin said, speaking quieter into the phone, "I didn't say I had anything on underneath them."

"I'll be there in five minutes," Wes said urgently.

Chapter 11

V alentine's Day proceeded just as Izzy had expected it from the time she rose in the morning. She considered wearing something red and vibrant to mark the day but instead opted for a black t-shirt and blue jeans. She tied her long red hair back into a ponytail and even spurned putting any makeup on before she made her way downstairs.

Izzy walked into the kitchen and was greeted by love songs playing over the speakers, Molly dressed in a cute white dress with red hearts all over it, and Melissa making heart-shaped pancakes for everyone. Izzy did her best to hide her revulsion for the outward displays of romance that seemed to be everywhere, even with her father and Kristin kissing each other at the table.

"Hey, Happy Valentine's Day," Wes said to Izzy. Wes rose from his chair and gave his daughter a kiss on the cheek. He reached underneath the island in the kitchen and grabbed a heart-shaped box of candy to present to Izzy.

"Thanks, Dad," Izzy said, before tossing the box onto the counter. "I can't eat it, though. I have to be careful about my weight so I can be sure to fit into the costumes for the musical. If they must do last-minute alterations, Ms. Higgins will have a fit."

"Well then, it's a good thing I got this!" he exclaimed, reaching underneath the counter again to pull out a stuffed yellow duck with a ribbon around its neck. Wes held it in front of Izzy, who just stared at it.

"I appreciate the attempt, Dad," Izzy said as she moved past her father and slumped into one of the kitchen chairs.

"What?" Wes said. "Molly loved it when I gave her one, didn't you Molls?" Wes waved the duck in front of Molly, who smiled widely and held up her hands, covered with mashed bananas, to try to grab the duck.

"She loves it when you hold up a napkin to her, Dad," Izzy said as she grabbed some sliced melon from the plate and shunned the pancakes.

"Okay, I tried," Wes resigned. "I'll go get my stuff together so I can drive you to school." Wes then walked into the bedroom.

"He's trying to cheer you up, Izzy," Kristin offered as she finished her pancake. "You have to give him a break sometimes."

"I know," Izzy remarked. "I just don't feel much like fun today. Can't you drive me to school?" she asked Kristin.

"I can't, sweetie," Kristin said as she stood up. "I'm only working a half-day today, so I need to get in early to take care of things so your Dad and I can go out later. He's off all day. Besides, he likes the time with you."

Kristin gave Izzy a kiss on top of her head.

"I hope your day goes well," Kristin told her.

"Thanks," she said glumly.

Kristin then gave a big kiss to Molly, who tried desperately to grab her mother's dangling hair with her banana-crusted hands. Kristin was fast enough to grab Molly's hands first and hold them, making the baby giggle.

"See you later, my sweet," Kristin said. "Call me if you need anything, Melissa."

Melissa gave Kristin a wave goodbye as she placed dirty dishes in the sink.

Wes reappeared from the bedroom with his jacket on, holding his keys.

"Kris left already?" Wes asked, looking around.

"She just left," Melissa said as she sat down in front of Molly and began to wash her hands with a washcloth.

"I didn't even get a kiss goodbye," Wes said with disappointment. "Oh well, I guess I'll get kisses later," he said.

"Gross, Dad," Izzy said as she pushed away from the table. She walked over to Molly and gave her a kiss, blowing on her cheek to make her laugh.

"See you later, little sister," Izzy told her.

Izzy walked past her father, grabbed her backpack, and yelled, "let's get this over with, Dad," as she went out the front door.

Wes followed behind and got out to the truck with Izzy waiting impatiently for him to unlock the doors.

"Why do you have to lock your doors every night?" Izzy complained. "We live in a one-horse town, we're the only house around for miles, and you have security systems. It's ridiculous!"

Wes used the clicker to unlock the truck, and Izzy climbed in, slamming the door behind her.

Wes put his hands together in a praying motion and looked up to the sky for divine intervention.

"First of all," Wes said, "Chandler is not a one-horse town. I know for a fact there are plenty of horses here," he said as he pointed out towards the farm as they drove down the hill from the house.

"Second, there is another house close by," Wes indicated as they drove past his parents' home.

"And third, security systems won't stop everybody."

"Are you worried about Grandpa coming up the hill and stealing your truck?" Izzy argued.

"You never know," Wes lilted. "I've seen the way he looks at it sometimes."

"Your Dad humor isn't working this morning," Izzy said in an exasperated huff.

"Apparently," Wes said softly as they drove the rest of the way to school in silence.

Wes pulled up to the school, and Izzy went to jump out right away before he placed a hand on hers to stop her.

"Hey," Wes said, smiling at his daughter. "Things do get better, I promise."

"I know you're just trying, Dad," Izzy said. "Thanks."

"Don't forget," he added before the door slammed shut, "Melissa is picking you up today. I'll see you tomorrow."

"Yep," Izzy acknowledged. "Have fun."

Izzy strode through the school hall, determined not to be distracted by all the teens giving cards, flowers, and balloons to others, and people opening presents. She put her Air Pods in and turned up her music, putting Metallica on, so she was sure not to hear any love songs.

Amber and Allison both met Izzy at her locker when she arrived there. They were each wearing red and had red ribbons in their hair. Izzy did her best to control her temper.

"No red today, Izzy," Allison noted as Izzy put stuff in her locker. Amber shot Allison a glare to get her to keep quiet as Izzy slammed her locker door closed.

The three girls walked down the hall, with Amber and Allison noticing all the romantic gestures around them. At the same time, Izzy focused on just getting to class without punching someone. When they got close to Eden's locker, it was difficult to miss the bouquet of twelve red and white heart balloons she held. Eden made no pretense of walking right in front of Izzy to stop her in the hall.

"Isabelle," Eden said loudly and formally, "Did you notice what I got for Valentine's Day?"

"I'm pretty sure the whole school has by now, Eden," Izzy grumbled as she tried again to pass.

"Why, I don't see anything that you got," Eden said, pretending to look all around Izzy. "Is that because you are all alone on Valentine's Day?"

Izzy stood up straight and looked right into Eden's green eyes. Eden smirked, and that was all Izzy needed to see. A boy passing Izzy in the hallway, the same one that Izzy took milk from the other day, had a pencil sticking out of his pocket. Izzy reached over and plucked it out of his pocket, checked its sharpness against her thumb, and proceeded to press it firmly into one of the red heart balloons, popping it instantly and causing everyone to jump back.

Izzy grinned at her success as Eden looked shocked.

"Keep it up, Eden, and the next jab goes into your knee," Izzy said as she looked at the bare knees Eden's short skirt exposed.

"Well, I never!" Eden shouted as she stepped back.

"That's not what I heard," Izzy told her before she kept walking down the hall with Amber and Allison scrambling behind her.

Focusing on classes throughout the day was challenging, with girls everywhere fawning over gifts they got. Izzy knew it would be even worse at lunch, where the tradition of delivering flowers bought at school as a fundraiser existed.

Izzy did her best to eat her sandwich and ignore the circus in the cafeteria. Amber had flowers delivered to her from her boyfriend, while both Allison and Brianna got single roses from secret admirers. When Izzy thought everything was done, she pulled off her Air Pods so she could rejoin the conversation. Before she could say a word, a girl with long, curly brown hair walked up to the table with her red wagon in tow with flowers. Izzy recognized her as Cassie from the Drama Club they were both parts of.

"Hey Cassie," Amber said as she smelled her flowers.

"Hey," Cassie said. "Uhm, Izzy?"

"What's up?" Izzy asked without even looking up from her phone.

"I have flowers for you," she said with a smile.

Izzy looked over at Cassie with surprise.

"Did one of you send me a pity flower?" Izzy asked. Her girlfriends all shook their heads no.

"Okay, let me have it," Izzy sighed. She wondered if someone, maybe even Bradley, sent her one because they felt sorry for her.

Cassie reached into the wagon and took out a large bouquet of red roses and handed it to Izzy.

"Happy Valentine's!" Cassie said as she marched away, rolling her wagon behind her.

"Holy crow!" Brianna said. "There must be two dozen flowers in there. Who are they from?"

Izzy scouted around for a card before she saw one tucked between two flowers. She plucked the card out and opened it:

Happy Valentine's Day. You deserve to have the best. I hope these make your day better.

"Well?" Amber asked.

"The card doesn't say," Izzy said as she passed it to Amber, who then gave it to the other girls to read.

"Wow, you really have some secret admirer," Allison said. "First all that money, and now this. I wonder who it could be."

Izzy hadn't thought much about the money for the last two days, but she knew it was still there. She had contacted PayPal about it, afraid that it was some kind of scam or phishing, but PayPal assured her that it was legitimate and that it came from the email and account of J. Smith LLC. They couldn't or wouldn't give her any more information and trying to search for J. Smith LLC online turned up about 200 million results on Google.

Izzy leaned her head forward so she could smell the flowers, and the faint sweet scent she loved leaped out at her. She turned her head from side to side, even standing up slightly, hoping to catch a glimpse of someone looking at her with her flowers so she could figure out who they were from, but no one stood out from the crowd.

Izzy sat back down, content to have been remembered, but puzzled at what was going on.

***

When noon rolled around, Wes could barely contain himself anymore. He had put bags in the car as soon as he got back from dropping Izzy at school in the morning, and now was just biding time until he could leave. At one point, he sat in the kitchen with his jacket on, twirling his keys on his index finger while he watched Melissa give Molly her lunch.

"Mr. Martin, please don't take this the wrong way..." Melissa said politely.

"Melissa, please, call me Wes," he said as he sat.

"Okay, Wes," Melissa said as she turned around. "Why don't you just leave now and go pick up Kristin?" she said with a tinge of frustration in her voice. "It's fine if you want to get on the road. Molly and I will be okay, and I'll get Izzy at 2:30 like I promised."

"If you're sure," Wes said.

"Yes!" Melissa yelled. "I mean, yes," she said more calmly and with a smile.

Wes walked over and gave Molly a kiss.

"See you tomorrow, Princess," he told Molly.

"Okay, you have our cells if you need anything," Wes stated.

"Yes, I do," Melissa said as she took a deep breath. "And I have Wyatt's number too if I need anything. You guys have a good time. We'll see you tomorrow."

Wes hurried out the door to his truck and sped off on the short ride to the Chandler Library. He parked the car and walked into the library, which was all decorated with Cupids and hearts for the occasion. Karen sat behind the counter, talking to one of the patrons when she spied Wes walk in. She just pointed to Kristin's office as she kept nodding and smiling.

Kristin was at her desk on the phone when Wes entered. He sat down in one of the chairs across from her, looking around at the books she currently had piled all over the place. He toyed with a few of the items Kristin had on her desk before she slapped his hand away. Wes then proceeded to point to his wrist to indicate it was time to go. Wes saw the angry look Kristin developed and instead snuck back out the door to stand by the front desk.

"Heading out for a romantic day?" Karen asked as she fiddled with paperwork.

"Yeah," Wes said, "If I can get her out of here."

"She's on with an author about a presentation next week," Karen explained. "I'm sure she'll be done soon. Is this your first weekend away from Molly?"

Wes nodded.

Karen broke out in a big smile.

"Planning on getting some, then?" Karen said with a straight face.

"What? Huh? I mean..." said Wes, all flustered.

"It's okay, Wes, I get it," Karen said, speaking quietly to him. "I'm sure Brian is expecting the same thing from me. You know, it's Friday night, it's Valentine's Day, all the stars are aligning... why not, right?" Karen jabbed lightly at Wes.

"Yeah, sure, Karen," Wes said.

Kristin walked out, carrying her bag and wearing her coat.

"Okay, I'm ready," Kristin said, placing some papers down on the desk for Karen. "If Henry Adams calls again with more requests for his presentation, tell him whatever it is can wait."

"What were you two up to?" Kristin said as she looked at Wes.

"Oh, nothing really," Karen added. "I was just about to give Wes some pointers for when he puts the moves on you tonight, right Wes?"

Kristin tried to stifle her laugh.

"Let's go," Wes said, taking Kristin by the arm.

"Let me know how he does," Karen shouted as the couple walked out the door.

"You know," Kristin said as she got in the car and put her seatbelt on, "she does that just because she knows it will rattle you."

"It works every time then," Wes responded as he started the car and left the parking lot.

The drive to Pittsburgh was a pleasant one and a surprise for Kristin. Wes had given no indications of what he planned for the night, and Kristin was thrilled to go into the city for something different. She was awed when they pulled up in front of the Mansions on Fifth, a luxury hotel in the Shadyside area of the city. The beautiful neighborhood had the ideal atmosphere for the couple. When the setting combined with the unusually warm weather for Valentine's Day with the sun shining, it made everything even more romantic.

Valets rushed over to open the door for Kristin, take the bags from the trunk, and the keys from Wes so they could park the car. Wes took Kristin's hand and walked with her to the lobby and front desk. While Kristin took in the immaculate view of the interior of the hotel. Everything about the space screamed elegance and opulence, from the beautiful walnut wood walls to the classic light fixtures and chandeliers, Kristin stepped into another world.

Kristin followed Wes to the front desk, where he was greeted by an older, gray-haired gentleman with the name tag of Gerald.

"Mr. Martin," he said in his practiced, refined voice. "it's so nice to see you again. It's been a while since you have been here."

"it has been too long, Gerald," Wes agreed. "This is my fiancée, Kristin Arthur," Wes said.

"Fiancée?" Gerald said with a happy surprise. "Well, congratulations to both of you, and it is a pleasure to meet you, Ms. Arthur. I hope we can assist you in having a fantastic stay with us."

"Thank you," Kristin said politely.

"Your room is all arranged for you, Mr. Martin. Your bags have already been brought upstairs as well. Please let me know if you need anything else," Gerald said as he handed the card keys over to Wes.

"Have all my requested plans been handled?" Wes inquired.

"Of course, Mr. Martin," Gerald said with a nod.

"Fantastic. Thank you, Gerald," Wes said as he hurried Kristin to the elevators.

The two darted into the elevator and began the trek upward to the top floor.

"Wes, this place is pretty swanky," Kristin said to him. "You know, I would have been just as happy with a night out at Angelo's or staying home and having Chinese food."

"No way," Wes insisted as they got off on their floor. "You deserve a special time, even if it is just for one night, and we may as well take advantage of having someone to watch Molly when we can. I'm pulling out all the stops tonight."

Wes stopped in front of the door to their room, placed the card key in, and opened the door. Kristin walked through to see the Presidential Suite that they were booked into for the night. The room had everything she could have wanted and more, including the king-size bed in the center. When Kristin walked into the bathroom, she ran her hands across the high-quality towels and noticed the jetted tub.

"This is some room," Kristin noted. "I'm pretty sure this place is bigger than my old apartment."

Kristin hopped onto the bed to feel the comfort of it, and then kicked off her shoes as she sprawled across the comforter.

"So, what do you want to do?" Wes said as he sat down on the bed next to Kristin. He bent down to kiss her.

"Hmmm," Kristin purred. "I know where to start," she said seductively.

"Oh yeah?" Wes said hopefully as he got his face close to hers again so that they were nose to nose.

"Yes," Kristin breathed. She gave Wes a quick peck on the nose and shot up off the bed. "I'm going to take a bath in that tub!"

Kristin raced into the bathroom, and Wes heard the running of water. Wes untied the laces to his sneakers and slipped them off so he could get comfortable on the bed, alone. No sooner had he raised his feet off the floor and onto the bed when Kristin appeared in the doorway to the bathroom, wrapped only in one of the bath towels.

"Are you waiting for a written invitation, Mr. Martin?" she said with a wink. Kristin disappeared into the bathroom and tossed the towel out the doorway so that Wes could see it lying in a heap on the floor.

Wes dashed off the bed, stripping off his shirt and pants before he ever got to the doorway of the bathroom. Even though he made it to the room in seconds flat, Kristin was already nestled in the tub, covering herself up with the bubbles she created using the soap provided by the hotel. The room smelled of lilacs, but Wes was more focused on other things.

Kristin scooted forward in the tub so that Wes could get in behind her. The bathtub was spacious and cozy at the same time, providing enough room for both adults but keeping them close together so they could enjoy the intimacy created. Wes picked up one of the washcloths positioned next to the tub, soaked it in the sudsy water, and then began to dutifully wash Kristin's back. The warm cotton caressed her shoulders, and Kristin had tied her hair up so that Wes quickly did her neck before leaning in to give her neck light kisses. Goosebumps shot through Kristin's body, causing her to shiver and giggle as Wes continued the downward path of the washcloth on Kristin's body.

Wes followed along the delicate curves of Kristin's back and hips, never letting his hands linger too long in one place before the cloth found the top of her backside. It was then that Wes placed his firm hands on Kristin's hips and pulled her body closer to him. He pressed up against her and started his washing routine down the front of her body. Kristin craned her neck as Wes gently passed over it before slowly reaching the tops of her breasts. Upon the initial move, Kristin arched her back, causing her backside to glide against Wes's body.

Wes continued guiding his soapy hands down to the undersides of Kristin's breasts, circling them slowly, before he moved his fingers ever closer to her erect nipples. His index fingers grazed across the tips, and that elicited a gasp that quickly transitioned into a drawn-out moan from Kristin. It only took just the slightest of touches from Wes to make Kristin extra-sensitive to every movement and feel and to bring her longing to a fever pitch. Wes continued, adding more kisses to Kristin's neck before she reached up to Wes's right hand and began to guide it even lower on her body.

Kristin had been self-conscious about the scar left on her body from the C-section and hernia surgery. Wes noticed right away as Kristin lifted his hand from her body when it reached that area of her abdomen so that she could move beyond it. Wes halted her movements, instead pressing his hand close to her body again.

"It's okay," Wes whispered into her ear in between kisses. "I love all of you and want all of you, just the way you are."

Kristin relented and allowed Wes to move his fingers to where the scar laid so he could touch it. Kristin trembled lightly as Wes touched the small bumps of the scar tissue, feeling the contours of it.

"It just shows me how strong you are all the time, no matter what," Wes told her before he allowed his hand to pass from her abdomen down to the curve of the top of her thigh.

Wes' fingers inched ever closer before Kristin ached for him and moved his hands to where she wanted them to be. He traced the outline of her sex slowly under the warm water, making Kristin boil over inside. Wes kissed Kristin's shoulder before he slowly slipped a finger inside her, quickly followed by a second. Kristin shut her eyes tightly and groaned, and as she pressed her back tighter against Wes, she felt the apparent state of firm arousal he was in.

"Wes, please," Kristin gasped.

"Not yet," Wes added playfully as his thumb went to work on her swollen clit as he moved his fingers inside her.

Kristin's hands were now gripping the sides of the bathtub as her breathing rate escalated more and more. Kristin found herself grinding her back against Wes's body at first, but as she got closer and closer to climax, her body became still. She reached over and held Wes's hand tightly in place, fingers inside her before she cried out in pleasure.

Kristin's body melted into the water, and she released her tight grip on Wes's hand as she dunked her entire body under the water in the oversized tub. When she emerged, she got to her feet, feeling wobbly at first and taking hold of the grab bar on the wall. She turned and grinned down as she stood over Wes's body that stretched out in the water.

Kristin had bits of bubbles and suds strewn across areas of her body as she eyed Wes hungrily. She slowly lowered herself onto him, sending shockwaves and sensitivity through her still-recovering body and she enveloped Wes. Kristin rocked her hips steadily as her hands pawed over Wes. Wes gripped her hips tightly as she moved, and he ran his hands back and forth over her tight buttocks and back to her hips.

As he got closer, he pulled Kristin towards his body more and sat up so that they were chest to chest, trunks intertwined. Kristin's hands gripped Wes's broad shoulders tightly, and she brought her mouth to his roughly. Her lips moved from his rapidly and kissed hungrily at his neck, over his Adam's apple and back up, sensing the slight stubble on his chin.

Kristin moved to wrap her legs around his waist, squeezing her whole body against Wes. She heard a deep groan building in Wes as he thrust, and again she closed her eyes, this time putting her head to Wes's shoulder and stifling her own moans as they both climaxed.

The two held each other, kissing over and over as the suds in the tub evaporated, and they noticed puddles on the floor from their whirlwind movements.

"I hope this floor is solid," Kristin said with a laugh as she lay her head on Wes's chest. "It looks like there is more water on the floor than what is left in the tub."

"Is it weird that I need a shower after taking a bath?" Wes smiled. Wes stroked Kristin's damp hair that had come undone during their escapades as she lay against him.

"I could stay here all day," Kristin added as she snuggled closer to Wes.

"As much as I would like to stay here all day, I do have other things planned," Wes replied.

"I hope some of it includes more of this," Kristin told him. She lifted her head from his chest and gave him a lingering kiss on the lips.

"Oh yes," Wes said insistently.

"Fair enough," Kristin told him. She slowly pushed away from her embrace and stood up in the tub. "Then, you let me take a shower, then you can have your turn."

"What about if we just take a shower together?" Wes asked.

"If we do that, you can forget about going anywhere tonight. My body will turn to Jell-O."

"That might not be so bad," Wes answered. His hand started snaking up Kristin's left leg as she turned to face the showerhead.

Kristin's knees weakened as Wes's touch got closer to her thigh.

"Wes," she sighed with pleasure. "We have all night for that. You're the one that said you had plans."

"Okay, okay," Wes said as he got out of the tub. "Is it okay if I stay in here and shave while you shower? At least then, I can spy your silhouette through the shower curtain while you wash."

"It's fine with me," Kristin replied, turning the shower on. She pulled the curtain around the tub, peeking her head out just a bit to talk to Wes.

"I don't want to hear about it, though if you cut yourself because you got distracted," she added.

"No complaints from me," Wes indicated. He lathered his palm with shaving cream as he watched Kristin's shadowy form glide her hands over her body.

***

Izzy was never more thankful for the end of a school day or the end of a week as she was this day. Even the surprise of the two dozen roses from an unknown admirer wasn't enough to make the day more palatable for her. It did help soften the blow somewhat, but watching all the happy couples strutting around the school together turned her stomach sour. The one joy she received was when she walked past Eden in the hallway later in the day after receiving her flowers. Knowing she had twenty-four roses in her hands while Eden was there with the eleven balloons that she now had to wrangle everywhere she went for the rest of the day made her grin, especially when Eden and Bradley both looked shocked to see Izzy holding the flowers.

Izzy walked out of the school and cradled her bouquet as she scanned the parking area for Melissa's car.

"Izzy!" Melissa waved from across the lot to get her attention.

Izzy slowly made her way toward Melissa's vehicle, an older red Subaru Outback that she had been driving for years. A couple of fellow seniors, Peter and Dylan, casual friends of Izzy's, walked up to her in the parking lot.

"Who's your hot friend, Izzy?" Peter said as he kept looking at Melissa, standing with her jacket open to show the V-neck Cage the Elephant t-shirt she was wearing.

"That's Melissa," Izzy said as she kept walking. She never cared much for Peter or Dylan and knew they only spoke to her to find out more about Melissa.

"She's my baby sister's nanny."

"Ooh, a hot nanny," Dylan added as they walked on. "I'd let her take care of me," he laughed.

"You're a disgusting perv, Dylan," Izzy added.

"Better a perv than a stuck-up rich girl prude," Dylan shot back.

Izzy had reached Melissa's car and got to the passenger side with Peter and Dylan not far behind her.

"Everything okay, Izzy?" Melissa asked.

"It's fine," Izzy said. "Let's just go."

"Hold on there, Melissa," Dylan said as he strutted closer to her. "So, you're the nanny, huh? I'll bet you're good at taking care of things. Probably much better than Izzy, from what I hear." Dylan turned to Peter as both laughed out loud.

Melissa walked over until she was right in front of Dylan. The teenage boy had not realized just how tall Melissa was, and she looked him right in the eyes.

"You think so?" Melissa said with a smile. She then quickly reached down and grabbed Dylan's crotch, squeezing until he whelped in agony.

"Doesn't seem like you have enough worth taking care of, friend," Melissa said as she released her grip, and Dylan fell to his knees.

"Next time you want to talk to a woman, try using some respect. It goes a long way. And stay away from Izzy. Trust me – you won't want to talk to me again if I hear otherwise."

Melissa gave a wave to Peter as he rushed over to help his friend up.

"You didn't have to do that," Izzy said to Melissa as she got back into the car, "but I'm sure glad you did."

Izzy cracked her first smile of the day as she watched Dylan writhing on the ground when they pulled away.

"Don't let those idiots bother you," Melissa said as she watched the road.

"They are teenage boys," Izzy lamented. "They are all idiots."

"True enough," Melissa answered. "It looks like you had a good day, though. Who are the flowers from?"

"I don't know," Izzy answered, still perplexed by them. "They got delivered to me, but no one signed their name to them. It's kind of weird. Just like the other day when..." Izzy cut herself off.

"The other day, when what?" Melissa asked, turning the car towards Martin Way.

Izzy was unsure about how to proceed, but she did need some advice.

"Okay, I'll tell you, but you have to promise not to tell Dad and Kristin."

"Izzy, we've already been down this road," Melissa cautioned. "I'm not going to lie for you."

"I'm not asking you to," Izzy said as the car arrived at the house. "I'm just asking you to withhold information until necessary is all."

"I don't like the sound of this," Melissa said as she got out of the parked car and started to take Molly out of her car seat.

"Please, Melissa," Izzy asked. "I need to talk to someone about all this, and if I tell Dad, his head will explode."

"That doesn't make me feel any better," Melissa answered.

The ladies made their way up the front steps and into the house, shedding coats and bags along the way until they arrived in the kitchen. Melissa sat at the kitchen table with Molly in her lap, and she bounced the infant on her knee to elicit smiles and laughs. Izzy walked over to one of the lower cabinets and grabbed the most giant vase she could find to fill it with water and then her flowers.

"Okay," Melissa sighed. "Tell me. But if I think it's way out there, you know I'll have to tell them."

Izzy walked over in front of Melissa, pressed a few buttons on her phone, and then held up the screen for Melissa to look at. It was Izzy's PayPal account, and it showed the large amount that was in there.

"Wow, don't take this the wrong way, but you must get some allowance," Melissa said.

"That's just it," Izzy explained. "I don't, and the money isn't from my Dad. I don't know where it came from. I got this cryptic deposit of $10,000 on my birthday from J. Smith LLC. I have no idea who that is or why they gave it to me. The note just said Happy Birthday, and that was it. Then today, all these flowers show up with a note and no signature."

"That doesn't sound kosher to me, Izzy," Melissa said. She rose from her seat with a restless Molly in tow and headed toward the living room. Melissa sat on the floor and placed Molly next to her so she could play with her toys.

"I don't know what it sounds like, or if I should be flattered or frightened." Izzy sat next to Molly and began to slowly turn the jack-in-the-box on the floor.

"You didn't find anything about this LLC? Maybe it's a relative or someone your Dad knows?"

"Dad's an only child, I've never met anyone from Kristin's family, and I barely know any of the guys Dad played baseball with. I can't imagine any of them would give me that kind of money. If they sent me flowers, it would be downright creepy," Izzy said as she slowly got closer to the end of "Pop Goes the Weasel."

"Maybe the two are completely unrelated. Just a coincidence in timing," Melissa added. "You still should tell your Dad about it. That's a lot of money."

"Come on, Mel," Izzy begged. "Give me a little time to try to figure it all out. If I don't in a few days, then I will tell him and ask for help, I promise."

Izzy crossed her heart with her index finger as she completed the turn of the Jack-in-the-box, so the clown came popping out, causing Molly, Melissa, and Izzy all to jump in surprise. Molly started laughing uncontrollably, causing the older two to join in.

"Okay, it's a deal," Melissa said as she shut the clown back in the box. "Let's move on to better things. Instead of sitting around moping all night about staying home, why don't you join Miss Molly and me in a little girl's night party and sleepover? We can order pizza, watch a movie, dance around, whatever that will take your mind off boys and everything about them."

"Sounds good," Izzy smiled widely. "Thanks, Melissa."

"You bet. I'm going to go change Molly and finish up a few things in the kitchen before getting her dinner ready, so we can meet back down here around five or so."

Melissa snatched Molly off the floor and ran with her towards the bedroom where her changing table was. Izzy picked up her bag and headed upstairs to her room to put her things away. She tossed the bag on her chair at her desk and then sat on her bed and stared at the PayPal screen again.

"Who are you?" she said aloud.

Chapter 12

K ristin took her time as she got prepared for the evening out with Wes. Nights like this were few since she first got pregnant, and even fewer since Molly's birth, and she wanted to pamper herself, so she felt her best. Kristin spent more time styling her hair than usual, so it looked just right, adding just the hint of curl to her blond locks. She made sure to put on her favorite perfume as well, giving her the beautiful jasmine scent that she knew Wes liked. Kristin had just the perfect dress for the occasion as well – a red, off-the-shoulder, gown with an embroidered lace bodice and mesh skirt. The dress also featured a sexy cutout at the waistline that was embellished with crystals. Kristin had ordered it weeks before Valentine's Day with the hope of getting to wear it for just an occasion like this.

When Kristin emerged from the bathroom, she noticed Wes putting the finishing touches on the tie he chose to wear for the evening. As always, he looked dashing in his traditional, tailored black suit with a white shirt. The red tie he wore matched Kristin's dress perfectly, almost as if they had planned it. Wes even finished off the outfit with a matching red pocket square.

After completing the Windsor knot in his tie, Wes turned to face Kristin. Kristin could see his jaw open slightly as he took in the vision she created. She sauntered over to Wes, stood on her toes since she hadn't slipped into her heels just yet, and gave him a quick peck on the cheek.

"You look amazing," Wes said with awe as he watched Kristin step into her heels.

"Why thank you," she offered, giving a slight mock curtsey. "You clean up pretty nicely yourself, Mr. Martin."

"Nowhere near as nicely as you do. That dress is... well, it's..." Wes fumbled as he tried to find the right words.

"You not being able to say anything lets me know it was the right choice," Kristin smiled as she did a slow turn in the room for Wes to take it all in.

"Maybe we don't have to go to dinner," Wes said as he pulled Kristin towards him quickly.

"I don't know, I'm pretty hungry," Kristin whispered. She stared directly into Wes's eyes.

"So am I," Wes growled. Wes bent and planted soft kisses along the nape of Kristin's neck.

"Hmmm, I think you are a different kind of hungry than I am," Kristin sighed.

"Always," Wes stated.

Kristin stepped back from Wes to move away from his seductive kisses and gaze.

"Let's go," she indicated. "I am so ready for a night out with you."

Wes inhaled deeply so he could compose himself and then took Kristin's hand to lead her out of the hotel room. It took all his restraint to keep his hands off her as they entered the elevator and took the slow ride down to the lobby.

"Just smelling your perfume is making me crazy," Wes told Kristin before the elevator doors opened, and an older couple joined them on the ride down to the lobby. Kristin moved closer to Wes so she could press her side against his for the rest of the journey.

Upon exiting the elevator, Wes walked over to the front desk to speak with Gerald, who was still on duty. They chatted for a moment before Wes moved back towards Kristin.

"All set," Wes indicated as he retook Kristin's hand.

"Do we need to get the car from the valet?" Kristin asked as they went out the front doors of the hotel.

"Not tonight," Wes replied as the black stretch limousine pulled up to the sidewalk in front of the couple.

"That's for us?" Kristin said with surprise.

"Tonight it is," Wes smiled. The driver, an older gentleman, dressed in a dark blue suit, scurried over to open the door.

"Good evening, Mr. Martin, Ms. Arthur," the chauffeur stated. "My name is James. I'm here to drive you this evening."

Kristin climbed into the limo and awed at the interior right away. The elegant leather seats, plush carpeting, full bar, and other amenities were more than she had ever seen in a vehicle before.

"Wes, this is too much," Kristin said as Wes got in and sat next to her.

"You said you had never had a limo ride before, so I wanted to make your first time the best it could be," Wes replied.

James drove the vehicle along the route as Kristin and Wes cuddled in the back seat. Kristin could see the lights throughout the city of Pittsburgh as they drove along, passing the Carnegie Museum of Natural History toward the Liberty Bridge and across it before they speedily arrived at their destination. James hurriedly came around to the passenger side to open the door and let Wes and

Kristin out. Kristin stepped out of the car and craned her neck to attempt to see the top of the building they were entering.

"Where are we going?" Kristin asked.

"You'll see in a minute," Wes answered, and then led Kristin into the building.

The two were whisked up to the top floor by elevator again, and when they emerged, Kristin realized they were at the top of the building where the restaurant was. Wes greeted the host at the podium, and, within moments, the couple was led to their cozy table. Kristin was astounded by the view they had out the large windows next to the table. The entire city of Pittsburgh seemed to lay before them, lit up in all its glory. The glorious view of the confluence of the Ohio, Allegheny, and Monongahela Rivers only added to the beauty of the scene.

"This view..." Kristin offered as she was lost for other words.

"Pretty amazing, huh?" Wes said as he too looked upon the panorama below. "I never get tired of looking at the beauty of this area."

The ultra-attentive wait staff sprang into action, providing the couple with water, a wine list, menus, and offers of cocktails. Wes ordered his customary Grey Goose martini on the rocks, while Kristin opted for a gin and tonic. The two then began to peruse the menus for the evening before their waiter, a young man named Daniel, arrived to introduce himself. Daniel presented himself cordially as he brought the drinks each person had ordered.

"Welcome to Altius," Daniel said proudly. "Is this your first time dining with us?"

Kristin smiled at Wes, unsure if it was his first time at the establishment.

"It's my first time here," Kristin smiled.

"I have been here," Wes indicated, "but it's been a few years for me."

"Well, it's nice to have you back, sir," Daniel said graciously, "And for you, miss, we are glad you chose to join us, especially on Valentine's Day. Now that you have your drinks, I'll give you some time to look over the menus to see if you have any questions."

Daniel excused himself while Kristin took a sip of her gin and tonic before glancing at the menu. She briefly perused it before bending it slightly so she could look at Wes, who was scanning the list of dishes himself.

"So, when were you here?" Kristin asked him.

"Hmmm?" Wes answered, distracted by the delectable descriptions on the page in front of him.

"Oh, here? Back when they first opened in 2014," Wes replied. "The stadium is right across the river there. See?" Wes said as he pointed towards PNC Park off in the distance. "I thought it would be a nice place to come to with you."

"And who did you come with back then?" Kristin asked curiously.

"Me? It was with a couple of the guys from the team. I don't remember who exactly."

"You came to a place like this with a couple baseball buddies?" Kristin said. "Seems more like the kind of place you would bring a date," she said teasingly.

"It does look like a good date place," Wes conceded. "That's why I'm here with you now. I've told you I never dated much after Rachel left."

"Just checking," Kristin said with a laugh.

Daniel reappeared tableside, ready to answer any questions about the food offerings.

"I think I will have she-crab bisque and the sea bass," Kristin said.

"Very nice," Daniel said as he jotted down the information. "And for you, sir?" he said, turning to Wes.

"I'll have the salmon poke and the strip steak, medium," Wes told the waiter.

Daniel was ready to leave the table before Wes stopped him to order a bottle of pinot noir to go with dinner.

Kristin let out a big sigh as she gazed out the window again.

"I'm so glad we got the chance to get away like this, even just for a night," Kristin told Wes.

"I know things have been a bit hectic at home, with Molly, work, Izzy, hiring a nanny, the wedding, and everything else," Wes said. "Tonight, we can be selfish for a bit and just be together. Any movement on the wedding front I need to know about?" Wes asked before helping himself to a piece of bread from the basket on the table.

Kristin rolled the ice in her glass and sipped her drink.

"Not really," she frowned. "Every time I think I have a few minutes to work on stuff, something comes along. I feel like I am running out of time to do things. We only have a little over six months left, and all I know is that the wedding is going to be on the farm."

Wes saw the stress on Kristin's face and reached to take her hand.

"Hey, we don't need to do anything fancy," Wes told her. "We can have Judge McGuirk come down to the farm and just do the ceremony, no fuss or anything. It doesn't matter."

Wes knew he had made a mistake as soon as the words left his mouth.

"It does matter, Wes," Kristin indicated. "I know I don't need a big, lavish wedding, and I don't want that. But I do want my friends and family there to see it, and I want it to be a special day."

"I'm sorry," Wes said. "I didn't mean it to come out that way. Of course, it should be unique. I just meant the important part is that we are together. I love you, no matter what. We can get married on the farm, in a church, in an office, or a hot air balloon. I just want to marry you. We'll figure it out."

"I know," Kristin said as she twirled her swizzle straw in her drink. "I just wish it was coming easier than it is."

"Let me know what you need me to do, and I will take care of it," Wes stated.

"Oh, I will, don't you worry," Kristin laughed.

Daniel appeared with the bottle of wine and opened it for the couple, pouring for them into their red wine glasses. Wes and Kristin carefully clinked their glasses in a toast to one another.

"Happy Valentine's Day," Wes said sincerely.

"Yes, Happy Valentine's Day," Kristin added.

Wes and Kristin thoroughly enjoyed their meal from start to finish. They spent their time leisurely dining and drinking, enjoying each other's company in a way that they had not done in a while. By the time dessert came around, Daniel had made sure to bring Valentine's special dessert of a vanilla bean semifreddo wrapped in milk chocolate and in the shape of a heart with vanilla bean whipped cream and fresh strawberries. Wes and Kristin both savored every bite of the decadent dessert as they ended their meal.

"Daniel," Wes said as he wiped the last bit of chocolate from the corner of his mouth, "that meal was amazing."

"I'm glad you enjoyed it," Daniel said with a proud smile as he cleared the dessert plates away. "Can I get you anything else?"

"I couldn't eat or drink another thing," Kristin indicated.

Wes dutifully paid the check, and Kristin took his arm as they left the crowded restaurant to head back down to their ride. James waited outside for them and opened the door for them immediately.

"Did you enjoy your dinner?" James asked as he climbed in the driver's seat and started the car.

"It was fantastic," Kristin said.

"Anywhere else you two would like to go this evening?" James waited for Wes to answer before pulling away.

Wes looked over at Kristin and grinned, and she quickly smiled back at him.

"I think just back to the hotel is fine, James," Wes replied.

"Very good," James said, closing the privacy panel between the back and the driver.

Kristin lay her head on Wes's shoulder as they drove along, making their way back to the Mansions on Fifth. There was a bit of traffic on the bridge now that slowed down the ride slightly and stopped the limo. Wes placed his index finger under Kristin's chin to raise her face towards his, and he kissed her. The delicate kiss steadily progressed into a deeper one as Wes wrapped his left arm around Kristin and pulled her to him.

Wes found his hands roaming down, past the cutout in Kristin's dress where bare flesh peeked at her waist until he found the bottom hem of the skirt. His right hand slid up her right leg, caressing the silky nylon of her stockings up to her thigh.

"Wes, what are you doing?" Kristin said coyly. Her head pressed back against the leather of the seat as Wes kissed her neck and moved his hand further up her leg.

"I thought that was fairly obvious," Wes added before he returned to kissing.

"What about the driver?" Kristin gasped. Heat rapidly moved through Kristin's body, and her thighs were closing on Wes's hand.

Wes glanced over to see the smoky partition up as the car moved along.

"He can't see," Wes answered. His lips swept down Kristin's neck as his hand and fingers kept sliding up and over her thigh. His fingers reached the lace covering Kristin's crotch, and a soft moan escaped from her.

The vehicle came to an abrupt halt that jolted Wes Kristin out of their world and back to the car. Wes heard the partition starting to lower and scrambled back to sitting up while Kristin straightened her dress, pulling it back down to cover up more of her body.

"Sorry it took so long to get back," James told his passengers.

"Not long enough," Wes noted quietly to Kristin.

The couple exited the vehicle, and Wes tipped James well for the driver's efforts for the evening. Wes and Kristin entered the hotel lobby, with only the sounds of their shoes echoing across the floor. They gave a quick wave to the young man behind the front desk for the evening before scrambling to the elevator so they could get upstairs as quickly as possible.

Wes had barely opened the hotel room door before he grabbed Kristin by the waist and kissed her passionately. Kristin then broke the kiss and took two steps back from Wes, smiling as she worked to take off her shoes. Wes bolted the room door, remembering to put the "Do Not Disturb" sign out so they would not be interrupted. Kristin then turned slowly, so her back faced Wes.

"Can you unzip me?" she said with a wicked grin.

"With pleasure," Wes said as his hand took hold of the zipper, and he slowly watched her dress unfold before his eyes. The zipper stopped at the small of Kristin's back, and Wes could just see a glimpse of the lace Kristin had on beneath it and that he had brushed earlier.

Kristin turned, her hands holding up her dress at her chest before she let it all fall to the floor so she could step out of it. She now wore nothing except for the red satin and lace strapless bodysuit she had chosen for the occasion, and she saw by the hungry look in Wes's eyes that he approved of the vision.

"I don't remember seeing this before," Wes stated as he pressed his body up against Kristin's.

"It's new," Kristin replied as she helped Wes out of his suit jacket and began to untie his necktie. "I bought it weeks ago, but I have been too afraid to wear it.

I didn't think it would fit at first after the baby, and then, with everything else... well, I just wasn't feeling very sexy."

"You never have any reason not to feel sexy, Kris," Wes told her. He placed his hands on Kristin's shoulders and slowly ran his fingertips down her arms, forcing goosebumps to appear there and all over her body. Wes then quickly moved his hands to Kristin's waist and scooped her up in his arms, carrying her over to the bed. Kristin laughed as she bounced lightly on the mattress. She propped herself up on her elbows and watched Wes as he took his clothes off, leaving his muscular body with just a black pair of boxer briefs on it.

Wes crawled up the bed and came to rest, so his head was at Kristin's waist. His hands gently moved up and down Kristin's sides before stopping at her hips. Wes planted soft kisses on Kristin's inner thighs as she looked on. Kristin closed her eyes slightly, reveling in the feeling of Wes's touch. Wes slid his hands beneath Kristin, taking her buttocks in his palms and lifting her a bit as he squeezed her while kissing. Kristin let loose with an audible gasp as she felt Wes's lips moving up her thighs and ever closer to where she desired them most.

Wes kissed the soft, damp lace fabric that covered Kristin, and it was then that he took notice of the snaps of the bodysuit.

"This is convenient," he said slyly as his left hand made quick work of opening the bodysuit. Kristin held her breath with anticipation at what Wes might do at this point, and when she felt his mouth come in first contact with her, heat spread throughout her body. Kristin tossed her head back into the pillows beneath her and enjoyed each kiss, tongue movement, and touch that followed. Wes's tongue darted in and out slowly while his thumb just barely moved over the top of her clit, causing Kristin to buck against his mouth and hand.

The stimulation was almost more than she could handle, and Kristin gripped the sheets tightly in the palms of her hands the more Wes teased and touched her intimately. Kristin knew she was teetering on edge, and it wouldn't take much to push her over. Wes moved from his position between her legs as his kisses went over her midsection, still covered in lace. His right hand eased down the cups of her bodysuit to free her breasts, allowing Wes to give them attention as well. The first touches on her chest and the flick of his tongue across a nipple made Kristin groan loudly.

Wes positioned himself over Kristin and made quick work of shedding his briefs. He slid himself into her, becoming enveloped by her warmth and wetness. Their bodies meshed and moved in unison, immediately finding a rhythm that brought each of them to a fever pitch. Kristin moaned and gripped Wes's back as she arched upward to hold him as close as possible, keeping him still as she experienced him pulsing and filling her simultaneously.

Kristin and Wes' were both bathed in sweat as their bodies started to calm. Wes moved to the side and took Kristin in his arms, holding her so that he could feel her soft flesh and rapid heartbeat pressed against him. The two lay silently, holding each other as they caught their breath for several minutes before Kristin spoke.

"That's a way to celebrate Valentine's Day," she offered as she snuggled closer to Wes. Her body shivered slightly as the combination of the air in the room, and the drying sweat on her body took hold. Wes reached the down blanket on the bed and pulled it up, so they both were covered.

"I have to agree," Wes told her.

"Hmmm, I could spend all night just like this," Kristin told him.

"Are you sure?" Wes asked. "We might have other things we want to do. It's still early."

"What other things are you referring to, Mr. Martin?" Kristin asked with mock unknowing.

"I can think of one or two," Wes told her as he rolled with Kristin to the other side of the bed, eliciting giggles from her as his hands traversed her body again.

***

Once Molly had settled down for the night and was sound asleep in her crib in Wes and Kristin's room, Izzy and Melissa set about setting up for their "slumber" party. Melissa made sure to bring the baby monitor downstairs with her so that they could listen in if Molly awoke. The young ladies arranged pillows and blankets on the wraparound couch in front of the big screen so they could watch movies. Melissa and Izzy both carried down piles of snacks and some bottles of iced tea that they could put in the fridge behind the bar where cans of soda already resided. After making sure they had all they needed, Izzy plopped down on the couch to relax.

Melissa came over, holding a cosmetics bag with some nail polish in it.

"Pick a color," she said, tossing the bag to Izzy. "I'll do your toes."

Izzy sorted through the choices before settling on a metallic blue. She held up the bottle for Melissa to see.

"Okay, your choice," Melissa told her. Melissa took off the robe she was wearing before she sat down. Izzy noticed not just the pajamas she wore, which were a simple plaid pair of pants and a white cotton cami, but the tattoos that were now visible on Melissa's body.

"You have tattoos?" Izzy said with keen interest.

Melissa took a cursory glance at her right shoulder and shrugged.

"Oh, yeah, I guess you haven't seen them before," Melissa indicated. "They are usually covered up. They're no big deal."

Izzy scooted over on the couch to get a better look at the ink on Melissa's shoulder. It was a simple green shamrock with three names on it, one on each clover.

"What are the names for?" Izzy asked.

"One is my brother, Tommy," Melissa said as she pointed. "This one is my Dad, Derek, and this one is my Mom, Maureen. It helps keep them with me all the time wherever I go."

"Cool," Izzy said. "Do you have any others?"

Melissa laughed. "I have one other one." Melissa rose from the couch and lowered the waistband of her pants to reveal the red heart on her right hip. The heart had a white banner under it that read "Sisters 4 Ever" in black script.

Izzy marveled at that one as well.

"No one really gets to see that one," Melissa smiled. "Three of my friends from college and I all got them one night. It was kind of a solidarity thing for all of us."

"I would love to get a tattoo," Izzy said, "but I think Dad would completely lose it."

"You have time when you are older," Melissa responded as she gently shook the bottle of nail polish.

"How old were you when you got those?" Izzy asked.

"I just got the shamrock last year, when I found out my Dad was sick," Melissa said as she began to work on Izzy's toenails. "The heart... I guess I was nineteen."

"I'm close to that," Izzy replied. "Maybe I can go and get one now."

"I thought you said your Dad would lose it," Melissa answered as she painted Izzy's big toe.

"He probably would, but I feel like I need to do something. I've always been the "good girl" who does her chores, does her homework, helps everyone, and always has a smile and follows the rules. Sometimes I just want to get away from that and do something... be something different."

"There's nothing wrong with being a good person, Izzy," Melissa told her. "We all go through stuff like this. You're in your senior year, you have lots of decisions to make, you broke up with your boyfriend... it's natural to feel this way right now. Don't start doing things you're going to regret later just because it feels right to rebel."

"Done," Melissa said proudly. Izzy looked down and could see the shine that the polish gave to her toes. "Want to do mine?" Melissa asked, passing the bottle to Izzy.

"Sure," Izzy said, still contemplating the advice Melissa had given her. Melissa had picked up her phone and was looking at it.

"I'm going to order pizza," Melissa said as she stretched her legs out so Izzy could start doing her toes. "What kind do you want?"

"Plain cheese is fine with me," Izzy said mindlessly.

"Good," Melissa told her as she typed in the order into one of the food delivery apps. "I'm a plain cheese girl myself, too. It should be here in about twenty minutes."

Izzy went ahead and began painting Melissa's toes in the same blue she had done while Melissa gazed at her smartphone. Izzy broke the silence first.

"Mel," Izzy started, "can I ask you something personal?"

"Sure," Melissa said.

"Do you have a boyfriend?"

Melissa chuckled at the question.

"Is that it? I thought you were going to ask something tougher. No, I don't have a boyfriend right now. I haven't had a boyfriend in a while. First, there was school, and then nursing, and then my Dad got sick. I haven't had free time for socializing like that in a while. To be honest, I haven't missed the drama that goes along with it either. I had a steady boyfriend when I was in college for a year or so, but he graduated and moved on. I don't think I've even been on a date since I came back to Chandler, and I'm okay with that. I get to spend some time taking care of me and doing what I want to do for a change now."

"I wish I felt that way," Izzy bemoaned.

"You're just getting over being in a long-term relationship," Melissa consoled. "Trust me, after a little bit, you won't be worrying about what Bradley is doing. There will be plenty of boys that come looking to ask you out, either now or once you go to college. Pittsburgh has a pretty active social scene, and the campus there..."

"What if I don't want to go to Pittsburgh?" Izzy interrupted, not even looking up at Melissa.

"Really? I thought you had already decided all that."

"My Dad has already decided all that," Izzy replied. "I've been accepted there; that's not the issue. There are other places I am interested in that have the programs I want most."

"Like where?"

Izzy took a deep breath.

"NYU. I want to study drama there."

"That's a great school," Melissa offered as she popped open a bottle of iced tea. "But haven't schools already done their acceptances by now?"

"They have. I applied to NYU; I just didn't tell Dad that. The application was completed last month, I submitted my portfolio and did my audition electronically."

"Did you get in?" Melissa asked with anticipation.

"I haven't heard anything back yet," Izzy added with disappointment. "I don't know if that's good or bad. I know Pittsburgh has a theater arts program, but NYU... The Tisch School, the location, the instructors... it would be a dream come true, and it might open opportunities for me that I can't get here."

"Izzy, you should just tell him," Melissa stated. She sat facing Izzy on the couch and pulled the blanket up over her legs. "I think he would understand."

"You obviously haven't been around my Dad long enough yet," Izzy answered. "He's been talking about me going to Pittsburgh since I was twelve. He keeps saying he wants me to go since he passed up on college and went right into playing baseball. You know, the whole 'first in our family to get a degree from Pitt' kind of thing. He won't go for it."

"Maybe I haven't been around your Dad long enough to know him that well," Melissa added, "but in the end, it's your decision where you go to school. You would instead go and spend four years at Pitt being unhappy than talk to him about going to New York? You keep saying you want him to treat you more like an adult. Well, this is your perfect chance to start doing that and have a serious discussion with him about your future and what you want to do."

"I know you're right, Mel," Izzy said as she tied her hair back into a ponytail. "I just don't know if I am ready to do it yet. Besides, I haven't been accepted there. Maybe nothing will come of it, and I'll end up at Pittsburgh. I've got enough to worry about right now between that, the musical, school, boys, and who knows what else."

The girls heard the familiar ring of the doorbell chimed through the house, and both were startled. As soon as the chime stopped, the baby monitor crackled, and Molly was heard fussing in bed.

"You get the door, I'll take care of Molly," Melissa said. "There's money on the bar for the pizza."

Melissa dashed upstairs to get to Molly in the bedroom before she fussed too much and woke up entirely while Izzy meandered toward the front door. She had just finished tying her robe when there was a knock on the door as well.

"I'm coming!" Izzy said with exasperation.

Izzy pulled the door open to see the delivery person standing there holding a white pizza box and a small brown bag. She recognized the driver as Tony, a classmate of hers.

"Hey Tony," Izzy said. She watched as she could see Tony's eyes gaze over her, and she pulled the top of her robe closed more to avoid his peering.

"Hi, Izzy," Tony said, still staring at her. "I've never been out to your house before. It looks really nice," he said, popping his head just inside the door frame to catch a glimpse of the darkened living room.

"Thanks," Izzy said at the intrusion before stepping in front of him and guiding his body back out the door. She held her hands out to take the pizza.

"Oh yeah," he said with a laugh. "One cheese pizza and an order of mozzarella sticks. $19.50."

Izzy took the pizza box and handed Tony thirty dollars.

"Keep it," she insisted as she saw him digging in his pockets for change. Izzy just wanted him to leave at this point.

"Wow, thanks, Izzy," Tony said. He leaned his arm on the door frame and smiled. "You know... I heard you and Bradley aren't together anymore, and I..."

"I've got to go, Tony, I'll see you at school," Izzy rushed and closed the door. She had just started to make her way back towards the staircase to go downstairs when there was a knock on the door again.

"Grrrr," Izzy growled, hauling the food back with her towards the door. She slammed the box down on the side table next to the front door before opening the door.

"Tony, I really don't want to get into this right now..." she started in as the door flung open. Instead of seeing her friend standing there, there was a dark-haired woman in a black fur coat standing before her.

"Can I help you?" Izzy asked with some confusion.

"I'm sorry," the woman started. "I guess Tony is that nice young man heading down the driveway," she said as she pointed. Izzy heard the beat-up car loudly make its way towards the end of Martin Way. She also noticed the unmistakable outline of a Lincoln Town Car now parked in front of the house.

Izzy instinctively closed the front door a bit, wary of who was standing before her.

"What... what can I do for you?" Izzy said, her guard up now.

"I dropped by to see you if that's alright," the woman smiled, revealing perfectly white teeth framed with her ruby red lipstick.

"Me? I'm sorry, but I don't know who you are or what you want..." Izzy began to close the door before the woman stopped it with her black leather-gloved hand.

"You do know me, Isabelle... better than you think," the woman told her.

Izzy looked at the woman with a mix of fear and curiosity.

"I hope you didn't mind that I gave you the money. I just thought it was the least I could do after missing all those birthdays."

Izzy peered into the woman's eyes profoundly and then pulled the door open some more.

"Mom?"

Chapter 13

Izzy just stood in the doorway, her feet glued to the ground. The instant she had taken a closer look at the woman at the door, she could see some of the familiar features that she remembered about her mother. Even though it had been almost eleven years since Izzy had seen her face, the bold green of her mother's eyes was hard to forget. Izzy hadn't been able to place her voice because she now had a more pronounced New York accent. Not the New York that you might hear at the ballgames, but the New York you only noticed when you were on Park Avenue, shopping at Tiffany's or dining at Per Se.

"Can I come in?" Rachel asked her daughter. The question jolted Izzy out of her trance.

"Well, my Dad isn't here..." Izzy started as she tried to get her brain straight.

"Isabelle, for goodness sake, I'm your mother," Rachel huffed as she stepped into the house. "I lived here for seven years. Your father isn't going to mind if I come in for a few minutes to see you."

Izzy closed the front door and flipped on the light switch to illuminate the living room.

"I see your father's taste in décor hasn't improved much," Rachel said with disdain. "So, let me look at you. My, you have grown into a beautiful young woman. What's with the red hair, though? Your hair was always lovely before when you were younger." Rachel ran her fingers through the ponytail before Izzy turned her head and took two steps back.

"I dyed it for the musical last year and kept it because I liked it," Izzy said. She worked to try to maintain composure.

"Oh yes, that's right," Rachel replied with a nod. "The Little Mermaid. You were fantastic."

"Wait... how did you know... were you there?"

"No, I wasn't there," Rachel admitted, "but I did get a DVD of the production. Not the best recording I have ever seen, but I did enjoy it. You have a lovely singing voice."

"How did you get a copy?"

"I do still have friends in this town, Isabelle. I called the office and asked if I could get one, and they sent it to me. Not everyone in Chandler thinks I am a complete monster, despite your father."

Anger coursed through Izzy and worked its way from her clenched fists up through her mouth.

"Dad has never said a bad word about you to anyone," Izzy shot back. "If anything, he has been more than understanding about it. You're the one who was having an affair and ran out on him... and me. What is it you want? You want me to rush over and hug you because you gave me a bunch of money? That's not going to happen. In fact, I don't want your money. I don't need anything from you. I've survived the last eleven years without having you around, I think I can make it the rest of the way."

Rachel nodded her head and let Izzy speak.

"I understand how you feel, Isabelle, I do. I didn't think I would just walk through the door here and get forgiveness from you right away. I know I don't deserve that. I just wanted you to know that I am trying to make amends. Look, do you know where my parents' house... your grandparents' house is over on Wagner Place? I'm staying there right now, and I'll be there for a bit tidying up my father's estate."

"Your father passed away?" Izzy asked softly. She had vague memories of her mother's parents since she rarely saw them even though they lived in the same town. They had always looked down on her father's baseball career and thought he wouldn't amount to anything.

"Yes, he did, about a week ago. Mother passed away several years ago as well, so I have to take care of everything over there now," Rachel sighed. Izzy couldn't tell if her mother was upset at their passing or annoyed that she had to come back to Chandler.

"I'm sorry," Izzy told her mother.

"Thank you," Rachel added in a matter-of-fact tone. "In any case, I will be there, and I would like you to come and see me if you get the chance so we can talk some more. I do want to get to know you better, Isabelle. You're all the family I have left."

"Sorry, Izzy," Melissa said, entering the room. "Miss Molly has been fussing, so I think she will be joining us for pizza." Melissa stopped short and stood next to Izzy, looking at Rachel.

"Who is this?" Melissa asked. Molly had reached out for her sister, trying to grab hold of the ribbon Izzy used to tie her ponytail.

"Are you the girlfriend librarian?" Rachel asked with surprise. "A lot younger-looking than I thought."

"No, no, I'm not," Melissa said. "I'm Melissa. I'm the nanny."

"Seriously?" Rachel guffawed. "Kind of cliché for your father to hire a gorgeous nanny, don't you think?"

"I'm sorry, I didn't get your name," Melissa said as she handed Molly to Izzy and stepped towards Rachel.

"I'm Rachel, Rachel Hebner," Rachel told her, extending her gloved hand. "Well, technically, Rachel Hebner-Martin-Adams, I guess."

"Melissa, this... this is my mother," Izzy said.

"Oh, well, it's nice to meet you, Mrs. Hebner," Melissa said as politely as she could. "But Mr. Martin and Ms. Arthur are not here, and it's my job to make sure that Molly's taken care of above all else, so it might be best if you left... now."

Melissa walked toward the front door and began to open it.

Rachel stepped towards Izzy, who held Molly close.

"Think about what I said, Isabelle," Rachel said calmly. Rachel placed her leather-clad palm on Izzy's cheek and held it there. She then moved her hand over to Molly and tickled her under her chin. Molly giggled lightly and then drooled onto Rachel's glove.

"Adorable child," Rachel commented. She plucked a tissue from the box on the table next to the sofa and wiped her hand as she turned and walked toward the door.

Rachel grinned at Melissa as she walked out the door and down the front steps, her high heels clacking on the steps as she made her way down to her car. As she neared the vehicle, Melissa could see that there was a driver who jumped out to open the rear door of the Town Car.

Melissa closed the door and bolted it.

"She's... pleasant," Melissa said to Izzy.

"Yeah, I'm sorry about that." Izzy shook her head as she handed Molly over to a waiting Melissa. "My mother has never been one to mince words, at least from what I remember of her."

"When was the last time you saw her?"

"About eleven years ago, when I was seven. I went to school one day on the school bus, came home, and my grandparents were waiting for me, and she was gone. I got a few phone calls from her after that until I was about nine, and then she just stopped altogether."

Izzy went over and picked up the pizza box and went into the kitchen with it. She sat herself down at the table, opened the box, and pulled out a still-warm slice, the cheese stretching far before it snapped off the pizza remaining in the box. She started munching before Melissa got to the kitchen to place Molly in her highchair.

"What does she want?" Melissa asked as she strapped Molly in her chair.

"I don't know, she didn't really say," Izzy stated through chewing pizza.

"What do you think your father will say about this?" Melissa questioned.

Izzy sat and gnawed on a piece of crust.

"Do we have to tell him?"

"Izzy, how many things do you think you can keep from him? You have to tell him," Melissa stated emphatically.

"I know, I know. But give me a few days to figure it out, please? I need to know what she is doing here and why she came and contacted me like this."

Melissa rubbed her temple with her right hand.

"Alright, I will give you some time. If you don't tell your father, I'm going to. He deserves the truth, and so does Kristin. It's not fair to them."

"Thank you, Mel," Izzy said as she gave Melissa a hug. "I promise I will figure it all out."

How am I going to figure this out? Izzy thought.

***

After their night in Pittsburgh and the romantic bliss they experienced, Wes and Kristin returned home refreshed and reinvigorated. Both fell back into their work routines quickly, but they were conscious about trying to spend more time together when they could, even if it was just for an hour or so after dinner and Molly had gone to sleep so they could catch up, be with each other and do simple things like listen to music, watch a TV show, or just be together and talk about the day.

The calendar days rapidly went by, and the winter thaw took place in Chandler, getting rid of much of the ice and snow that is typical for the time of year. March brought surprisingly warmer days to the town, and the sunshine had Wes thinking more and more about the upcoming season and how he would do as a first-time manager. He had undertaken a lot of promotional work since the manager's job became his. He didn't remember the previous manager doing this much work with the local community, doing interviews, or commercials to help promote the team. Wes, being something of a local celebrity already, knew the team was using him to help bring in fans and promote the upcoming season.

As spring approached, it also meant long hours working with the team to start planning for workouts to get everyone ready. There were times where Wes spent twelve hours or more at the stadium offices going over everything, looking at the player stats, going over the other teams and what they looked like, and more. Many times, he ended up getting a room nearby the stadium instead of driving home because he was so late.

Likewise, Kristin found herself occupied with more work as well. Spring programs at the library needed to be coordinated. Karen was a big help to Kristin as always and shouldered more responsibility to help. The two worked together to come up with schedules that would keep the community interested and coming back to what they had to offer. They arranged new speakers to come in and talk about their books, that would be an appeal to young and old alike. They started a weekly movie night that coordinated with books that they would highlight each week. Kristin even convinced Izzy to help with movie nights not just because she needed the help, but because it got Izzy out of the house more even though she was still dealing with the grounding Wes had imposed.

After a free showing of Snow White that had a full house, Kristin and Izzy arrived back home. It was after ten by the time they had cleaned everything up at the library, and Kristin was exhausted after a twelve-hour day. The two walked through the door, and both collapsed on the couch. Melissa walked into the living room from the kitchen to see the two tired ladies sprawled on the sofa.

"How'd it go tonight?" Melissa asked.

"It was great," Kristin said with a stretch of her arms. "There wasn't an empty seat, and I think everyone had a good time. The movie and book combo has been very popular. We may have to keep it up even after the weather gets nicer. I was thinking about finding out if we can clean up the empty lot over on Oak Street and use that for outdoor movies. It would give us more space and people could come in the summer, bring a picnic, and watch the show."

"That sounds great," Melissa said, "but it might be a lot of work to just organize it, round up volunteers to clean the lot and get it ready. Are you sure you have time for all of that?"

Kristin leaned her head back on the couch and considered the question. She thrived on the work she did and always wanted to do more, but she also knew Melissa was right. With all that she had been involved in, with having Molly, taking care of her, then the surgery, and work, Kristin had little to no free time as it was. Here it was, into March, and she had less than six months left to plan the wedding.

"I know, and I have done nothing about the wedding," Kristin lamented. "I don't know when I am going to have time to get it all together. I'm drowning in things to do right now. I feel like I don't get enough time with Molly as it is lately."

"Maybe you need a wedding planner," Izzy said through a stifled yawn and with her eyes closed.

Kristin turned her head to look at Izzy. Izzy felt the stare on her and cracked one eye open to look back at Kristin.

"You know, a wedding planner," Izzy said, explaining herself. "Someone to coordinate the wedding for you and take care of all the details so it goes the way you want and you don't have to put in a ton of hours doing everything. You see them on TV and in the movies all the time."

"I know what it is," Kristin said, "I just never thought I would need this much help. Besides, we're in Chandler, not New York City. I don't believe there are even wedding planners around here to work with."

"Actually," Molly said as she sat down on the couch next to Kristin, "I know someone who might be able to help. A friend of mine has a small business, and she does event planning, including weddings. She's terrific and has a great eye for things. I'll bet she could help you plan it all."

Kristin considered the notion.

"I don't how I feel about turning everything over to someone that doesn't know me and what I want for the day."

"It doesn't work like that," Izzy responded, sitting up. "The planner works with you to help you get the day to be perfect for you. She takes your ideas and makes them a reality. It would save you from having to spend hours talking to caterers, bands, DJs, decorators, and everything else, and you would still be able to get what you want. I think it's the best way to go."

"How do you think Wes would feel about it?"

"I think Dad just wants you to have what you want for the wedding," Izzy told her. "I don't think he would be upset if someone else took over organizing and planning the day."

Kristin peered over at Melissa.

"Okay," Kristin said as she stood up and stretched again. "Do you think you could call your friend and set up a meeting so I could talk to her?"

"I'll send her a text now and see what I can do," Melissa replied.

"Thanks, Melissa." Kristin gaped a giant yawn. "I'm going to get ready for bed. Thank you for all your help tonight, Izzy. I know it wasn't how you wanted to spend a Friday night."

"You're welcome," Izzy said, now mimicking the contagious stretches and yawns. "I had fun."

"Goodnight, ladies," Kristin offered with a bow and then headed off to the bedroom.

Izzy rose from the couch herself and worked her way up to her bedroom. She tossed her backpack on her desk and got into a short set to wear to bed. It was after she had finished brushing her teeth and tying back her hair and climbed onto her bed that there was a knock at her door.

"Come on in," Izzy said as she sat Indian style on her bed and looked at her phone.

"It's just me," Melissa said as she walked in and quietly closed the door behind her. Melissa sat on the bed and faced Izzy.

"It's been a few weeks, Izzy," Melissa began. "I haven't heard anybody say anything about your Mom. Have you told them you saw her that night?"

"No, I haven't, but..." Izzy was cut off by Melissa.

"Izzy, you promised," Melissa said sharply. "You should at least let your father know that she's around and wants to see you. I mean, it was only that one time, right?"

Izzy didn't answer immediately and looked down at her phone again.

"Izzy? Have you seen her since then?"

"Just a couple of times," Izzy confessed. "She stopped by during practice for the musical and talked to me a few times, and once we went out to dinner. And then I went to her house once."

"I thought you didn't want to deal with her?" Melissa said with surprise.

"I didn't think I wanted to either. I was mad and still am at what Mom has done, but I spent a lot of time explaining that to her and... well, I think she has changed. She's my mother. I guess I owe her a chance. I haven't had her in my life for so long, Mel, and it's something I have missed. I never told my Dad that or anyone. Kris is fantastic, and I love having her in my life, but..."

"But she's not your mother," Melissa added.

"She's not," Izzy said with resignation. "I have to find out if my mother is sincere about changing and being part of my life again. Once I know that for sure, I will tell Dad and Kristin."

"Izzy, I can't tell you what to do," Melissa answered. "The decision is ultimately yours. I think they deserve to know now. Your Dad would just try to protect you, you know that."

"I believe Dad's version of protection would be to tell me not to see her at all, and I don't know if I'm ready for that."

"Are you sure about that? You might be underestimating him, and Kris," Melissa advised.

"I have to do this my way for a bit longer, at least until after the musical is done, and then we can see how things go."

"Okay," Melissa nodded. "I hope you know what you're doing. Goodnight, Izzy."

Melissa rose from the bed and left the room, leaving Izzy alone. She looked down at her phone and saw text messages from her mother that had come in while she was talking to Melissa. The notes were to let Izzy know that she had already bought a ticket to the school musical for next week. A lump formed in Izzy's throat when she read the information. Enough stress existed now with the final dress rehearsals before opening night, and just keeping this secret from her father was difficult. Izzy's only hope was that her mother would just come, stay back, watch the show, and then leave. Her gut kept telling her that it would not all go this smoothly.

Chapter 14

Crunch time at the team offices was here, and know that the team roster had been completed, Wes was spending time working out strategies, potential lineups, and what workout days would be like. The problematic part was arranging everything on the limited budget that they had to work with. Wes's unfamiliarity with how the front office ran meant he had a bit of a learning curve as he worked closely with Tom Killian on arranging things.

As Tom had suggested, Wes had gone to visit with the local pitcher, Joe Johnson, and met with his family. His parents lived in a small house just outside of Washington, and it was there that Wes learned the reasons behind Joe leaving junior college and disappearing. Both of his parents had health issues and needed Joe around to assist them. While Wes knew he couldn't promise Joe a big salary like major league ballplayers would make, he could do his best to offer him a pathway to greater success.

"I make decent money working construction, Mr. Martin," Joe told him politely. "To be honest, I would be taking a pay cut to come and play ball right now, and I don't know if I could afford to do that."

"I hear you, Joe," Wes answered as he sipped the glass of iced tea Joe had offered him when they went to sit on the back porch. "I know what that is like. When I first signed out of high school, my salary was $700 a month playing ball. I worked on my Dad's farm during the offseason to make up for it where I could. The bonus money I got helped too, of course, but it wasn't easy. I know I can't match the money you are going to make doing what you do now. Still, I have seen how talented you are. I can tell you have that special something few have that can take you places. I know if you play for us, that scouts will see you and be impressed by you. That can lead you to the financial success you want to help your family."

Joe sat back, pushing the ball cap he always wore off his head and rubbed his short-cropped black hair.

"Let me talk it over with my folks," Joe insisted. "I need to do what's best for them right now."

"Absolutely," Wes said, rising from his patio chair. "If you have any questions or need anything else, give me a call. Here's my cell number. Call me at home if you want."

This was one of several meetings Wes had like this. He made it a point to travel around to meet with players that were close by before practice started so he could speak with them, let him know his thoughts, and to find out where he could help. Wes had placed most of the local players with families in the Washington area that were willing to provide living quarters for players to help them save money. He had also secured off-season jobs for more than a few of them who needed work right away before the season began.

Wes knew as manager his role was more than the guy to fill out the lineup card each day. His team was comprised of young players, kids in their teens and early twenties looking to catch a break or just play because, like him, they loved the game. Wes wanted to teach them about baseball, but he also wanted to help them develop life skills that would help them now and beyond, whether they ended up with a career in baseball or not.

Wes's computer at the stadium office and his cell phone were now filled with contact information for players, their parents, girlfriends, jobs, places they lived, and more, and he let each player know they should reach out to him if they needed help or advice. Some of the players he knew from the team last year, like Felix Machado and Emil Stanton, had already found it easy to call Wes when they had a question or found themselves needing something.

As it got close to the end of March, Wes had his roster assembled and wanted to get the team together before practices began in a few weeks so guys could meet face to face. He arranged for a party at his home and invited all the players to come. Wes's room downstairs was built for just such an event. He made all the arrangements for the party using Melissa's friend Kim, the local party planner, so that food and beverages were aplenty for the event. Kim had even arranged for rooms at a hotel in Washington near the stadium for the players and a bus to escort them back and forth to Wes's home, so no one needed to worry about driving.

When the players arrived, they were greeted outside the house by Wes, and he made sure to shake the hands of each man and thank them for coming. The players were escorted into the house, where Kim guided them through the foyer and downstairs to where the party was. Players were in awe not just of Wes's house, but of the presence of Kim, Melissa, Izzy, and Kristin.

"Do you only have beautiful women around you?" Emil mentioned as he spied the ladies gathering in the kitchen, entertaining Molly in her highchair.

"Keep walking, Emil," Wes insisted as he guided him down the stairs.

Wes was most happy to see Joe Johnson had decided to come. While Joe had signed his contract with the team just days earlier, Wes knew he was still working hard and was having second thoughts about playing.

"Joe, I'm thrilled you are here," Wes beamed as they shook hands.

"Thanks, Mr. Martin," Joe smiled. "This is some house you have here."

"Thank you, Joe," Wes replied. "It's the product of hard work and dedication, two things I know you take to heart. And you can call me Wes, please. Calling me Mr. Martin makes me feel even older than I do when I am around all you guys."

The players gathered and enjoyed the snacks and buffet that was presented to them. Since much of the team was still under twenty-one (something that made Wes cringe when he was putting the party together), it was a mostly soda and iced tea affair, though the few that were older were offered alcohol by the bartender Kim had brought in to work behind Wes's bar.

Once everyone had settled in, and all were chatting, Wes stood at the front of the room in front of the big screen and got the attention of the group so he could speak.

"I want to thank all of you for coming out tonight," Wes began.

"Why wouldn't we come?" Emil shouted. "Look at this place, man! This is paradise!" The crowd all laughed and clapped.

"It is paradise," Wes said with a smile. "it's that way for a lot of reasons. It's my home, where my family and loved ones are, and that makes it perfect. But it's also an example of what you all can accomplish and strive for if you want it. I worked hard for what I was able to attain as a ballplayer. It didn't come easy, and I spent time in the minors working on my skills until I made it to the bigs. The same chances are here for you now. Each one of you has the skills to be a pro ballplayer. You wouldn't be here if you didn't. Now is the time for you to prove it to me, to scouts, and to yourself so you can allow yourself to go further. Let's be honest – Washington is just a stepping stone here. It's a place to hone your craft, to learn, and to improve so you can move on to something else. Will all of you do that? I hope you all do, but you need to be dedicated to make it happen."

"It's my job to make sure you make the most of what is in front of you. You're going to work hard, but you're going to have fun too. This is a game, after all, and we play it because we love it. And we are here to support each other. We're a team and a family. Never forget that. The more we work like that, the more we will win and have fun. So tonight, let's have a good time, get to know each other a little better, and enjoy this great food we have, but then, starting tomorrow, we are getting down to work. We have about six weeks until the season starts, and we need to be a team before that first game."

Emil led the team in rousing applause for Wes, and Wes gave a slightly embarrassed wave to the team before going over to the bar to get a drink.

"Nice speech, Skip," Emil said. He slapped Wes on the back and asked for a bottle of beer from the blonde bartender.

"Thanks, Emil," Wes laughed as he raised his vodka martini on the rocks to Emil, who clinked his cold bottle of beer against the glass.

"You're twenty-one now, right?" Wes asked cautiously.

"You bet," Emil smiled as he sipped the beer.

"Emil, I know this sounds funny, but you are one of the veteran leaders of this team right now. We have a bunch of new people – kids, really – on this team, and I am going to lean on you for help to guide and lead this team. Are you up for that?"

"Wow, Wes, thanks," Emil said sincerely. "You know I've got your back. I can whip these guys into shape, no problem."

"Okay, I'm not asking you to do that," Wes stated. "Just help out when you can. Lead by example on and off the field, okay?"

"Got it," Emil said with a thumbs up. "You can count on me."

Wes heard a hush come over the group of guys in the room and saw they were all turned towards the staircase. Izzy and Melissa had come down, carrying a couple of more trays of food that the caterers had left upstairs in the kitchen. The ladies placed the food on one of the catering tables arranged and smiled at all the attention they garnered.

"Are those two with the caterers?" Emil said as he placed his beer down so he could run his hands through his hair.

Wes grabbed Emil's shoulder before Emil could move away from the bar.

"No," Wes chided. "One of them is my daughter, and the other is the nanny of my infant daughter."

Izzy walked over to where her father stood as more of the young men stopped and stared.

"How's it going?" Izzy asked her father, looking around at the attention she had garnered.

"Good, good," Wes told her. "Maybe you and Melissa should go back upstairs, though."

"We just came down to deliver the rest of the food and to grab Kim so Kristin could talk to her about the wedding."

"Please tell me you're not getting married," Emil said, covering his heart in feigned pain.

Izzy giggled at the sight and the thought.

"Me? Heck, no," Izzy laughed.

Emil quickly reached over and took Izzy's hand in his so he could shake it and hold it briefly.

"I'm Emil Stanton," he crowed proudly. "I'm sure Wes has told you all about me. We're like best buds."

Izzy laughed some more.

"No, I don't think he's ever mentioned you," Izzy replied. "I'm Izzy, his daughter."

"His 18-year-old daughter," Wes emphasized, getting Emil to release Izzy's hand.

"It was a pleasure to meet you," Emil said, glancing over at Wes. "I guess I'll go get some more of those empanadas."

Emil sauntered away, making sure to look closely at Melissa and Kim as they came over to Wes.

"It might be safer if you ladies stayed upstairs for a while until the horde has had their food. These guys live on next to nothing, so eating is the next important thing to them after baseball, but eventually, the focus will turn to the women in the room," Wes cautioned.

"It's nothing I haven't dealt with before," Kim replied. "I can deal with them, and Melissa here has taken enough self-defense classes that she can protect all of us."

"I kind of like the attention," Izzy said as she looked around the room.

"Upstairs," Wes ordered, pointing towards the staircase.

Melissa and Kim led a dejected Izzy up the stairs as all eyes followed them once again.

"Focus on the food," Wes yelled, directing the group back to the tables.

***

Melissa and Kim herded Izzy upstairs and closed the door. They walked back into the kitchen, laughing and smiling at flustering all the young men downstairs. They reached Kristin, who had just finished wiping Molly's face clean from all the pureed plums she had just polished off as part of her meal.

"What's so funny?" Kristin asked as she completed removing purple from Molly's chin.

"Oh, just the way those 'boys' reacted down there to Izzy," Melissa laughed.

"Boys is right," Kim said as she sat down at the table. "That room is filled with raging hormones right now. You're better off not being down there."

Melissa had come back to the table carrying a tray of coffee mugs and cookies, and then retrieved the coffee pot and teapot and placed them on the table.

"So, Kristin," Kim began as she picked up a chocolate chip cookie, "Melissa tells me you are looking for some help planning your wedding."

Kristin sighed and brushed a stray blonde hair from her face.

"I thought I would have more time to do everything myself," Kristin lamented. "With work, and Molly, and Wes being so busy, I just haven't had time to pull much of anything together, and we want to get married in September."

"Okay," Kim replied. "What have you got done so far?"

"Um... I know we want to have it here on the farm," Kristin admitted. "That's pretty much it."

Kim sat forward in her chair, expecting to hear more, but that was all Kristin had to offer.

"Well," Kim answered, "the good news is we still have five months to pull it all together. Not to brag, but I am really good at what I do. The venue can be the hardest part, and since you already have that planned, we can go to work on the rest of the day. All I need from you is to point me in the right direction of things you like and things you don't, and I can start putting together some packages that will appeal to you. We can have things like food, flowers, decorations, music, and the cake selected in practically no time at all, and I know some fantastic vendors we can work with. Have you thought about a dress for you and something for the bridesmaids?"

Kristin stared forward like she was a deer caught in headlights.

"You would think I would have done that already, wouldn't you?" Kristin said, her voice cracking. "I haven't even looked at anything yet. I haven't asked anyone to be in the bridal party! This is a mess!"

Kristin reached across the table and grabbed an oatmeal raisin cookie and bit into it.

"Hey, it's okay," Kim said calmly. "We'll get there. Let's take small steps first. Have you thought about who you want for bridesmaids?"

"Well, I would have Karen, she's my best friend," Kristin said. "And my sister in Georgia." Kristin turned and looked at Izzy.

"I want you part of it too, Izzy, if you want to be."

Izzy grinned widely.

"Of course! I would love to!" Izzy exclaimed.

"And you too, Melissa," Kristin said.

Melissa gasped and had a shocked look.

"Are you sure?" Melissa questioned. "I mean, I would be honored, but you don't have to pick me for anything. It won't hurt my feelings. I mean, we have only known each other for a little while and all..."

"Melissa," Kristin stated, "even though we haven't known each other for very long, you are an important part of my life, and I feel like we have grown close quickly. I want you to be with me... with us... for that day."

Melissa choked out a "Yes!"

"See, now that was easy and only took five minutes!" Kim laughed. "Make sure you talk to Karen and your sister tonight, and we can have that much done, and then we can see about setting up a day for dress shopping. I promise you, Kristin, I will make this fun and more comfortable for you. You will have more time to focus on other things."

Izzy's phone buzzed in her back pocket as a phone call was coming in. She plucked the phone out and answered it without thinking anything about it.

"Hello?" she asked, trying to block out the background noise combination of the loud kitchen and even more deafening din coming from downstairs since Wes had just come up and opened the door.

"Hello, Isabelle," her mother said with pleasant correctness.

"Oh, hi," Izzy replied, trying to give no indication of who she was talking to. Melissa gave her a glimpse and could tell by Izzy's face who was on the phone. Izzy's eyes widened more as her father walked over towards her.

"Izzy, can you run out to my car and get my notebooks off the front passenger seat? I have some things to go over with the team," Wes asked.

Izzy stood frozen, not responding to either her father or her mother, even though both were trying to get her attention.

"Izzy?" Wes said, moving closer to get her attention. "Did you hear me?"

"Huh? I mean, yeah, I'll go get it," Izzy answered, still frozen with her phone in her hand.

"Who are you talking to?" Wes asked.

"Oh... Oh, it's just Amber... nothing important," she said as she hurried out the front door towards her father's truck.

Izzy closed the front door behind her and heard her mother laughing into the phone.

"Why didn't you just tell him who it was? Are you embarrassed, Isabelle? You can talk to me, you know," Rachel said.

"I know I can," Izzy answered in a hushed tone. "But I haven't talked to him about you being here yet, and I don't know how he would react to it. We have a house filled with people tonight, and now was not the best time to get into it. He's got ballplayers here, and Kristin and I were talking about the wedd..." Izzy cut herself off before she finished that thought.

"Ahh, yes, the royal wedding in Chandler," Rachel said. "I am sure Princess Kristin is ready to have quite the elaborate affair."

"You don't even know her," Izzy spat back. "Why would you say that? She's nothing like that. And you're the one that ran off with a billionaire because Dad's money wasn't enough."

The phone was silent for a moment.

"I deserve that," Rachel conceded. "Anyway, I was calling to see if you wanted to swing by tonight, but I see you are busy. I will let you know I am excited about the show next weekend. I can't wait."

"Yeah, it should be fun," Izzy answered quietly. "I really need to go. I'll talk to you another time."

"Whatever you say, dear," Rachel stated politely. "Goodbye, Isabelle."

Izzy hung up as she stood in front of her father's vehicle. She tugged on the passenger side door several times without it opening. Each pull got harder and harder, and frustration reached a fever pitch.

"Shit!" Izzy yelled, slamming her fist into the passenger door.

It was then that the car lights flashed and an audible beep was heard as the door locks opened. Izzy jumped back with surprise and turned quickly to face the house, praying her father hadn't been standing there the whole time through her conversation with her mother. Instead, she saw a tall, thin figure moving towards her. When the figure hit the light in the driveway, it clearly was not her Dad, but one of the young men from his team. This man was dark-haired, blue-eyed, and built, unlike the teenage boys Izzy dealt with at high school.

"Your Dad sent me out here," the man said as he got closer to the car. "He realized the car was locked after he sent you out."

"Oh, thanks," Izzy said as she nervously bent into the car to gather up her father's books. She turned and looked over her shoulder as she saw the young man watching her as she bent and then rose. Izzy spun around and handed him the books. It was then that Izzy could see just how tall he was. Izzy was always the one towering over all the girls and a lot of the boys she knew, but she felt short next to this person.

"Here you go," she said as she looked up and into his eyes.

"Thanks," he said shyly. "I'm Joe, by the way," he said, extending his right hand.

"Izzy," she replied and took Joe's hand to shake it. Joe nervously dropped the notebooks he was holding onto the ground at their first touch. Both bent down to pick up the fallen notebooks, and Izzy not only got a better look at Joe's bright blue eyes, but she could see just how strong his arms looked.

"Sorry about that," Joe said. "I can be a little clumsy sometimes."

"Maybe not the best trait in a baseball player," Izzy said, trying to be funny. She realized maybe it didn't come out that way, however.

"I'm sorry, I wasn't trying to be rude or anything, I just thought..."

"It's okay," Joe said with a smile. "I know it's not. It doesn't go over too well when I'm working construction either. I need to be better about picking my jobs, I guess."

The two stared at each other for a moment without saying anything before Izzy's phone buzzed. She lifted it quickly and saw a text from Melissa:

Where'd you go? We're looking at bridesmaids' dresses. You need to get in here!

"I've got to get back inside," Izzy stammered. "We're talking about wedding stuff."

"If you don't mind me saying, you seem a little young to be getting married," Joe said as they strolled towards the front door.

"Me? Oh, it's not me. Why is everyone saying that tonight? No, it's Kristin... my Dad's fiancée... we're going over plans."

"Good to know," Joe said as he closed the front door behind them.

"Thanks for your help, Izzy," Joe said as he turned to go down the stairs while Izzy walked into the kitchen.

"Sure, no problem," Izzy told him as she walked right into Melissa, who was standing in the doorway waiting for her. Melissa closed the downstairs' door behind Joe and then grinned at Izzy.

"What was that all about?" Melissa asked.

"Oh, he came out to Dad's car to get books, and I was out there," Izzy said. She fussed with her hair as she tried to hide her red cheeks.

"Don't give me that," Melissa said as she elbowed Izzy. "You're blushing like crazy, and you were making goo-goo eyes at him."

"I was not," Izzy replied indignantly.

"Do you two want to stop gossiping and come look at dresses?" Kim said, calling them over to the table.

Izzy strode over and realized bridesmaid dresses were now far down on her list of things to think about.

Chapter 15

I zzy nervously paced backstage as the cast and crew readied for the opening curtain. She had spent time getting into costume, doing her hair and makeup, and going over the first song in her head, so she was ready. It wasn't her performance she was most worried about. Instead, it was the thought of her Dad running into her mother at some point before, during, or after the show. Izzy knew both were going to be in the building tonight, and she had made sure to reserve seats upfront for her father, Kristin, and her grandparents. She hoped this lessened the chance of them seeing Rachel come in or leave.

Once the curtain went up and the show began, Izzy was a true professional in action. Her love of the stage kicked in, and she put everything else out of her mind. She spoke, sang, and danced with the energy each scene required, smiled when she had to, and appeared heartbroken when it was needed. Even the quick costume change needed to slip into the grand ball gown she wore for the famous dance scene with the Beast went flawlessly, unlike in dress rehearsals where she and her helpers fumbled with all she had to put on in a short amount of time.

All the effort, hard work, and rehearsals Izzy and the entire cast had put into the show paid off. A rousing standing ovation followed the final reprise of "Beauty and the Beast." When Izzy appeared to take her bow, there was thunderous applause. She smiled widely and could see her father standing, clapping, and beaming proudly next to Kristin, who had tears running down her face as she smiled as well.

Once all was done, and the cast had assembled backstage for hugs with each other, and to change was when Izzy started to tense again. She slipped back into her blouse and skirt, took a deep breath, and began the walk out to the auditorium. Many people stopped to tell her how much they loved her performance before she eventually reached where her Dad and Kristin had stayed positioned. Her father gave her a big hug.

"Izzy, you were amazing!" he crowed. He reached over to his seat and picked up a bouquet of roses that he had purchased for her. "I am so proud of you."

"Thanks, Dad," Izzy blushed.

Kristin rushed over and followed up Wes's hug with one of her own.

"You were fantastic, Izzy. The whole show was wonderful," Kristin told her before she hugged her some more.

Izzy spied her grandparents standing just behind Kristin and her father and smiled back at them.

"Great stuff, Izzy," Wyatt told her as he kissed her cheek.

Izzy walked over to her grandmother so that Jenny did not have to try to maneuver over with her cane and gave her a kiss.

"Thanks for coming, Grandma," Izzy said softly.

"I wouldn't have missed it," Jenny told her granddaughter. "Now I'm just waiting to see you in a big-time show somewhere!"

"Come on, Jenny," Wyatt said, taking hold of his wife's arm. "Let's get you out to the car before we get trampled by all the fans looking for her autograph. Are we meeting at Angelo's for dinner?"

"I reserved a table," Wes told him. "We won't be far behind you."

Wyatt and Jenny worked their way up the aisle towards the exit, and Izzy turned back to face Kristin and her Dad. What had been her smiling face turned to one of shock and fear as she saw her mother coming up behind Wes and Kristin.

"A truly fabulous job, Isabelle," her mother said as she clapped her hands.

Wes slowly pivoted, expecting just to see another parent or teacher giving congratulations. However, he instantly recognized Rachel and stood in stunned silence for a moment before gathering himself.

"What... what are you doing here?"

"Why shouldn't I be here?" Rachel said with mock surprise. "Oh, and this must be the librarian," Rachel faced left and looked Kristin up and down.

"Wes?" Kristin asked with confusion on her face.

"Kristin, this is Rachel..." Wes hesitated, unsure of how to continue.

"Rachel Hebner, dear," she said, thrusting her gloved hand forward. "I've gone back to my original maiden name now."

"Rachel, as in your ex-wife, Rachel?" Kristin put her hand out without much force, still confused by what was going on.

"How did you know about Kristin?" Wes asked defensively as Rachel pulled her hand back.

"Come on, Wes. Chandler is still a small town, and I do have friends here, even if my family is gone now. People tell me things. Congratulations on your engagement by the way. When's the big day?" Rachel turned her attention back to Kristin, who was clearly flustered by the scene and the question.

"Well, September, but we haven't actually pinned down a day yet," Kristin said without thinking.

"Really? That's interesting," Rachel commented. "It must be stressful for you with a career, a new baby, planning a wedding, and keeping a man like Wes happy."

"I..." Kristin started to answer before Wes stepped in.

"You don't owe her an explanation, Kris," Wes said abruptly. "It's none of her business. You still didn't answer my original question, Rachel. Why are you here?"

"I'm here because it was my daughter starring in a show, that's why. I am in Chandler right now at my parents' house, taking care of it, and I knew Isabelle's musical was going on, so I came."

"It just seems odd to me is all," Wes said, moving closer to Rachel now. "Izzy starred in three other shows, and you never came to any of those. In fact, you have been absent from her life for eleven years, and then, out of the blue, you make an appearance on the night of her show?"

"It was hardly out of the blue, isn't that right, Isabelle?" Rachel said, looking at her daughter.

Izzy froze on the spot, unsure of what to do next.

"Izzy? What is she talking about?" Wes asked.

"Tell him, Isabelle," Rachel nodded.

"I... I knew she was in town," Izzy admitted.

"For how long?" Wes said.

"Since my birthday." Izzy could no longer look Wes in the face and turned her glance down towards her shoes. She kept thinking if she could just click her shoes together and disappear back to her bedroom, this would all end.

"You've known for six weeks and never bothered to say anything about it? Have you seen her before today?"

"Of course she has, Wesley," Rachel added. Rachel knew how much it got under Wes's skin when people called him Wesley. "I'm her MOTHER, after all," she said with emphasis, glaring at Kristin when she said it. Kristin was nowhere near as bewildered by the events as they unfolded as Wes was. In fact, she was now peering back at Rachel, aware of what Rachel was trying to do to manipulate the situation in her favor.

Kristin tugged on Wes's arm to get his attention as he kept his gaze shifting back and forth between Izzy and Rachel.

"Wes, this isn't the place to get into all of this," she said calmly. "Let's go and meet your parents, and we can deal with all this later."

"Fine," Wes growled before regaining his composure. He tugged on the lapels of his suit jacket, turned away from Rachel, and put his arm around Kristin as they moved toward Izzy.

"A family dinner at Angelo's tonight?" Rachel guessed. "Oh, and I didn't get an invitation?"

"You have got to be kidding with this shit, Rachel," Wes stated as he scowled at his ex-wife.

"Wes, let it go," Kristin emphasized.

"It's okay, dear," Rachel coddled. "I always knew how to get under his skin. I'm not one for Angelo's anyway. It seems rather pedestrian after dining in Manhattan for all these years."

"Maybe you should just go back there," Wes barked, "and leave us alone."

Wes marched Kristin over to Izzy and corralled her as they led her up the aisle toward the exit. Izzy glanced back at her mother and saw Rachel give a casual wave of her fingers with a Cheshire Cat grin on her face.

By the time the trio had arrived at Wes's truck, Wes's blood boiled. He opened the doors for Kristin and Izzy politely, but the way he slammed them shut and then the driver's side door shut let both ladies know how annoyed he was.

Everyone was silent for the first few minutes as they waited to get out of the jammed parking lot. Wes rhythmically tapped his fingers on the steering wheel progressively harder and harder until Kristin thought he would smash right through the steering column.

"Wes!" she finally shouted.

Wes looked over and saw the concern on Kristin's face. They could also hear Izzy gently sobbing in the backseat.

Wes pulled the truck out of line waiting to exit the parking lot and instead tore across the grassy dunes of the front of Chandler High School. He swerved violently to avoid oncoming and exiting traffic before he got out onto Route 5 and headed toward the center of town.

"Pull over!" Kristin yelled. Wes moved onto the shoulder of the road and stopped the vehicle.

"Are you out of your mind?" Kristin said. "You're so mad at your ex-wife that you're willing to risk all of our lives like that? Have you forgotten we have an infant daughter waiting for us at home?" Kristin took off her seat belt and got out of the car. She marched around to the driver's side and pulled open the door.

"What are you doing?" Wes asked.

"You are moving over, and I am driving the rest of the way. You are in no state of mind to do this right now."

"Kris, I can..." Wes said as he tried to argue his case.

"No, you can't, and I won't let you. Now either move over, or Izzy and I are getting out and calling for a ride. Your choice. I'm not taking chances."

Wes resignedly slid over to the passenger seat, and Kristin climbed behind the wheel. Naturally, the truck was set up for Wes to drive, and Kristin could not get her feet to reach the pedals, nor could she see over the steering wheel since Wes had the height of the seat set low. It took her a moment to adjust everything before she safely pulled out into traffic and drive the rest of the way to Angelo's, all without a word from anyone.

They arrived at the restaurant later than anticipated, but Angelo greeted them with his usual smile and graciousness. He fawned over Izzy, remarking about how lovely she looked and how he had heard nothing but wonderful things about the job she did in the musical. Izzy attempted to remain social and polite, but putting on a happy face proved difficult.

Angelo led the group to the table in the back room where Wyatt and Jenny sat waiting. Wyatt dutifully rose from his seat when they arrived and ushered Izzy to sit next to him, pulling her chair out for her.

"Thank you, Grandpa," Izzy said, forcing a smile.

Wyatt watched to make sure Wes showed the same courtesy to Kristin before sitting down himself.

"What took you so long?" Wyatt asked. "I already went through a basket of Angelo's bread. Traffic bad getting out?"

"Among other things," Wes groused.

"What's that supposed to mean?" Wyatt inquired.

"Let's just say we ran into an issue leaving," Wes said. He pulled the menu up from the table and started to look it over.

"Did you have car trouble?" Jenny remarked. She looked over at Kristin and then at Izzy, and neither gave any indication of what was going on. "Wesley?" she asked.

Wes nearly crumpled the menu when he heard his mother say this.

"No, Mom, we didn't have any car trouble," Wes snapped.

"Hey, don't talk like that," Wyatt said, reaching over to force the menu down from in front of Wes's face. "She's your mother, dammit... pardon my French."

"Dad, don't do this right now, okay?" Wes said with a raised voice. The few other patrons in the back looked over at the table.

"Wes," Kristin insisted.

"Can everyone please stop?" Izzy yelled. "You know, this was supposed to be a great night. My last opening night in high school. I rehearsed and worked hard and poured my heart out, and it all got ruined in about sixty seconds. I'm sorry that she came back and reached out to me, Dad. I didn't ask her to. I didn't ask her to send me flowers, or give me a birthday present, or come to the show, or invite me to her house, but she did all those things. What was I supposed to do?"

"She gave you a birthday present?" Wes said, trying to remain calm.

"Who are you talking about?" Wyatt asked, trying to catch up.

"Rachel was at the show tonight," Kristin said softly.

Wyatt and Jenny were both taken aback by the announcement.

"Yes, she was there," Wes added, "and apparently, she has been in town for six weeks seeing Izzy, and I knew nothing about it. So, what did she give you for a present? After eleven years, it had to be a whopper, right? Is it a Picasso? Or a Lamborghini? Maybe diamond earrings?"

"Wes, please," Kristin begged, taking hold of his wrist.

"She gave me $10,000, okay, Dad?" Izzy shouted.

Wes nodded.

"Of course, nothing but cold cash from a cold heart. How much of it have you spent?"

Izzy stared at her father.

"I haven't spent any of it," Izzy said, trying to hush her tone.

"Well, that's good," Wes said. He picked his menu up again. "You have to give it back, and you shouldn't see her again. You know she has some ulterior motive for all this Izzy. It's the way she is now."

"Why do I have to give it back?" Izzy asked. "And why can't I see her again? She's my mother."

"Because it's the best thing for you. It's the right thing to do. Because I'm telling you to. Those are all good reasons."

"Dad, I'm eighteen now. You can't tell me I'm not allowed to see her anymore. If I want to, I can. That's my choice, not yours."

"Oh, I see," Wes said as he looked at his daughter. "You have such a good track record of making good decisions since you're eighteen that I should trust your judgment now? Do you remember what happened six weeks ago? I tried to give you leeway, Izzy, but it didn't work."

"You know what?" Izzy said as she got up from the table. "I don't feel much like celebrating anymore. I'm sorry, Grandma and Grandpa, and I'm sorry Kris, but I need to go."

"Izzy, don't," Kristin said as she got up to try and stop her. Izzy, however, turned and ran from the room and out the front door before Kristin could get far. Izzy ran into a waiter carrying a tray of plates of calamari and sauce, knocking him to the ground as she fled.

"Wes, you need to go after her," Kristin pled.

Wes got up from the table and sprinted through the front of the restaurant, nearly running into the same waiter as he tried valiantly to clean up the mess. Wes got out the front door and went to the parking lot but saw no sign of Izzy. He moved to the sidewalk and looked up and down the street. There were groups of people out on the street since it was a lovely evening, but Wes saw no signs of Izzy anywhere.

***

Izzy hurried down the street and then ducked into the doorway of the closed barbershop not far from Angelo's so that she could hide for a moment and go unseen. She struggled to catch her breath from the running and the crying she was doing. However, once Izzy regained her composure, she stood still for a moment. She waited to make sure her father, Kristin, or her grandfather were not chasing after her. Izzy peeked around the edge of the building and saw no one coming her way, and she raced down the rest of Main Street before taking a left turn and heading up the street there.

Chandler was not a big town, and the area just off Main Street contained several other businesses scattered on the side streets that did not get the level of foot traffic those on Main Street did. Izzy gazed into a couple of closed storefronts as she got closer to a couple of the local bars in the area. She received more than a few glances from so of the younger guys coming out of the bars there as she passed.

After struggling to clear her head with all that had happened, she noticed she was walking by Altered Ego, the lone tattoo parlor in town. Izzy stopped and stared into the window, looking at some of the design work and photos the business displayed to lure customers in. Without a second thought, Izzy pushed open the door and walked in.

The Altered Ego was small, even by Chandler standards. There were two areas where chairs were for the artists to do their work, a couple of aluminum chairs with torn red vinyl seats along the far wall, and not much else. Art designs covered the worn walls of the place, and Izzy looked at different options and thought about what she might want. Her mind raced with ideas of getting something substantial or tawdry just to piss off her father more, but she then decided she might like something more meaningful to her instead.

"I can be with you in a little bit, honey," said a hefty, burly, bearded man that was working on some ink for an equally large man lying back in one of the chairs. The way the artist had grinned at Izzy made her more than a bit uncomfortable and made her feel like she was way out of her element. It was then that a young woman walked over to where Izzy stood.

"Leave her alone, Earl," the woman shouted. The dark-haired girl turned to Izzy and smiled. "Don't be afraid of him, he's all talk," she said. "What can I help you with?"

"I'm... I'm not really sure..." Izzy stammered. "I don't know what I want, or if I really want one, I guess."

It was then that Izzy spotted artwork on the wall that caught her eye. Plain as day, there was a red heart with a banner underneath that read 'Sisters 4 Ever.'

"I want that one," Izzy said authoritatively.

The woman looked at it and smiled.

"Are you sure? That's a pretty specific design I came up with for a group of girls that came in a while back. Usually, girls come in together and want that one."

"Well, I'm kind of on my own, I guess," Izzy said. "Maybe you could just do the heart for me and leave out the rest."

"Sure. Are you old enough to be doing this on your own? You have to be eighteen, or you need a parent here with you."

"I'm eighteen," Izzy stated firmly, reaching into her purse to pull out her driver's license.

The woman examined the license and handed it back to Izzy.

"It's going to cost $125," she told Izzy.

"You take PayPal?" Izzy asked.

"Sure."

"Then let's do this," Izzy determined. Izzy walked over to the empty chair and laid down.

"Where do you want it?" the woman asked as she slipped on her protective gloves.

Izzy pulled down the waistband of her skirt and pointed to her right hip.

"Are you sure you want it there?" the artist questioned. "I have to tell you; it's going to hurt more right near the hip bone."

"Yes, that's where I want it," Izzy stated as she tried to keep her voice from cracking. "How... how long do you think this is going to take?"

"For something like this, it's not very big," the artist told her as she prepared everything. "Maybe an hour at most, but probably shorter. Just try to relax."

Izzy gripped the sides of the chair tightly as she braced for the first touch of the needle. She was shocked by the coolness of the rubbing alcohol the artist applied to her hip first, and then maintained control when she felt the first scratch of the needle.

Throughout the process, Izzy concentrated on the conversation, no matter one-sided, it seemed to her, that she had with her father. Izzy knew that withholding the information about her mother was bound to cause problems. Still, her hope all along was that her mother would come to the show, leave quietly, and then go back to New York without causing a fuss.

"The best-laid plans," Izzy whispered through gritted teeth.

"What's that?" the artist asked.

"Nothing... how's it going?" Izzy asked, afraid to look down to watch.

"It looks good so far. How are you holding up?"

"Great, just keep going," Izzy insisted.

"There's no turning back now anyway, honey," the artist laughed through her mask.

Izzy resorted to all kinds of mind tricks – saying the alphabet, singing songs internally, counting ceiling tiles – all to help herself along. Time went faster than she thought when the artist told her she was almost finished.

Izzy heard the door to the parlor open, and her chair was positioned closest to the entrance. She noticed a few heads peeking over the wall separating where she was and the waiting area. It wasn't until one of the heads disappeared and then re-appeared quickly that she got concerned.

"Izzy?" the familiar voice asked. The face peeked further over the wall this time, and she saw that it was Joe, one of the players on her Dad's team. Panic started to fill her chest and work upwards to her throat.

"Hi, Joe," Izzy squeaked as she felt the tattoo artist start to wipe the tattoo area again and begin to put the bandage on.

"What are you doing here?" he said with a puzzled look on his face.

"What do you think she would be doing here?" the artist asked sarcastically. "She's not picking up her dry cleaning."

"I mean... I guess I never expected to see you here," Joe said, trying to catch a glimpse of the artwork of the tattoo that resided on Izzy's hip now.

"Is it okay if your boyfriend here gets a look or should I chase him out?" the artist asked Izzy.

"Oh, he's not my boyfriend," Izzy said quickly. "He's just... well, just a friend. It's okay if he looks."

Joe walked over to the artist's side to get a look at the work done.

"Very nice," Joe said as Izzy noticed his gaze working down her leg and then up to her face.

"Perfect." The tattoo artist gently bandaged the area for Izzy and reminded her to keep the bandage on for the rest of the night before using a gentle soap to wash the site tomorrow and pat it dry.

Izzy tugged her skirt back into place while Joe kept a keen eye on her. The artist tapped out an invoice to send Izzy on PayPal, which Izzy paid. She made sure to add a hefty tip for the job done, figuring she had nothing else to spend all this money on anyway.

"Hey, thanks, honey," the artist said with glee. "When you're ready for another one, make sure to come back and ask for me. I'm Andi."

"Thanks, Andi," Izzy acknowledged and walked around the wall to see four players from the Washington team that was just at her home a few weeks ago sitting there looking at possible tattoos.

"I guess I'll see you around," Izzy said to Joe, hoping to hustle out as fast as she could before anyone else recognized her. She went out of the shop door and started down the street without even thinking about where she was going or how she was getting there.

"Izzy!" a voice shouted behind her.

She turned around and saw Joe running up to greet her.

"What is it?" Izzy asked, worried that her father might show up at any moment. "You should go back inside with the other guys."

"Nah, I didn't really want to go and get another tat right now anyway," Joe said. "Those guys can take care of themselves. Can I... can I walk you to your car?"

"Umm... the thing is... I don't have my car here. I don't really know what I am going to do."

"Is everything okay?" Joe asked with concern. He could see Izzy wrinkling her brow as she worked to figure out what she was doing.

"It's kind of a long story," Izzy said as she began to walk away. She did not want to break out in tears in front of Joe and seem like the helpless damsel she felt like inside right now.

"Wait!" Joe jogged to catch up to her again.

"Why don't you come to my car and let me give you a ride then. I drove myself over here. My car is just up the block by the bar up there."

Izzy hesitated, but the thought of having a friend right now gave her comfort, and she nodded in agreement.

The two walked along the sidewalk without saying much of anything to each other. Izzy noticed out of the corner of her eye how Joe kept glancing at her, almost like he was trying to come up with something to talk about. Eventually, Izzy shivered as the cooler night air gave her a chill.

"Are you cold?" Joe asked.

"It's just a little cooler than I thought it would be, and I left my jacket..." she was about to say, 'in my Dad's car,' but thought better of it and just left it alone.

"Here," Joe said as he unzipped the olive-green hoodie he was wearing and handed it to Izzy.

"No, really, it's okay," Izzy balked, but Joe had stepped in front of her to stop her from walking. He placed the sweatshirt on Izzy's shoulders so that she could guide her arms through the sleeves. It was difficult for Izzy not to notice his strong arms and upper build, along with the hint of fragrance from whatever cologne Joe wore.

Once Izzy had pushed her arms into the sweatshirt, Joe began to zip it up for her. His fingers moved slowly, coming to a stop just beneath her chest as Joe was reluctant and too modest to go any further.

"Thank you," Izzy said with a blush.

The two kept walking toward Joe's car, a beat-up white Ford pickup that sat just outside the front door of Bream's Brewhouse, a relatively new addition to Chandler. Just as Izzy and Joe were reaching his truck, the entrance to the Brewhouse opened and out walked Karen and Brian. Karen stopped suddenly at the sight of Izzy.

"Izzy! I'm surprised to see you over here," Karen remarked. "How was the show? I thought you guys were having dinner at Angelo's tonight."

"Oh, hi, Karen," Izzy answered quickly. Izzy couldn't help but feel defeated by her string of bad luck tonight of having people she least wanted to see randomly appear. "Yeah, well, plans kind of changed, I guess."

"Who's your friend?" Karen asked with a smile.

"This is Joe Johnson," Izzy answered. She wanted more than anything to just get into the truck and disappear. "Joe, this is Karen. She works with Kristin at the library."

"Nice to meet you, Ma'am," Joe said, offering his hand.

Karen tried not to laugh too hard. "Ma'am! Brian, he called me Ma'am," she said to her husband. "I don't think I'm much older than you, Joe. What are you, nineteen?"

"Twenty," Joe answered with a laugh.

"We should get going, Joe," Izzy said, taking Joe by the arm and getting him closer to the truck. Joe opened the passenger side door, so Izzy could climb in. "Nice seeing you guys," Izzy said with a wave as the door closed.

Joe got into the driver's seat and started up his truck. They pulled away with Karen and Brian watching them on the street.

"They seem nice, though the guy is kind of quiet," Joe remarked as he drove.

"They are nice. The problem is that Karen will tell Kristin she saw me tonight," Izzy told Joe.

"Why is that a problem?" Joe quizzed as he turned onto Main Street and began making his way towards Route 5 to get to Martin Way.

"It's complicated... wait, you can't take me home! Stop the car!" Izzy exclaimed.

Joe pulled over to the side of the road and stopped the truck.

"Why can't I take you home? What's going on? I want to help you, Izzy, but I feel like I need a little more information."

"Can you please take me over to Wagner Place? It's in the other direction," Izzy pleaded.

"Okay," Joe said as he turned the truck around. "Who lives on Wagner Place?"

"It's my Mom's house," Izzy replied.

"I didn't know your Mom lived around here," Joe told her as he looked at street signs to find his way.

"It's a recent thing," Izzy said as she pointed when Joe should turn onto the correct street.

"Here... her house is right here," Izzy stated. Izzy went to get out of the truck, but Joe grabbed her hand.

"Are you going to at least tell me what is going on? If you are in trouble, maybe I can help."

"Joe, the less you know, the better it will be for both of us, I promise. Thank you so much for the ride tonight," Izzy said as she got out. She slammed the door shut and then walked around to the driver's side of the truck. She tapped gently on the window so Joe could take the glass down.

Izzy leaned in and gave Joe a soft kiss on the lips.

"Thank you," she said before she hustled off inside the front gate and up the walkway to the front door before Joe could react in any way.

Joe was the first guy Izzy had kissed who wasn't Bradley, and even with all the drama that had gone on, that quick kiss was enough to elate her.

Izzy knocked on the front door and waited patiently for someone to answer. She glanced down towards the end of the driveway, and she could see the headlights of Joe's truck as it sat idling there. She sensed he was watching to make sure she got inside safely, causing her to inhale and smile.

When the front door creaked open, Izzy was surprised to see her mother answering instead of the housekeeper. Rachel stood wearing a long, beige silk robe.

"Isabelle, what a pleasant surprise," Rachel smiled.

"Is it... is it okay if I stay with you for a few days?"

"Of course, dear, come on in," Rachel said as she guided Izzy into her home before shutting the door.

Chapter 16

D inner ended abruptly, with Wes going back to the table after he was unable to locate Izzy anywhere on the streets around Angelo's. He issued his apologies to his parents and to Angelo before he and Kristin hurried out to the truck to leave. Wes circled the immediate streets around Main Street for any sign of where Izzy might have gone, going slowly past anyplace that might still be open to see if she was around. He also went into a couple of the local bars to see if Izzy had managed to sneak her way in. Even though she was just eighteen, Wes knew Izzy could easily pass for older, and that might lead to more trouble.

When Wes exited the last bar in the area, he came back to the vehicle and slammed the car door shut loudly, making Kristin jump a bit in her seat.

"No luck?" Kristin asked with concern.

"No... I don't know where she disappeared to," Wes said. The combination of anger, fear, and guilt mixed his voice so that it cracked.

"I called the house, and Melissa hasn't heard from her either. I asked Melissa to call me if Izzy showed up there."

"Maybe I should swing by the police station," Wes contemplated.

"I don't know how much help they would be right now, Wes," Kristin offered as she tried to calm him down. "It's only been about an hour or so since she left us, and she is eighteen. She's allowed to not come home legally if she doesn't want to."

"This is nuts," Wes barked, slamming his hands on the steering wheel. "I'm sorry," he added. "I'm just upset is all. I'm sure all of this is Rachel's doing in some way. I thought after she left me and stopped contacting Izzy, that was the end of it, and we wouldn't hear from her again. I don't know why Rachel chose now to come back and stir things up. I don't understand why Izzy didn't tell us Rachel had contacted her and that she was seeing her. It doesn't make sense."

Wes started the truck and drove around some more along Main Street. The streets had begun to thin out even more since it was later, and few people circulated around the entrance to the diner, the only place still open, as Wes drove back towards home.

"Wes, I know Izzy has gone through a lot lately. She has dealt with her break-up, school, our chaotic family life at home, the wedding, and goodness knows what else. I think she's just a little confused right now," Kristin reassured. "It all just came to a head tonight. I think we need to hear more of her side of things than we have been letting her."

"When you say we, you mean me, don't you?" Wes asked, full knowing he was the primary cause. "I know I have been hard on her lately, but Izzy has to realize she has a lot of responsibility in her life right now, and the decisions she makes now can have an impact on her life in the future and on other people. I think she has lost sight of that, primarily based on her behavior over the last six weeks or so."

"Wes, I'm not condoning some of the decisions she has made and things Izzy has done," Kristin added, "but eighteen-year-olds are confused, they make mistakes, and come to decisions that may not be the best. I know that happened to me and I am sure, if you think about it, you did the same thing. All we can do is be there for her to help her out and guide her. Trying to force her into situations will just drive her away more."

"Force her into what?" Wes said as he pulled onto Martin Way. "I've given her a lot of leeway. If anything, she gets more than what most kids her age get, including chances. I think asking her to follow some rules is reasonable."

"It has nothing to do with rules, Wes," Kristin told him. "You can't force her to be someone she isn't. Pushing the University of Pittsburgh on her is part of it. The way you treated Bradley every time you saw him..."

"Well, that was clearly for a good reason," Wes interrupted. "You see how all that turned out."

Wes got out of the car and walked toward the front steps before Kristin grabbed him by the arm.

"That's what I mean, Wes. You can't make every decision for her. She has to live her life."

"Let's just find her first, and then we can worry about the rest of it," Wes said as he opened the front door.

Wes walked straight to the kitchen, where he found Melissa talking on her cell phone as she sat at the table.

"Is that Izzy?" Wes said as he moved toward Melissa. Melissa looked up at Wes, but before she could say anything, Wes had grabbed the phone from her hand.

"Wes!" Kristin yelled.

"Izzy, is that you?" Wes said into the phone. There was silence on the other end for a moment.

"Yes, it's me." Izzy's voice was softer than usual, but it also contained a coldness in it that Wes was unaccustomed to.

"Where are you? Are you alright?"

"I'm fine," Izzy answered, "and where I am doesn't matter right now. I'm safe, and I won't be home tonight."

Wes worked to show more considerable restraint and control in his voice.

"Izzy, I know what I said was wrong, and I'm sorry," Wes told his daughter. "I was out of line and upset. Please, just come home so we can talk about it."

"Dad, I know you mean it when you say you're sorry, but I don't know if it would change anything right now. I think we both need a little time apart from each other."

"What does that mean?" Wes asked. "Isabelle, you need to come home... now."

"Good night, Dad," Izzy said as she cried. "I do love you." She then hung up the phone.

Wes stared down at the cell phone before he absently handed it back to Melissa.

"Did she tell you where she was?" Wes asked Melissa.

Melissa looked at Kristin and then back to Wes.

"No, honestly, she didn't," Melissa admitted. "She didn't want to tell me and put me in a position where I would have to tell you about it. I called her a few times before she answered. Izzy told me what happened and that she was okay and not to worry about her, that's it."

Wes sat down at the table and tossed his keys, so they skittered across to the other side.

Kristin walked behind Wes and put her arms on his shoulders before she wrapped them around him and held him. The three of them sat in silence for a moment before there was a light knock heard on the front door. Melissa, Kristin, and Wes all perked up, and Kristin headed toward the door first.

Kristin flung the door open, hoping to see Izzy on the other side. Instead, there stood Joe Johnson.

"I'm sorry to bother you this late, Ms. Arthur," Joe said politely. Wes had walked behind Kristin at this point, also with the hope that Izzy was at the door.

"Joe, what are you doing here?" Wes asked.

"Hi, Coach," Joe said. He looked down at his sneakers, scuffling them along the concrete of the front step. "I didn't want to bother you, but I thought I needed to. Can I come in?"

"Sure," Kristin invited. Joe walked into the living room and sat down on one of the chairs while Kristin and Wes sat on the couch.

"I thought you should know that I ran into Izzy tonight," Joe told them.

"Where?" Wes asked excitedly.

"We ran into each other over near Bream's," Joe told him.

"What was she doing in Bream's?" Wes wanted to know. Wes's anger was rising again.

"Oh, no," Joe said calmly. "She wasn't in there. A few of the guys and I were coming out of there when I saw her, and I went up to her because she looked upset. She didn't get into what happened, but she asked me to give her a ride."

"Where did you take her?" Kristin said. Kristin took hold of Wes's hand to hold it and calm him down.

"Well, it was a house over on Wagner Place," Joe replied.

"That's Rachel's family house," Wes added.

"Izzy said it was her mother's place," Joe admitted.

Wes stood up from the couch and start patting the pockets of his suit pants.

"Wes, what are you doing?" Kristin asked.

"I'm going over there," he answered, "if I can find my damn keys."

"Maybe that isn't the best idea," Kristin warned.

"Kris, I need to talk to her, and to Rachel," Wes insisted. "Where are my keys?" he yelled.

In the distance, Molly was heard starting to cry.

"I got her," Melissa yelled from the kitchen.

"Coach, I can give you a ride," Joe told Wes.

"Good, let's go."

Wes began to lead Joe toward the front door and out onto the steps.

"Wes, give her the night to calm down," Kristin pleaded.

Wes was too focused on finding his daughter to consume what Kristin told him, and in seconds he and Joe were in Joe's pickup and on their way to Wagner Place.

"Coach, I don't want to get her into any trouble or anything," Joe stated.

"Joe, you did the right thing by letting me know. We've been worried about her since she left," Wes replied.

Joe did his best to remember just where the house was on Wagner Place, but he needed a little assistance from Wes to point the way to get the exact location. Wes had the door to the truck open before Joe came to a full stop.

Wes marched up the path to the front door and knocked loudly several times. It had been many years since Wes was at the front door to this home. The last time was likely when Izzy was a small child, and they came over to see Rachel's parents, something they infrequently did.

Wes pounded his fist on the door once again, but still, no one answered. Joe now appeared behind Wes to see what was going on.

"Coach, maybe we should go," Joe said tentatively.

"Not if she's in there," Wes roared. "Rachel, open the fucking door!"

Wes thumped his fist some more on the door and saw a light flick on in the foyer. Rachel opened the door a crack and peered out to see Wes standing there.

She then pulled the door open more fully, revealing herself in her open silk robe and low-cut silk negligee.

"Why, Wes, what brings you here at this hour?" she said demurely.

"Knock it off, Rachel," Wes growled. "Where's Izzy?"

"It's a bit late for gentleman callers, don't you think Wes?" she asked, spying Joe standing a few feet behind Wes.

"I know she's here," Wes said as he moved toward the front door.

"I didn't invite you in," Rachel said seriously. "I would hate to have to phone the police and tell them you were entering illegally. It wouldn't look suitable for the local hero, I'm sure you would agree."

"I don't know what you think you're up to, Rachel," Wes said, bewildered. "You walk out on me, leave me with our daughter, move away, and we never hear from you. Now, suddenly, you show up and think it's okay to just throw our lives into turmoil? Why are you bothering us? Don't you have a life in New York to live?"

"I think the only one I am bothering is you," Rachel answered, "and maybe that little fiancée of yours. She seems a bit young for you, Wes, I have to say. I mean, she's practically our daughter's age. How the people in Chandler must gossip about that."

"Enough of this," Wes barked. He pushed past Rachel into the foyer and yelled.

"Izzy, I know you can hear me!" he shouted.

"Coach, don't," Joe said, trying to keep his manager from getting into trouble. Joe pulled Wes back out onto the front porch.

"Rachel, you don't want to do this," Wes said as he peered at his ex-wife.

"Are you threatening me now, Wesley?" Rachel chirped. She put a hand to her chest to feign fear.

Wes saw a shadow moving behind Rachel and then saw Izzy standing there, wearing a t-shirt and a pair of sweatpants.

"Dad? What are you doing? How did you..." Izzy started and then spotted Joe with her father.

"Joe, did you bring him here?" Izzy asked, crestfallen.

"Izzy, I'm sorry," Joe said as he moved forward now. "I didn't know what to do, and it seemed like you were in some trouble and needed help."

"I don't need anyone's help, not yours, or his," Izzy said emphatically.

"Izzy come out and let's go," Wes said, trying to regain control of the situation.

"I'm not coming, Dad," Izzy answered. "I'm staying here for a bit until I can figure things out. Go home."

Izzy backed away and returned to the shadows. As Wes made another move towards the front door, a flash of blue and red lights appeared behind them.

Joe turned and saw the familiar shadows of two police officers moving up the walkway towards them. Wes turned slowly to see the police getting closer before he pivoted back to look at Rachel.

"I guess I already called them when I heard pounding on the door late at night," Rachel admitted. "You can't be too careful these days, Wesley. I have a young girl inside to protect."

"Do you really have to be this much of a bitch?" Wes asked. "What did I do to you?"

One of the officers was already leading Joe off the property while the other walked up to Wes.

"Officer, please escort this gentleman off my property," Rachel insisted. "He is threatening my daughter and me."

"Come on, Mr. Martin," the officer said quietly, putting his hand on Wes to guide him. The officer immediately recognized Wes and wanted to make the situation as easy as possible for all involved.

Wes glared back at Rachel, who gave a grin as she watched Wes get led back toward the squad car.

***

Izzy watched the scene from the steps of the staircase as her mother spoke to the police for a bit before closing the front door and returning inside.

"Did you really have to call the police?" Izzy asked her mother. "He wasn't going to do anything."

"Isabelle, a lady alone can never be too careful," Rachel cautioned. "It could have been anybody out there trying to get into my home to rob me or worse. I was looking for your safety and mine."

"You knew it was Dad," Izzy insisted. "You heard him yell. I heard him yell."

"The police won't do anything to him, dear, don't worry," Rachel consoled. "They will just make sure he goes home. Come on, let's get you back to your room."

Rachel put her arm around Izzy and led her up the spiral staircase and to the large bedroom at the end of the hall that Rachel had designated as Izzy's room. The room was already nicely decorated and outfitted when Izzy first arrived earlier in the evening, almost as if Rachel had been expecting her to show up. A large bed in the center of the room took up just a fraction of the spacious area that held a dresser, an armoire, and a walk-in closet, along with a vanity and an entrance to its own bathroom.

"Thanks for letting me stay here," Izzy said as she climbed onto her bed.

"Of course, Isabelle," her mother told her. "You can stay as long as you like. It's wonderful to have someone else here. You're the only family I have left."

"What... what about your husband in New York?" Izzy asked, treading lightly.

"Who, William?" Rachel said with a laugh. "Oh, William was a nice man for years, but we started to drift apart. He spent more time working and in the office, and then more time in his admin assistant if you know what I mean. That was when I divorced him."

"Oh, I'm sorry," Izzy said sincerely.

"Don't be, dear," Rachel replied. "It was all for the best, and I got half of his money plus the inheritance from my father. I've done alright, and in turn, you will do well also."

"What do you mean?"

"You're all there is, Isabelle, at least for me," Rachel explained. "I want to make sure I can make up for the lost time and be with you, but I also have made sure you are taken care of. You are my sole heir, so at some point, everything will be yours."

Izzy didn't know what to say.

"I don't need you to do that," Izzy said. "Dad takes good care of me and makes sure I have what I need."

"Sure, he has in the past," Rachel added, "but now with a new wife-to-be and a new baby, I'm sure his focus will be more on them than it is on you. He has a new family to look after. Once they are wed, and you got to college, it might be like you aren't even there at all anymore."

Izzy recoiled at the harshness of the statement.

"I don't mean to be crude about it, dear," Rachel assured. "I'm just honest. That will be the reality of the situation. I wouldn't be surprised if they have plans for several other little ones, or maybe even move to a bigger house and leave Chandler."

"Dad would never do that," Izzy contended. "His parents are here, he loves that house, and Kristin works right here."

Rachel let out a small laugh.

"Isabelle, you still have a lot to learn about the world outside of this small town. If they have other children, do you really think Kristin will keep working? She'll stay home with the children and make sure they get the best of everything, and they can't do that in Chandler. And not to be cruel, but Wes's parents aren't getting younger, and Jenny, well, her health is not good as it is. At some point, things must change. You should be prepared for it now so you can start thinking more about yourself and your future instead of worrying about them. I only wished I had seen it sooner. I regret not taking you with me so you could have had a better life."

"My life has been fine," Izzy answered. She began to feel confused about what her mother told her.

"Has it?" Rachel questioned. "You were basically raised by your grandparents on a farm without a father around most of the time. Then, when he finally is around, he latches on with a young woman to spend time with instead of you, and they have a child together right away, hire a nanny instead of asking you to help. It's like they brought her in to replace you. Suddenly you are the outsider looking in. If I had taken you with me, you would have lived in a beautiful home, gone to the best schools, and been the center of attention all the time. We could have traveled the world together. We can still do that. It might be even more fun for both of us now."

Izzy stared at her mother and tried to process all that was said. Izzy didn't want to believe it was true, but a lot of what her mother told her did fit what had happened.

"I can see that this has been a trying day for you, and that was a lot of information for you to process. We can talk more about it in the morning. Get some rest, dear."

Rachel leaned in and gave Izzy a hug, the first real intimate contact she had with her mother in almost eleven years. Izzy hugged her tightly, feeling like she needed a hug from someone who cared about her now more than ever.

Chapter 17

The sunlight streamed across Izzy's face through the curtains as her eyes blinked open. She sat up with a start, momentarily forgetting where she was and not recognizing the surroundings before she remembered all that had occurred the night before. She dragged herself out of bed and into the bathroom so she could wash up and splash water on her face. She marveled again at the size of the bathroom, the lavish sunken tub, and separate shower, the large mirrors, and the different toiletries that filled the large counters around the double sink. The thought of sinking herself into that tub to soak was inviting until Izzy realized she didn't have any of her own clothing.

She walked out of the bathroom and gasped loudly at the sight of someone making her bed.

"Oh, I'm sorry, Ms. Isabelle," the older woman noted. "I knocked, but you didn't answer, and I peeked in and didn't see anyone. I should have knocked on the bathroom door first. I was just tidying up."

"That's okay," Izzy said. "I can make my bed myself, though. That's kind of you."

"Nonsense," the woman insisted. "That's my function in the household. I'm Adrian, one of the housekeepers."

"One of... how many housekeepers are there?" Izzy said softly, but loudly enough, so Adrian heard her.

"There are four of us, Miss," Adrian answered, "but we don't all work at the same time. We also have Terrance, the cook, and then there is Arthur, Ms. Hebner's driver."

"Okay," Izzy said. She instinctively went over to the dresser drawer before she remembered her clothing dilemma.

"The dresser is empty, but Ms. Hebner had purchased a couple of dresses and skirts and such. They are hanging in the closet," Adrian said, pointing to the closet door.

Izzy tentatively went over and opened the closet door. Lights came on automatically as soon as she set foot into the large area. Most of the closet was empty, though there were some dresses, skirts, and blouses hanging. Izzy pulled a hangar holding a yellow floral dress down and held it up against herself as she stared into the large mirror. The dress looked like an ideal fit, which surprised Izzy. She pulled off the t-shirt she wore and slipped the dress over her head and saw it clung to her form perfectly. Izzy then shimmied out of the sweats she wore and emerged from the closet.

"Oh, that looks quite nice," Adrian said as she readied to plug in the vacuum. "Here, let me zip it up for you, and then you can go down to breakfast. Ms. Hebner is already in the dining room."

Adrian zipped the back of the dress, and Izzy smiled at her and said thanks before heading down the stairs barefoot to breakfast. She found her way to the dining room and saw her mother seated at the head of the long oak table that was adorned with a bevy of breakfast items.

"Good morning, Isabelle," Rachel said as she sipped tea. "Did you sleep well?"

"Not bad, all things considered," Izzy said as she sat to her mother's right. No sooner had Izzy sat down than another of the staff was at her side, asking if she wanted coffee, tea, eggs, or anything else.

"Just some coffee, please," Izzy said politely. "I can fix a plate for myself."

"Don't be silly, Isabelle," Rachel insisted. "Maria can fix your plate for you. Just let her know what you want."

"Really, I can do it myself."

Maria looked at Rachel, and Rachel gave her a quick nod to send the young woman off into the kitchen for the coffee.

Izzy went over and placed some fresh fruit onto a plate for herself.

"You don't want anything else?" Rachel asked. "Terrance can fix you anything. He is an amazing chef."

"Mom, I don't need people to do everything for me," Izzy insisted, silencing herself as Maria returned with a cup of coffee.

"They aren't here to do everything for you," Rachel answered. "They assist with the smaller things, so your time is freed to do what you please."

Izzy stirred some cream into her coffee and munched on a fresh strawberry.

"That dress looks lovely on you," Rachel said with a smile. "I'm glad it fits well. I guessed at sizes, so you would have a few things here if you ever wanted to spend time here."

"Thank you," Izzy answered. "I didn't really think everything through last night. I don't have any sneakers or casual clothes, or even any underwear here. I'm going to have to go back to Dad's."

"Ridiculous," Rachel scoffed. "We can get you whatever you need. Would you like to go out shopping, or should we have things brought in for you to try on?"

"Mom, I need my stuff for school for Monday anyway," Izzy told her. "My car is at home, my cell phone charger, my computer, everything."

"It's nothing we can't take care of for you. We'll get you a new phone, a new computer, new clothes, even a new car if you want one. Or you can have Arthur take you anywhere you want to go in one of mine. There's no reason for you to go back there and have to deal with your father."

"At some point, I'm going to have to talk to him," Izzy said. "I can't just not go back there."

"Why not?"

"Because he's my father," Izzy stated. "And Molly is my sister, Kristin and Melissa are my friends."

"If you go home now, it will all start over again, Isabelle," Rachel explained. "He is in no state to be reasonable about whatever you want to do right now. And the baby, well, she is too young to really remember anything that is going on now. As for those two young ladies, are they really your friends? It seems to me they are more likely to side with your father than you. Let's just finish breakfast, and then we'll have Arthur drive us to Pittsburgh. I know some fabulous boutiques we can shop at; we can go for a nice lunch, maybe go to the spa, and just pamper ourselves all day today. What do you say?"

Izzy thought about it, and the notion of having a day to spoil herself after all the mounting stress of the last several weeks sounded inviting.

"Sure, why not?" Izzy answered. "Let me go grab my phone and my shoes from yesterday."

"Wonderful!" Rachel clapped. "I'll let Arthur know to get one of the cars ready. This will be so much fun!"

Izzy went upstairs and peeked into her room to make sure Adrian was finished cleaning before she entered. The room looked as untouched as it had when she showed up last night. Izzy slid into the shoes that were beside her bed and picked up her phone. She glanced and saw she had a slew of messages from friends, but she also had texts from Melissa and Kristin, imploring her to contact them and let them know she is okay. One of the last texts she saw was from Joe:

Just checking in on you. I'm sorry if you are mad about me going to your father, but I was worried about you. I hope you'll forgive me. I wish I had gotten more time to spend with you. Reach out to me if you need anything.

Joe's message was one of the many that Izzy read, but the only one that she was glad to see. As disappointed as she was that he had gone to her father, Izzy felt like at this time, he was someone that she wanted to see more than anyone else. After thinking for a moment, she punched out a quick reply to him.

I know you meant well. I'm okay. I hope last night wasn't too much trouble for you. TTYL.

Izzy kept it short and didn't want to lead Joe on too much, but she hoped more than anything he would reply at some point. Seconds later, there was a smiling emoji staring back at her, along with an emoji of a heart that was similar in design to that tattoo she got last night. Izzy had almost forgotten about it all and laughed to herself, her hand instinctively going down to her hip to rub the slightly tender spot. She stared down at the text, smiling and biting her lower lip until she heard her mother call out.

"Isabelle? Are you ready? The car is waiting?"

Izzy tossed her phone into her purse and headed out for a day that she thought would be all about her for a change.

***

The tension and stress Wes experienced on the night of the big blow-up carried with him throughout the following week. His attempts to reach out to Izzy so he could speak with her routinely fell on deaf ears. She didn't answer phone calls and exchanged basic text messages occasionally, if at all so that he knew she was okay. Wes thought for sure it would just last for the weekend, and Izzy would come home before school started up again on Monday. He was shocked when she didn't come back. It was only through messages Izzy had sent to Kristin that he learned she had gotten what she needed for school, clothing, personal items so that she could remain with her mother for now.

Concentrating on work with on-field practices beginning was more of a challenge. Wes couldn't focus and found himself lashing out at players for even the smallest mistakes or lapses in judgment. A missed groundball, failure to pick up a sign, a misplaced pitch, and more all ended with Wes raging at players to work harder. Even the players that knew Wes well, like Emil, were not spared from his wrath. When Emil tried to approach him about it, he was brushed off. Joe Johnson, who knew well the reasons for Wes's demeanor, kept to himself and went about his work.

Friday came, and the workout was grueling. An unusually warm weather streak for April had hit the area, and the players neared the end of the activities drenched in sweat and aching for relief. Wes retreated to his office in the stadium, avoiding the locker room altogether. He picked up his cell phone to see if Izzy had returned any of his latest text messages. When he saw nothing, he slammed his phone down in disgust and tossed his ball cap on the floor before slumping back into his chair.

Tom Killian walked into Wes's office just after this and sat in the chair across from Wes.

"How're things going out there?" Tom asked. Tom noticed the look on Wes's face and had concerns immediately.

"They could be better," Wes grumbled. "Some of the guys don't seem to have their heads in each practice. Fundamentals are a mess right now. The batters are missing signs, fielders are lackadaisical, and the pitchers are just leaving everything flat. We're a long way from ready."

"Really?" Tom asked. "I've watched the last couple of practices. Things haven't seemed so bad to me. We still have about a month before the season starts, so I think we will be in good shape by then."

"I sure hope you're right, Tom, because I do not see it," Wes replied.

A knock on Wes's office a door, and both Wes and Tom turn their heads. It was Tom's admin assistant Brenda standing there with a confused look on her face.

"What's up, Brenda?" Tom asked.

"There are two police officers here... they said they want to see you, Wes."

Brenda glanced down the hallway, and the two officers appeared in the door frame.

"Mr. Martin?" The one officer asked as he moved into the room.

"Yes?" Wes replied with puzzlement.

"This is for you," The officer said, handing papers to Wes.

Wes looked at the papers and saw that it was an order of protection filed with the Chandler police department, ordering him to stay away from Rachel and Izzy and providing him with a court date for an appearance.

"You have to be kidding me with this," Wes said, re-reading the order again.

"I'm just here to deliver it, sir, to make sure you received it," the officer said politely. "Have a good day."

"What is it?" Tom asked.

"It's a protection order taken out by my ex-wife," Wes said as he sat back down.

"What's going on with that?" Tom said with concern.

"Something that my ex is blowing way out of proportion for some reason," Wes told Tom. "Now, I have to figure out how to deal with it."

"Do you have a lawyer?" Tom asked him.

"One who handled my baseball contracts through my agent, but no one local I can use."

"Let me make a call," Tom suggested. "I can contact my lawyer. She'll be able to advise you, and she's right here in Washington."

"I can't believe all this." Wes leaned back in his chair and rubbed his neck, feeling nothing but tension.

"Wes... don't take this the wrong way," Tom started, "but is this something I need to worry about? I know it's insensitive to ask, but if this is already done, the local news might pick it up from the courts. I have to think about..."

"Tom," Wes said, cutting him off, "I promise you; I haven't done anything wrong. I don't know what's going on with this."

"Okay, let me give Sybil Crawford a call and see what she can do."

"Thanks, Tom. Can you close my office door, please?"

Tom nodded and shut the door as he left. Wes immediately picked up his phone and dialed Kristin.

"Hey there," Kristin answered sweetly. "I'm just leaving work. I'm going home, and Kim is coming over to go over wedding plans. If you get home on time, she'll probably be there still so you can get in on the decision-making."

"I don't know if I'll be home on time tonight," Wes said with a sigh.

"What's wrong, Wes? I can hear it in your voice."

"I got served with an order of protection. Rachel went to the courthouse in Chandler and got them to go along with it, I guess. It forbids me from contacting or going near her and Izzy."

"That's outrageous," Kristin replied. "You haven't done anything, and certainly not to Izzy."

"I know, I know, but I'm still going to have to appear in court regarding this. Tom is setting up a meeting with his attorney so I can get some advice. This is insane. It was terrible enough Izzy wasn't answering me, but now I can't even try to talk to her to fix things."

"We'll work it all out, Wes. Izzy will come around, I just know it," Kristin reassured. "I can't believe she would go along with this in the first place."

"I'm going to talk to the lawyer and see what can be done. I'll be home later and let you know what I found out."

Kristin could hear the disappointment ringing through Wes's voice.

"Hey... we'll get through this," Kristin told him. "I love you."

"I love you too," Wes replied before hanging up.

***

Kristin wasted no time after she got off the phone with Wes. Part of her wanted to drive over to Rachel's home and confront her and Izzy to find out what was going on, but reason got the better of her. Instead, she picked up her cell and sent a text to Izzy.

Call me. Now.

Kristin had never used any kind of authoritative tone with Izzy before. She never felt like it was her place to do that, but things had changed. Kristin saw how all this was tearing Wes apart, and she could not tolerate it any longer. Her first approach would be to see how much Izzy was involved in everything.

It took a few minutes, time that Kristin used to rehearse in her head just what she planned to say to Izzy before the phone rang. Kristin walked over and quietly closed the door to her office before answering. Karen gave Kristin a look of concern as the door shut.

"Hi Kris," Izzy said with more happiness in her voice than had been there lately. "What's going on?"

"That's why I'm calling you," Kristin said sternly.

Izzy hesitated before answering.

"What's wrong?"

"I've tried to be supportive of you, Izzy, throughout all of this with your father. I've stood up for you and attempted to get him to be reasonable, but if you and Rachel are going to keep pushing him like this, I can't stand by you any longer."

"What are you talking about?" Izzy said with bewilderment. "I haven't done anything. All I've done is stay away while trying to get to know my mother and figure things out."

"Then what is with the protection order?" Kristin said, raising her voice.

Izzy was unaccustomed to hearing Kristin react this way and was taken aback.

"Protection order? I don't know anything about it... what protection order?"

"The one your father was just served with while at work, in front of his boss. He's beside himself, Izzy. This is going too far."

"Kristin, I swear, I don't know what happened. Even though I am angry with Dad, I wouldn't do that," Izzy spoke.

"Well, you may want to have a discussion with your mother then, because your father needs to appear in court next week in front of a judge to go over it."

"I will, I promise I will talk to her," Izzy replied.

"Good," Kristin said, and she hung up abruptly.

Kristin's hands were shaking when she was done. Deep down, she knew she had taken the best steps. Kristin also had a feeling Izzy really did know nothing regarding the order and that it was just another ploy by Rachel to disrupt their lives.

Kristin rapidly packed up her things and walked out of her office, closing the door behind her.

"Everything okay?" Karen asked with concern.

"Lately, it never is," Kristin told her friend.

"Is there anything I can do to help?"

"Come to the house with me and look at wedding stuff," Kristin pleaded. "I need to get organized; Wes is going to be late, Izzy isn't around, and I don't know what I am going to do."

Karen walked over and put her arm around Kristin.

"You got it," Karen said. "I'll call Brian and tell him I'll be late, or maybe I won't be home at all if we can make some margaritas too! Besides, I get to play with that cutie Molly too."

"Thanks, Karen," Kristin said with relief.

Karen grabbed her cell phone as the two left the library.

"Brian, I'll be home late, maybe... it's girl stuff... do you need to know more than that? Good. I'll make it up to you, I promise. Bye, love."

Kristin looked at Karen as they moved to their own cars in the parking lot.

"Is Brian okay with it?" Kristin asked as she unlocked her car.

"He's fine," Karen assured Kristin. "He was just hoping for... a little something extra tonight, let's say," Karen laughed.

"Karen, if you need to go home..." Kristin offered.

"No way. Girlfriends come first. He can find his own way to pass the time. I'll meet you at your house."

***

After she hung up with Kristin, Izzy left her bedroom and went downstairs to find her mother. Her mother was sitting alone in the study. Izzy had vague memories of this room as being her grandfather's sanctuary. This was a place she was never allowed to go to when she was small.

"Mom?" Izzy interrupted. Izzy felt like she was seven years old again as she approached her mother, who sat in an oversized leather chair, reading a book.

"What is it, dear?" Rachel said, putting a bookmark in her book and placing it on the small table next to her. Rachel then picked up the wine glass next to her and sipped the red wine she had.

"Um... I just spoke with Kristin..."

Rachel was already interrupting with a deep sigh and eye roll.

"What did SHE want?" Rachel said, shaking her head.

"She was pretty upset, more than I have ever heard her before. She said Dad got served with a protection order."

"That sounds about right," Rachel assented. "He was supposed to get it today."

"Why would you get an order of protection? And why is my name included in it?" Izzy asked, trying not to raise her voice.

"Isabelle, have a seat," Rachel said. She pointed to the leather chair across from her.

Izzy felt the chill of the leather on her bare legs.

"After your father stormed over here last week, swore at me, tried to come into the house uninvited, and threatened me, I thought it was the safest thing to do. I need to protect myself and you. You said it yourself – he's snapped at you and made accusations several times in the last month or two. The safest thing to do is to make sure he stays away. It's in everyone's best interest."

"I'm not afraid of him," Izzy stated. "He would never do anything to hurt me. He's not like that. You're twisting everything around."

"I'm not, Isabelle. This is the right thing to do for now. Once we get that all settled, we can get on with the rest of our lives and do things like we have planned."

Rachel picked up her wine and sipped some more.

"What have we planned?" Izzy inquired.

"I thought we would do some of the traveling we talked about," Rachel said. "I've talked to a travel agent, and they are planning a month-long trip for us."

"I can't just pack up and go," Izzy insisted. "I have high school to finish. I still have a month left of school, final exams, prom, graduation. After that, I need to finalize plans about college."

"I already talked to the high school," Rachel said. "It took a bit of arm-twisting, but they have agreed that it is okay for you to miss the remainder of the school year, given the circumstances. Your grades are excellent enough, where graduating was never in question. As for college, well, I was saving that as a surprise for you when we were on our trip."

Rachel rose from her chair and went over to the large oak desk in the study. She picked up a manila folder and passed it to Izzy. Izzy looked at her mother and then flipped the envelope open. She read the letter inside, and then reread it before locking eyes with her mother again.

"What is this? How did you..."

"I have many connections in New York, Isabelle. It was effortless. All I had to do was make a couple of phone calls," Rachel said. She gleefully picked up her wine glass.

"This is an acceptance letter to NYU... to the drama school," Izzy said with surprise.

"That is where you said you wanted to go, correct?" Rachel added.

"Sure, but I never heard back. I assumed I got passed over, or on the waitlist, and I would go to Pittsburgh."

"You deserve much better than Pittsburgh, Isabelle. Now you can travel with me, we will come back and live in New York, you can go to school, have access to the best opportunities, maybe work on Broadway, or in the movies, whatever you would like."

"This is all happening too fast," Izzy said, dropping the envelope on the floor. Izzy got out of the chair and paced the room nervously.

"I can't just leave school... and my friends and my family... what about the wedding? I'm supposed to be in the wedding party. It's Dad's wedding."

Rachel walked over and took hold of Izzy by both arms.

"Do you really want to be part of that? Better yet, do you think they want you to be part of the wedding after all this? Nothing good can come of you going to that wedding. We can all move on in our separate directions. It's a much better solution, Isabelle. Trust me. I'm only thinking of what is best for you."

"I need to think about all this," Izzy said.

She marched out of the study before her mother could say anything else to her. Izzy raced up the stairs to her room, shutting the door and standing with her back to it. Her head spun with all that was going on.

At times like this in the past, she never had a second thought and would reach out to her father, her grandparents, or to Kristin. Now she felt like she had no one to turn to for help so she could make the right decision.

Izzy sat on her bed next to her nightstand for minutes before she reached over and picked up her phone. She hesitated before doing anything, but then pressed the dial button before she could change her mind.

"Hey, it's me," she said softly into the phone. "Do you... do you think we can meet somewhere? I need to talk to you."

Chapter 18

Izzy sat on her bed for more than a few minutes before changing out of her pajamas and into a pair of jeans and a t-shirt. She grabbed the green hoodie that she had surreptitiously stolen from Joe. She zipped it up before she started down the staircase quietly. Izzy was unsure if her mother would still be awake at 11 PM. Most nights, Rachel turned in early, but Izzy knew that she could not be too careful.

When Izzy approached the front door, she saw that the deadbolt was on, and all had been locked up for the night. Securing the doors was part of the nightly routine Rachel engaged in before she retired for the evening, so Izzy felt confident she could slip out of the house without being noticed. Izzy slowly turned the deadbolt, so the click quieted some, pulled the door barely open, and slipped out to shut it. Izzy had the foresight to grab her keys as well, and she re-engaged the deadbolt upon leaving so it wouldn't arouse suspicion if her mother happened to get up.

Once outside, Izzy realized she had no plan to move any further. Her car was still at her father's house, and walking into town from this distance, while not far, was not really an option either. Izzy looked left to right as she contemplated her next move. She saw a dim light coming from the guest house just to the right of the main entrance to the house. It was where Arthur resided, living on-site in case Rachel needed assistance during times when no one else was around.

While Izzy did not know Arthur well, she felt she had built up a rapport with him in the short time she had been at her mother's. Arthur had been her primary source of transportation back and forth to school, which initially caused Izzy some consternation. The image of pulling up to the high school in a Town Car, or worse, one of the more audacious vehicles her mother owned to flaunt wealth, was not something she relished. Arthur, a gentleman she guessed, was about the age of her grandfather, recognized Izzy's discomfort, and began to drop her off where no one would see her get out of the vehicle to avoid embarrassment. There had even been a couple of occasions where Arthur had driven her for ice cream on the spur of the moment when Izzy wanted to get out of the house.

Izzy walked as quietly as she could on the gravel on the walkway in front of Arthur's guest house. The crunching seemed deafening to her, and she worried when she stumbled a bit, and then one of the outdoor lights flipped on as she tripped the sensor for it. It was then that the front door to Arthur's residence opened, and he stood staring through the screen door before moving outside.

The surprise of seeing Arthur not wearing his customary black suit and tie kept Izzy in place as he approached her. He was clad in flannel pajama pants and a white t-shirt and a pair of moccasins. The casualness of the image made Izzy laugh a bit even though she was tense.

"Ms. Isabelle, are you alright?" Arthur said. Unlike Rachel, Arthur had a heavy New York accent from his years of being raised and living there.

Izzy raised her index finger to her lips to get Arthur to keep his voice down.

"I'm fine," Izzy whispered.

"What are you doing out here?" Arthur said, taking the hint and speaking softer.

"I hate to bother you this late... and you can say no if you want to... but I need some help."

"You need a ride somewhere?" Arthur asked, understanding the situation.

Izzy nodded, worried he might ask too many questions.

"Let me get my coat and keys," Arthur said. He gently guided Izzy out of the spotlight of the floodlights and the view of Rachel's bedroom window on the third floor of the house. Izzy ducked into the comfort of the shadows of Arthur's awning and front porch, and the light mercifully went off a few moments later.

Izzy nervously looked at her phone for messages, but there were none. Arthur startled her when he appeared from his home wearing his customary jacket and tie.

"Arthur, why are you wearing all that?" Izzy said in a hushed tone.

"Because I'm working," he said with a smile. "Come on."

Izzy began to walk towards the Town Car that was parked closest to his residence before Arthur tugged on her arm.

"Not that one," he whispered. "Your mother might hear it start and come across the driveway. It's right under her window."

Arthur quickly led Izzy up and around the front of the house, far enough out so that they did not trigger any lights. They reached the far side of the home where the garage was located, a secure and further point from the house.

Arthur opened the door to enter the garage and guided Izzy inside. He walked over to the silver Rolls Royce parked there and unlocked the back door. He held the door open for Izzy and waved his hand for her to enter.

"Nothing to be embarrassed about driving in this one this late at night, is there?" Arthur asked.

Izzy smiled and got in, settling into the elegant leather seat. Arthur started the car and crept the vehicle out of the garage as quietly as he could. He went out the side entrance of the property, one that was used primarily by the landscapers and delivery people, to avoid detection.

"Wow, Arthur," Izzy said as they pulled away from the house, "You're really good at this sneaking around stuff. You should be a spy or something."

"Who says I wasn't," Arthur commented with a smile into the rearview mirror.

Izzy let Arthur know where they were headed, and he was not surprised to hear her destination. It was a quick trek through town and out to Route 5 before they were coming up on Martin Way. Izzy directed Arthur to turn before they reached her grandparents' house so they could go towards the barn and stables. Arthur was hesitant to take the Rolls down in this direction, but he nodded to Izzy and went along the path until they reached the first building.

"I don't know how long I'll be," Izzy said apologetically.

"That's okay," Arthur said to her. "it gives me a chance to catch up on my favorite podcasts," he said, tapping the iPhone he had in his inside suit jacket pocket. "Take as long as you need, Ms. Isabelle."

Izzy got out of the car and strolled towards the stable. She reached into her sweatshirt pouch pocket and removed her keys, finding the one that opened the lock to the stable door. Izzy had access because she regularly was tasked with feeding and grooming chores when Izzy worked on the farm. She opened the latch and slid the large door open, and then hurried inside to shut off the alarm as it started beeping its countdown before going off. Luckily, the alarm code, set by her grandfather, was one that was easy for her to remember – 93072. It stood for September 30, 1972, the day of Roberto Clemente's 3000th and final hit.

Izzy took a quick look back to make sure no lights had come on at her grandparents' house before she entered the stable fully. The stable was eerily quiet, with all the horses long settled down. Each step Izzy took echoed loudly to her on the bare, clean floor. She used the flashlight feature on her phone to guide her way over to one stall and stood in front of it. She knew that Wanda, her horse of the last several years, was likely to be up and awake. Wanda, a chestnut brown filly, greeted Izzy quickly, nuzzling into her hand when Izzy held it forward for her. Izzy reached over to the basket where the staff regularly kept cut carrots so that she could get a treat for her friend, and Wanda happily munched while Izzy stroked above her nose.

"Hey girl," she said softly. "I know I haven't been down much in a while. I'm sorry. Things have been kind of crazy."

"Glad to see you still have your keys," a voice said behind Izzy, causing her to jump. "You know she shouldn't have a treat this late at night."

Izzy swung around to see her grandfather standing before her, wearing his sheepskin coat and cowboy hat even though it was nearly midnight.

"You didn't need to get all dressed to come down here, Grandpa," Izzy said as she hugged Wyatt tightly.

"You know when I come down here, I feel like I'm working," Wyatt said, returning the tight embrace. "These are my work clothes."

Izzy laughed after hearing this for the second time in under an hour.

"So, what is it that has you dragging yourself over here at this hour in a Rolls Royce?" Wyatt asked. He took Izzy's hand and led her over to a few stacked hay bales so they could sit down.

"Grandpa, I don't know what to do," Izzy lamented. "This whole situation is a mess, and it's all my fault. Now things are getting worse. Mom filed a protection order against Dad, and she wants me to leave Chandler with her, leave high school early, and go with her. I'm all confused about this."

"Yeah, I heard all about the court stuff from your father," Wyatt answered, stroking his gray mustache. "It's a mess for sure, but I wouldn't say any of it is your fault. Your mother sure isn't playing fair right now, and your father hasn't handled anything well since you... well, your indiscretion, let's say. Now, what's this about leaving school?"

Izzy went into the explanation of Rachel's plan to have Izzy forgo the end of high school, travel the world, and then come back to New York to live. She also explained all about NYU and how Rachel had arranged her acceptance and admission there.

"And how do you feel about all of this?" Wyatt asked bluntly.

Izzy leaned her back against the barn wall.

"I don't know, Grandpa. I always imagined going to prom and graduation, of course. Still, everything that happened at school and with my friends, sometimes I feel like I wouldn't miss anything. Traveling the world would be amazing to do for a month or two, but I would lose time with you and Grandma, with Molly, all the wedding plans, Kristin..."

"Don't forget about your father," Wyatt reminded. "Izzy, no matter how upsetting it may have been to have the arguments you have had, you need to remember he has always done what is best for you, and he loves you. It might not be easy to see that right now, but you know it's true, and he would be devastated if he didn't get the chance to see you graduate or spend time with you."

"I know he does," Izzy agreed. "There are a lot of times lately, though, where it feels like I am the odd man out. Kris and Dad are going to get married; they have Molly to focus on, they have Melissa in the house, and they have their own lives. What if they decide to have more kids? Or they want to move somewhere else?"

"That's bullshit, and you know it, Isabelle... pardon my French," Wyatt said emphatically. "Families grow and change all the time, but they are still families that love each other and look out for each other. Your father and Kristin might have full plates right now, but that doesn't mean they consider you any less. Molly needs more attention, but it won't always be that way. And so what if they have more kids or move to another house, town or city? Your grandmother and I would love to have more grandkids around, but you'll always be the first one, no matter where you go to school or where you live."

"So, what do you think I should do?" Izzy implored.

"Come on, Izzy. You don't really expect me to tell you what to do, do you? Why should now be any different than it has been for the rest of your life? What have I always told you?"

Izzy sighed.

"Your decisions are yours to make, and you live with them, right or wrong."

Wyatt smiled and nodded.

"You know, Grandma and Dad never liked that philosophy because it ended up with things like me falling into the pond when I stood up in the rowboat, or when I fell into the manure pile because I thought I could get shoveling done faster by using two shovels at once," Izzy reminded Wyatt.

"But you learned from both of those, didn't you? Your father was no different when he was younger. You two are peas in a pod. That's why you butt heads so often now. He realizes you're a young adult and he can't just use the 'because I said so' argument anymore."

Izzy rose from the hay bale and walked over to Wanda's stall to pet her some more.

"I guess I have some decisions to make," Izzy offered.

"Yep," Wyatt replied. "You know I'll support you whatever you choose, Izzy, and so will your grandmother. You just need to think about the possible consequences of what you decide either way."

"I know. Either I cut myself off from Dad and Kristin, or I cut myself off from a mother I was just getting to know."

"I understand that you want to connect with your mother again, Izzy, but you need to consider why she is approaching things the way she is right now. Why did she suddenly appear after years of no contact with you at all? Why is she going so hard after your father? I think there are still facts you don't know entirely," Wyatt said as he walked over to Izzy.

"That almost sounded like you were telling me what to do," Izzy commented.

"Nope," Wyatt insisted. "I just want you to know all the details before you make a decision. Now let's get out of here. It's late, and I have to get up in five hours to be out here with the horses again."

The two moved toward the stable door and back outside, where the night air in April was now much cooler than before. Izzy zipped her sweatshirt up all the way to ward off the chill while Wyatt turned on the alarm and locked the door.

"Where's the sweatshirt from?" Wyatt asked as they walked towards the waiting car. "Seems a bit big for you."

"Oh," Izzy remarked as she held the sleeves in front of her, so the cuffs dangled inches beyond her outstretched fingers. "It's a friend's. I guess I need to give back to hi..." Izzy cut herself off.

"Him, huh?" Wyatt chuckled. "I figured as much. Is he really just a friend?"

"I'm not sure yet," Izzy responded. "I don't know if I want to talk about boys with you, Grandpa."

"Probably better if you don't, for both of us," Wyatt agreed.

Wyatt and Izzy reached the Rolls Royce, and Arthur stepped out of the car to open the rear door. Izzy faced her grandfather and gave him a big embrace.

"Thank you," she said into Wyatt's ear before giving him a kiss on the cheek. "I needed some Grandpa time."

"Whenever you need it, I'm here," Wyatt answered.

"Arthur, this is my grandfather, Wyatt Martin," Izzy said as she climbed into the back seat. "Arthur is Mom's... I mean, my friend," she said, smiling.

"Pleasure to meet you, Mr. Martin," Arthur said as the two men firmly shook hands.

"You've got worker's hands," Wyatt noted. "How do you get that driving a fancy car all day?"

"I do whatever is necessary," Arthur smirked.

"You two have a lot in common," Izzy said as she watched the two men size each other up.

"Get her home safe and take care of her," Wyatt encouraged.

"I would do nothing less," Arthur assured before he got into the car.

Arthur worked the car up the pathway to Route 5 so that he could bring Izzy back to her mother's home.

"Mission accomplished, Miss?" Arthur asked politely.

"Kind of," Izzy answered. "Arthur, this outing... you're not going to..."

"You have nothing to worry about, Miss Isabelle," Arthur told her. "Consider it part of personal driver/client privilege. It stays with me."

"Thank you, Arthur," Izzy said with relief. "You know, you don't have to call me 'Miss Isabelle.' Izzy is what my friends call me."

"I appreciate the gesture, Miss Isabelle, but, to be honest, it makes me more comfortable to call you Miss. It's part of the job."

"Whatever is best for you, Arthur," Izzy laughed.

Arthur pulled the car through the service entrance to the property, the same way they left, before guiding the vehicle back to the garage, exactly where it sat earlier in the evening. The two left the garage and walked toward the front steps.

"Thank you for your help," Izzy said, giving Arthur a hug that startled him.

"You're welcome. Have a pleasant evening, Miss," Arthur said. He gave her a smile and nod as he went over toward his home.

Izzy paced up the front steps and reached inside her sweatshirt pocket for her keys. Unfortunately, they were not found there. She patted the pocket thoroughly and then the pockets of her jeans, but the keychain was nowhere to be found.

"Shit!" she shouted as she gently tugged on the door. Just then, lights went on in the foyer, and the light outside the front door came on. Izzy heard the deadbolt turn and was confronted by her mother in her robe, with a confused look on her face.

"Isabelle? What are you doing out here? I thought you were in bed. Why are you dressed?"

"I... I wanted..." Izzy struggled for words as she sought what to answer.

"Miss Isabelle requested I take her out, Ma'am," Arthur said as he appeared just beyond the front steps.

"Out where?" Rachel inquired. "Nothing in Chandler is open this late."

"No, Ma'am, nothing is," Arthur answered. "We went up toward Washington. She wanted a Whopper from Burger King."

"A Whopper? Really?" Rachel said skeptically.

"Yeah, I love them," Izzy answered. "Arthur tried to convince me to go to Wendy's because it's closer, and he thinks they are better, but I think I won him over with the 2 for $6 deal, right Arthur?"

"Absolutely, Miss," Arthur answered. "it was my first Whopper, but it won't be my last."

"Terrance makes elegant meals every night, and you have to go get a fast-food hamburger late at night?" Rachel remarked.

"Sorry, Mom. Sometimes you just need a burger. I guess I forgot my keys when I left. I didn't mean to wake you up."

"It's fine," Rachel gave in. "Let's all call it a night now, please. Isabelle, we need to meet with lawyers tomorrow to finalize a trust for you, and to talk about the hearing next week. You should get some rest."

Rachel walked back in the house, and Izzy turned toward Arthur to mouth 'Thank you' to him before she followed her mother in.

Izzy shut the door and locked it, and then turned and saw her mother standing on the staircase with her arms crossed. Izzy worried about what would happen next.

"Isabelle, I have to talk to you about this stunt you pulled," Rachel said crossly.

"What do you mean?" Izzy said, her voice shaking.

"Look," Rachel relaxed, "I understand that a young girl wants to go out sometimes. If you went to meet a boy, that's fine. You're a young woman who is going to have suitors. It's to be expected. Just be honest with me. I was the same way when I was your age."

"Mom, honestly, I wasn't meeting a boy," Izzy answered. "I just wanted a quick bite to eat, and Arthur was nice and took me."

"Okay," Rachel told her. "But I don't want you getting too friendly with Arthur or the other staff. They work for us; they aren't our friends. It might make it more difficult if you or I have to let them go one day if there are emotional attachments like that. Understood?"

Izzy nodded, but she knew inside that she could never take the same cold approach her mother seemed to have.

Chapter 19

An introductory conversation with Sybil Crawford, Tom Killian's attorney, gave Wes an idea of what he could expect at the hearing. Wes made sure to provide as many accurate details as possible about the recent incident in question, along with the history between himself and Rachel. Sybil was surprised when he mentioned that he had not seen Rachel in eleven years before all this happened.

"How long have you known she was in town?" Sybil asked.

"I only found out the night of Izzy's play when I saw her there, so it hasn't been long at all. And all hell broke loose that night. I haven't seen her since then, or Izzy."

"Well, it's not like there is a history of problems between the two of you, and you have been divorced for a long time. The problem is that it's next to impossible to get things like this overturned, Wes. Even if we get a compassionate judge if the judge sides with her, it could mean no contact for three years," Sybil warned.

"Three years?" Wes exclaimed. "Izzy will be practically done with college by then. There has to be something we can do."

"I can try negotiating with her lawyers, maybe get them to agree to a lesser amount of time."

"Any amount of time is too long to not see my daughter," Wes said as he pounded the table in the conference room.

"Let me read over the order," Sybil advised. "Let's make sure of what the complaint is and see what defense we might have. Then we can talk about whether a deal is the best move or not. In the meantime, just keep your temper in check, Wes, and do not try to contact your ex-wife or your daughter. You don't want any trouble before the hearing or to give Rachel any more ammunition than she already has."

"Okay," Wes agreed. He shook Sybil's hand before leaving her office so that he could begin his trek home. Wes still had a few days before the hearing was to take place, which left him some time to figure out what he could do to straighten everything out. Even though Tom did not come right out and say it, Wes knew it would be bad publicity for the team if word got out that he had an order of protection taken out against him. It might not only cost him his job now, but it conceivably would prevent him from getting another chance down the road, whether it was true or not.

Wes started his drive home from the lawyer's office. He worked to avoid getting consumed with all the thoughts about what might or could happen. The sharp ringing of his phone sounded over the speakers of the truck, and he pressed the Bluetooth button on the steering wheel to answer the call from Kristin.

"Hey," he answered somberly.

"I was calling to see how things went with the lawyer, but that doesn't sound so good," Kristin told him.

"She was helpful, but she was also honest," Wes explained. "Sybil didn't make it sound too optimistic. She said it's tough to fight, and that the order could stay in place for up to three years, according to the law."

"Three years? Wes, that's too long. There must be something we can do."

"I don't know," Wes answered. "Sybil is working on it. She said maybe we can cut a deal for a shorter amount of time."

"Do you really want to do that?"

"No, I don't want there to be any time at all, but I don't know if I will have any other choice." Wes's frustration was apparent to Kristin in his voice. He took a deep breath and let it out.

"How are things going with Kim?" Wes said, hoping the distraction of the wedding plans might be good for both.

"Are you sure you want to talk about that now?" Kristin replied.

"I need something to distract me," Wes admitted. "Tell me something happy about the wedding."

"We made a lot of progress tonight," Kristin started. "Kim set up appointments to meet a couple of caterers to talk about menus and decorations, and she gave me some information and music from a few bands that we can check out. We also made an appointment at a dress shop to look at dresses next weekend. I'm going to see if I can get something picked out soon for the bridesmaids so we can find a place in Georgia for my sister to go and get her dress since she won't be able to get here for a fitting. Then we'll just have to get..." Kristin stopped before the word 'Izzy' came out of her mouth.

"I don't know if we'll be able to count on Izzy being in the wedding," Wes said with resignation.

"She will be there, Wes," Kristin assured him. "We will find a way to settle all of this."

A text message alert popped up on the screen in Wes's console as he drove and talked.

Come and meet me at my home so we can talk about this.
Rachel

Wes was unsure of what to do. He wanted to do what he could to work all this out. Still, he also knew there was potential trouble if he were at the house in violation of the temporary order.

"Wes, you still there?" Kristin asked.

"Yeah, I am," Wes announced. "You have a good time with Karen and Melissa and Kim. I'm... I'm going to swing by my parents and check on them and pay them a visit before I head home. I'll be there later. Love you."

"Okay, give them my love. I'll see you later. Love you," Kristin responded.

Wes hoped he would not regret what he was about to do.

***

Wes slowed down and took his time getting over to Rachel's house. He wanted to give himself time to think about what he would say and do once he arrived there. The scenarios Wes ran through his head all ended badly for him, but he had to hear Rachel out and explain his side of the story. At the very least, he might get to see Izzy and speak with her before he would have to leave.

The truck pulled into the all too familiar drive, and he pulled up close to the house, just behind where a Town Car was parked. Wes took a moment to compose himself with a few more deep breaths, and he told himself the entire walk to the front door that he would not and could not lose his cool at all. He knocked lightly on the door and filled himself with the hope that Izzy might answer so he could give her a hug.

Instead, Rachel opened the door and smiled. She was clad in a little black dress that came down to midthigh and had a deep V-neck to reveal ample cleavage.

"Hello, Wes," Rachel purred. "Come on in."

"Rachel, I really shouldn't be here," Wes started before he entered the house.

"Oh, don't worry about that," Rachel said. "I invited you here. You can't get in any trouble for that. If you really thought you shouldn't be here, you wouldn't have come, would you?"

"I want to work this out and settle things," Wes insisted. "And, I want to see Izzy."

"Unfortunately, she isn't here," Rachel said as she strolled into the study. "She went out for the evening, so you are stuck with just little ole' me."

Rachel sat herself down in one of the oversized chairs in front of a fireplace that roared with flames. As soon as Wes entered the room, his memory was flooded with the few times he had come into the study to meet with Rachel's father.

"This room still smells like your father's cigars," Wes said as he stood looking around the dimly lit area.

"Daddy did have a fondness for fine cigars and scotch," Rachel replied. "The cigars are gone, but I can offer you a drink if you would like one." Rachel pointed her index finger adorned with a fire red fingernail at the chair across from her own.

"Sure, I'll have a scotch," Wes said as he sat.

"He always tried to get you to join him for an after-dinner drink and smoke," Rachel said as she poured two fingers worth of 12-year-old Macallan into a rocks glass for each of them. She clinked a single ice cube into each glass, bending over slightly and looking back to see if Wes was watching her.

Rachel paced slowly back towards Wes and extended a glass toward him. He took the scotch, and Rachel lifted her glass to his.

"Cheers," she said before sitting back down and seductively crossed her legs.

"Your father never did understand that I was an athlete and didn't smoke and wasn't drinking scotch," Wes added as he sipped his drink.

"Daddy never understood you period, Wes," Rachel said with a laugh. "He always thought you were just a distraction for me."

"Was I?" Wes asked, honestly.

"Were you a distraction? Maybe, at first," Rachel answered. "You were well outside of the box that my father wanted for me, that's for sure. But there was something about seeing you in that high school baseball uniform, those tight pants... I just couldn't resist you. I did fall in love you with you at one point, Wes. We did get married, after all."

"True," Wes replied. "But at some point, all that stopped, and you picked up with a billionaire hedge fund manager instead."

"I knew you were going to bring that up," Rachel said with an eye roll. "I was trapped in that big house with no one to talk to but your parents and an infant, Wes. My family was doing all these fancy things, going to parties, and galas and charity events, and I was missing out, and they made sure I knew I was. So, I finally went to one of the parties, and that's where I met him. He was nice and kind, and he listened to me, and yes, he had a ton of money. He offered me an escape."

"You mean another distraction," Wes said, raising his eyebrows.

"Call it what you want, but it gave me more opportunities than I was ever going to get staying in Chandler. One day he promised to marry me, and I took him up on his offer and left. I'm sorry if that hurt your feelings or your ego."

"Rachel, you didn't just leave me. You left our daughter. You were the constant in her life at that point, and then you were gone," Wes thundered.

"I'm well aware of what I did, Wes," Rachel stated. "It is one of the few things I regret in my life. I never should have left Isabelle behind. I should have taken her with me so she could have had a proper upbringing."

"There's nothing wrong with the upbringing that she had with me," Wes shot back. "She's a happy, well-adjusted, hardworking, kind young lady. I think I did pretty well."

"You?" Rachel snorted. "That's a laugh. You had about as much a hand in raising her as I did! Your parents are the ones who did everything; you just footed the bill. And then, the first chance you get to spend time with her, what do you do? You run out and find a girl practically her age to date, so you don't have to spend time with Isabelle. Then you take another baseball job, have a child, and plan to get married. How is all that doing what is best for her?"

Rachel's words stung Wes deeply, but he didn't want to show her they did.

"Is this why you wanted me to come over here?" Wes growled. "You could have saved us both the time and the lecture, Rachel. What do you want?

"I am willing to offer you a deal, so this ugliness goes away," Rachel said to him as she finished her drink and placed the glass on the table beside her chair.

"A deal? What kind of deal?" Wes asked warily.

"I'll make the temporary order go away. You can see Isabelle without any trouble or restrictions, and making the order go away will likely save your job."

"Okay... but what are you expecting from me?" Wes asked.

"It's simple, really," Rachel said as she walked over towards Wes and stood in front of him. It was challenging to ignore Rachel's shapely body in her form-fitting dress, but Wes wasn't distracted at this point.

"I want you to call off the wedding," Rachel said with a smirk.

"You're insane," Wes scoffed.

"I don't think it's insane at all," Rachel said coolly. "Think about it. You know this girl for what, a year or two at the most? You barely know her family, and what you do know tells you they don't have much. She gets pregnant, has your baby, and moves into your house? What do you think she really wants, Wes? She wants your money. It's plain as day. Save yourself the trouble and end it before it ends up costing you everything. You marry her, you lose Izzy, your job, and probably your money and your property once she decides to divorce you. That beautiful farm all gone."

"And you know this how? Because you did the same thing to your last husband and me?"

"If you want to look at it that way, sure," Rachel said casually. "I guess that does make me an expert."

"You might be able to pull this shit with other people, and they fall for it, Rachel, but it's not going to work on me," Wes insisted.

"Are you sure about that, Wes?" Rachel said with her hands on her hips. She quickly moved from standing in front of Wes to sitting on his lap. She draped her arms over his shoulders and brought her face close to his so their lips were barely separated.

"I'm sure you remember the fun we used to have in this office when my parents weren't home," Rachel said breathlessly. "Probably right in this chair, too. That could happen again, you know. It could be just you, me, and Izzy. We can give Kristin a pile of money for her and that baby and live the rest of our lives together."

Rachel leaned and pressed her lips to Wes's, pushing his head back into the chair. Wes immediately shifted his arms to push Rachel back and away from him so he could stand up. It took every impulse he had to hold himself back.

"If you think for a second, I would be willing to do any of that, to go back with you, then you really are deranged," Wes spat out. "Your second husband should be glad he got away, and it only cost him half a billion dollars. I don't know how you have managed to convince Izzy to go along with you on any of this, but I will fight you tooth and nail and spend every penny I have if I have to. You aren't getting your way this time."

"Wow, you have some fight and spark in you yet, Wesley," Rachel said, impressed by his stance. "I can even see by looking in your eyes that you would love to throw me across the room. I'll let you put your hands on me if you want. It's been a while since I've had a big, strong man do that."

Rachel took a step towards Wes, so she was in front of him again, and Wes instinctively put his hands up to stop her before he pulled them back down to his sides.

"I'm leaving now," Wes said as he slammed his glass on the table, causing the ice cube to jump out and onto the floor.

Wes stormed out of the study and headed toward the front door. Rachel trailed behind him, her high heels clicking on the marble.

"Last chance, Wesley," Rachel said to him from behind.

"Go to hell," Wes answered, opening the front door. Wes stopped cold as he opened the door and saw Izzy standing on the front steps about to come in.

"Dad?" Izzy said with a befuddled look on her face. "What are you doing here?"

"Izzy... it's so good to see you... your mother invited me over here to talk, but all I really was hoping for is the chance to see you. I'm so sorry about everything and I..."

Rachel interrupted Wes's speech by stepping between him and Izzy.

"Don't speak to her!" Rachel barked. "I invited you over; that's one thing. She did not. Technically you are violating the protection order right now. I can call the police and have you arrested this time. Isabelle, get in the house."

"Izzy, you don't have to do that if you don't want to," Wes said to his daughter.

"Dad, you better go before you get in more trouble," Izzy said sympathetically. Izzy slowly walked around her father to go into the house. She reached out with the pinky of her right hand to touch his, and they held it just for a second before she moved passed.

"Time to go," Rachel said with a steely look. She slowly closed the front door, leaving Wes on the porch for a moment before he moved back to his truck. Wes got in behind the wheel and sat for a moment as he wondered just how bad things might get now.

***

As soon as Izzy was inside the house, Rachel bolted the front door and looked at her daughter.

"What was that all about?" Izzy asked, trailing behind her mother as she went back toward the study.

"Your father and I needed to have a little chat about the future," Rachel remarked.

"Is that why you asked me to go out and get ice cream?" Izzy said. "I'm not six-years-old anymore; You can't just push me out of the house when you want something."

"I didn't think it was best for you to be here when we discussed things," Rachel said simply.

"Discussed what things?" Izzy felt more confused and annoyed by the second.

Rachel had walked over to the bookcase on the far wall, picking up one of the knickknacks in the shape of an old sailboat. She pulled the top off the boat and removed a small device from the inside.

"What is that?" Izzy said as she stared.

"A little bit of insurance," Rachel said with a smile. She went over to the table and picked up her smartphone.

"The camera was recording the interaction between your father and me and streaming it to the app on my phone. Now I just need to do a little editing and send it along," Rachel commented as she played with the video.

"What are you doing? And who are you sending it to?"

"I just want to make sure our little librarian knows what Wesley was really up to tonight," Rachel answered. "And send," she said as she gleefully pressed the button. "Now, let's see if she still wants to marry him."

"Why are you doing this?" Izzy said in disbelief. "Kristin didn't do anything to you. She doesn't even know you! You're sending her a doctored video to make it look like Dad was cheating on her... for what? I don't understand anything you are doing."

"Relax, Isabelle," Rachel said, trying to soothe her daughter by putting her arm around her. "I'm doing all of this for you."

"How is this for me?" Izzy yelled, trying to pull away from her mother.

"Because once you are away from these people, you will see how much better life can be for you. They are only going to drag you down, Isabelle. I gave your father the chance to be with us, but he turned it down. Now he'll have to live with the consequences of his decisions. We'll be able to get on with things after the hearing. I've already made plans to have the house closed. We'll go back to New York, get settled for a bit, get you everything you need, and your passport, and then we can begin traveling. Where would you like to go first? Paris? London? Morocco? South America? You name it."

Izzy stared at her mother as if she were seeing her for the first time.

"I can't do this," she said out loud, walking toward the door. "You're destroying lives... my family... like it means nothing. I need to tell them the truth."

Izzy turned away from her mother and paced quickly to the door. She tried the handle and felt it was locked, but even after unlocking the deadbolt, the door didn't open. A glance at the doorknob revealed that there was a new lock in place that only opened with a key.

"Why is the door locked like this?" Izzy asked. Panic worked its way through her body now. "Where is the key?"

"I had hoped it would go much easier than this, Isabelle, but I had to plan for all possible contingencies. I'm sure you understand that. I did worry that you might have a conscience about these things. Once it's all done, you will realize it was the right thing to do and accept it. So, for the next couple of days, we'll just be staying indoors, okay?"

After trying the doorknob a few more times, Izzy got scared and turned and ran. She stumbled and dropped her purse, and then went up the stairs towards her room, slamming the door shut. With her back to the door, Izzy tried to think about what to do. It was then she heard a loud click on the other side of her door.

"Isabelle," Rachel's voiced said, muffled through the heavy door, "be reasonable about all of this, please. In two days, the hearing will happen, and everything will be settled, and we can get on with our lives. If you look in your closet, there are some supplies in the basket in there – food, water, etc. You should have plenty there until the hearing is over."

Izzy tried the doorknob, and it did not turn. She then went to her closet and saw the wicker hamper of supplies in it. Izzy's first reaction was to go to the two windows in her room. Neither would budge open and even if they did, her room was on the third floor of the house. If she was lucky, she might only break a leg if she jumped.

"You planned to hold me a prisoner in my room?" Izzy yelled. "What is wrong with you?"

"Please," Rachel said snidely. "It's more comfortable there than any hotel room you may have stayed in before. Relax and make the best of it. Call me if you need anything," Rachel laughed. Izzy could hear her mother's footsteps go down the hall.

"Call me," Izzy said out loud and immediately started looking for her cell phone. It was nowhere to be found on her nightstand or desk, and Rachel had made sure to remove the laptop from her room as well. Izzy recognized that her phone was in her purse on the floor by the stairs and was now likely in her mother's possession. Izzy sat on her bed, fear coursing through her again.

"This is a nightmare," she said aloud, biting her lower lip.

Chapter 20

Kristin, Karen, Melissa, and Kim were all enjoying drinks, laughs, and wedding talk all at the same time. Karen had just finished mixing another batch of margaritas, gone over to the speaker on the kitchen counter and told Alexa to turn it up so they could dance to "Call Me Maybe."

"Karen," Kristin chastised, "Molly is sleeping."

"Oh, come on," Karen said, "she needs to learn about adult time and kitchen dancing at some point."

Karen walked over to Kristin's glass and filled it again with more margarita.

"This is supposed to be a fun time," Karen reminded Kristin. "We got a lot of wedding stuff done tonight. Let's just kick back and enjoy some downtime. There are no men here to worry about."

"Wooh, no men!" Melissa and Kim both shouted simultaneously and then broke out in giggles as they laughed.

"I know, you're right," Kristin agreed. "I just wish Izzy was here, too."

Karen put her arm around her friend.

"It will all get worked out. I'm sure Wes can figure a way to fix everything," Karen assured.

Kristin took a long sip of her margarita and smiled.

After another draw on her drink, Kristin heard the telltale beep of her phone to let her know a text message had come in. She walked over to her phone and picked it up to look at it, expecting a message from Wes that he was still down at his parents. Instead, she saw that it was from an unknown number with a video link. The only tag on the message was 'Kristin – you need to watch this.'

Under any other circumstances, Kristin would have stayed away from a message like this. She had been to enough training classes through the library to recognize a potential virus and phishing scams. However, underneath the play button of the video, it looked like Wes sitting in a chair. She hesitated for a moment before bringing her index finger down to press play.

She put her hand up to her mouth as she watched what was clearly a video of Wes sitting in a chair with Rachel on his lap. She then leaned in and kissed him as he put his hands on her arms. The video kept repeating over and over on a loop.

Eventually, Kristin dropped her phone, and it rattled on the table, drawing the attention of the other women in the kitchen.

"Kris?" Karen asked with concern. "What's wrong?" She could see the horrified look on Kristin's face.

"It's a video of Wes..." she said as her voice trailed off.

Karen walked over and picked up the phone to see the video looping.

"Who is he with?" Karen gasped.

Melissa and Kim came over to look at the phone.

"That's Izzy's mother," Melissa replied.

"This has to be faked," Karen said, trying to find a way to stop the video before she finally just turned the phone off.

Kristin sat down in one of the wooden chairs as Kim went over to the speaker to stop the music.

Kristin reached over and picked up her phone again to turn it on.

"Don't watch it again," Karen said, trying to grab the phone. Kristin angrily pulled it away so Karen couldn't reach it.

"I'm not watching it again," she said.

She dashed out a quick message to the sender of the video.

Who is this? Why are you sending this?

Kristin thought about everything for a second and typed again.

Rachel?? This must be from you.

A moment passed before a message came back of a winking emoji and nothing else. That was followed by another note.

U R missing all the fun!

Kristin looked up quickly from her phone and then looked down again. She pulled up her recent calls list and pressed Wes's number. The phone rang twice before he answered.

"Hey, honey," he said calmly. "How're the plans going?"

"Where are you? Right now," Kristin asked, trying her best to control her temper.

"I'm at my parents, like I told you," Wes answered. "Why? What's wrong?"

"Stay there," she commanded. "I'll be right down."

Kristin hung up and began to march toward the door.

"Melissa, listen for Molly, please," she remarked as she grabbed her jacket from the closet and kept walking.

"Kris, where are you going? Do you want me to go with you?" Karen asked. She did her best to slow Kristin down, but Kristin moved forward.

"You can stay here, Karen. I'm fine," Kristin said.

Kristin walked out into the darkness and made her way down the driveway towards Wyatt and Jenny's home. She strode quickly and was on the porch in no time at all. In the past, she always felt funny about just walking in without knocking, but this time she had no hesitation and threw the door open.

She found Wes and Wyatt sitting in the living room, sipping coffee together.

Wes saw the look of consternation on Kristin's face and knew something was wrong.

"How long have you been here?" Kristin asked, crossing her arms.

Wes looked at his father and hesitated before he answered.

"Just tell me the truth, Wes."

Wyatt rose from his chair calmly.

"I think I need to leave you two alone to talk," Wyatt remarked.

"I'm sorry to barge into your home like this, Wyatt," Kristin said, barely holding it together now. She turned her attention back to Wes. "Tell me, Wes."

"Not long," he said seriously.

"And why is that? Where did you go instead of coming here?"

Wes rose from his chair and stood in front of Kristin, looking down into her eyes.

"Tell me," Kristin said as she choked up.

"I was at Rachel's," Wes confessed. "I know I shouldn't have gone, and I ran a risk of getting arrested, but she said she wanted to straighten things out, so I went. I wanted to see Izzy."

"So, is that what you did? Straighten things out?"

"Not exactly," Wes said. "Rachel was... well, being Rachel, for lack of a better term."

"Is that what you call it?" Kristin said. She hit the play button on her phone and played the video for Wes, holding it up to his face.

Wes watched the video, unsure of what he was looking at until he figured it out.

"Kris, this isn't what it looks like," Wes insisted. "That video... I had no idea she was recording that..."

"I'll bet you didn't," Kristin retorted and turned to walk out the door.

Wes took hold of Kristin's arm and pulled her back to him.

"Hey... listen to me! You have to give me a chance to explain this. It is not what it looks like."

"It looks like you are getting cozy with your ex-wife and kissing her. Is there something more to it that I need to know about?" Kristin asked.

"Kris, I didn't kiss her... I mean, well, I didn't. She came over to me, sat on my lap, and kissed me. She cut out the part where I pushed her away and said to stop. She's setting me up... again. Because I didn't go along with what she wanted to do. You must believe me. I don't want any part of her, you know that. I'm in love with you. Please, Kris."

Kristin thought about what Wes was saying. She had no reason to distrust him, and plenty to doubt Rachel's veracity.

"Why," Kristin whispered. "Why would she do something like this?"

"Because she's twisted," Wes answered. "She said she wanted to make a deal with me. Rachel said if I called off the wedding, she would drop the protection order, and I could see Izzy again. When I told her no and pushed her away, I went to leave. I saw Izzy as I was leaving, but Rachel wouldn't let me talk to her. She threatened to call the police and told me I would regret my decision. She cut all the audio out of that exchange. I guess this was her way of trying to do that."

Wes stepped forward and gave Kristin a strong embrace, folding her into his arms.

"When I got that video, I didn't want to believe it," Kristin said, muffling a sob. "I knew in my heart there had to be something, but…"

Wes cut Kristin off.

"It's okay," Wes said, running his hands through Kristin's hair.

"What are we going to do about her?" Kristin worried.

"I don't know," Wes replied, "but we only have two days left to figure it out."

***

Try as she might, Izzy could not find any way out of the room. Rachel had thought of every conceivable answer, making sure there were no methods of communication or even anything Izzy could use as a tool to pry open the door or window. Even all the pens, pencils and paper were gone from her room. Rachel had made sure there were no wire hangers in the closet, no paper clips, nothing that was useful. Izzy plied her time over the next two days laying on her bed, working it all through her head. She watched every sunup and sundown out of her windows, and she barely had the appetite to eat any of the food left in the picnic hamper in the closet.

After showering on the Monday morning, since it was all she could really do, Izzy took a quick inventory of what she had available that might be useful. Outside of a toothbrush, deodorant, and the plastic spork and knife in the picnic hamper, she had nothing to work with.

"Where's MacGyver when you need him?" she asked herself.

Izzy looked at the alarm clock in her room and saw that it was nearly 9 AM. She knew the hearing was scheduled to start at 10, and once that happened, all might be pretty much lost. She determined that even when she got out of the room afterward, if she went directly to see her father, Rachel would simply have him arrested and who knows what would happen after that.

A slow knock on the door was the first contact Izzy had with anyone since Sunday morning when she finished calling out for one of the staff to please help her.

"Hello? Adrian? Maria? Can one of you please let me out of here? My mother... she's out of control..." Izzy pleaded, jiggling the doorknob.

"Lost control?" Rachel answered. "Really, Isabelle? If anything, I feel more in control than ever. I just wanted to let you know I am on my way to the courthouse. I'm not sure how long I will be, but once I am back, I will let you out, I promise. Everything will be done by then, and I will have Arthur drive us to New York. We can send for your things afterward. Just relax, and it will be over soon."

"Please... don't do this, Mom," Izzy begged.

"Oh, don't cry, Isabelle. It will be fine, I promise. You'll forget all about Chandler once we are enjoying life." Izzy heard the familiar sound of her phone buzzing when it got a message.

"You know, you are quite the popular lady," Rachel remarked. "You have been getting texts all weekend. Amber, Brianna, Melissa, Karen... they keep sending messages. And Joe... he is quite persistent as well. Is he that boy who was here with your father that night? It seems like he is smitten with you, but to be honest, you could do much better, Isabelle. You'll meet some nice young men in New York, you'll see. I'll be back later. Ta-ta."

"Wait! Please!" Izzy yelled, banging on the door with her fists, but to no avail.

Izzy kept hitting against the door, even picking up the chair in her room and slinging it against the door several times. After some effort, the chair finally splintered and broke, but did nothing to the door. Izzy was able to pull apart a couple of the wooden slats from the broken chair. She tried to attempt to wedge one into the door jamb, but it did nothing, and eventually, the slat broke into pieces. With just one other slat left and covered in sweat, she slumped to the floor.

It was then that she looked at the window and decided to try there. The windows were old since her mother had hoped to keep the natural look of the house, and there was a bit of a gap between the sill in the window in one spot that showed age. Even though nails had been driven in to keep the window shut, Izzy had nothing to lose at this point by trying to pry it open. She grabbed the one whole slat, and then picked up a piece of the broken one to use as a hammer. She drove the slat into the gap to form a lever and began to steadily start to pry at the window to lift it through the nails. Izzy could see that it was working, and some room had formed to get the slat underneath the window.

"Easy... easy," Izzy told herself. "Please don't break, please," she begged to the wood she held in her hand. Finally, the window budged past the nail as Izzy heard the window crack enough so Izzy could get her fingers underneath and feel the fresh air. She was able to wiggle three fingers in enough to grab the spring of the screen in there and push it forward, so the screen toppled out and onto the lawn below.

"All right!" she exclaimed and put both hands underneath to lift the large window. With all her force, she tugged, throwing the window up. The problem was it barely rose two or three inches. Izzy pulled on the window some more, but it wouldn't move, feeling like it was jammed. She looked up and saw that, above the window, Rachel had wedged a block of wood to prevent the window from being raised further.

Izzy rushed over to the other window in the room and saw that it, too, was wedged shut.

"Fuck!!" Izzy yelled, slamming her hand on the window, so it reverberated.

Izzy considered trying to break the glass at this point and went back over to the open window. She spotted one of the landscapers in the yard, blowing leaves and debris off the grass with a leaf blower.

"Hey! Up here! Help, please!!" she yelled as loudly as she could out the window. Izzy kept this up for minutes before she noticed that the landscaper was clearly wearing headphones to drown out the sound of the leaf blower. She kept yelling anyway, but he walked away and around the corner of the house to the front.

"Wait... please, don't go!" Izzy screamed as the gardener disappeared.

Izzy collapsed to the floor of her room exhausted and began to weep. She cried loudly, but then heard a faint voice outside the window.

"Izzy?" the voice questioned. "Are you here?"

Izzy sat up and then shot from the floor. She looked out the window, and there stood Joe, looking up at the window with a puzzled expression on his face.

"Joe!" Izzy yelled, banging on the window. She put her face down to the crack on the window. "Joe, please..."

"Izzy, I've been worried sick about you," Joe started. "I've called and texted you, and you haven't answered me at all. What's going on?"

"Joe, my mother has me locked in here, and there's no wat to get out. The window won't go up any further than this. I need to get out of here. Please, help me."

"Okay, let me think for a second," Joe said, looking around. "I've got my tools in my truck. Maybe I can get the front door open."

"She's got some special lock on it and its deadbolted. It would take too long to get through," Izzy lamented.

"Is there a ladder around somewhere?" Joe asked. "A high one, to reach up there?"

Izzy thought for a moment.

"In the garage!" she exclaimed. "I saw one in there when Arthur took me out the other night. That should reach. Get that!"

"Who's Arthur? And why is he taking you out?" Joe asked.

"He's the driver, he's sixty, and now isn't the time, Joe! His place is around the front of the house. Go and get him and get the keys. God, I hope he's there, and hopefully, she hasn't gotten to him, too," Izzy yelled.

Joe took off, running around the front of the house as Izzy paced back and forth, staring out the window. Every second that went by felt like an hour to Izzy at this point.

"Come on, Joe, hurry," she said to herself. She pressed her face to the glass to try to see around the corner. Arthur finally appeared walking towards the window.

"Miss Isabelle? What are you doing up there? What's wrong?" he yelled.

"Arthur, please, you need to help me. She locked me in here, and I can't get out. She's going to ruin Dad's life at the courthouse."

"Ms. Hebner told me you were staying with friends until the hearing and gave me time off until we headed back to New York today. I am so sorry. I gave your friend the keys to the garage to get the ladder," Arthur said.

"Arthur, do you have keys to the front door?" Izzy asked.

"Not for the new lock on there, no," he lamented. "I'll get it open, don't worry."

Joe finally came back, dragging the giant ladder behind him. Arthur helped to anchor the ladder, and Joe quickly began to climb.

"Go try the front door," Joe screamed to Arthur as he scurried up each rung.

In no time, Joe was outside Izzy's window. Izzy smiled through her tears as Joe tugged hard on the window, trying to free it. The ladder wobbled perilously each time he tried to do that. Once the ladder pushed back from the house, precariously going backward until Joe leaned forward to push it back to the house.

"It's wedged on the top," Izzy cried.

"I didn't bring anything up with me to help," Joe replied. "I can go back down and out to my truck," Joe said as he began to descend.

"No, please don't leave me!" Izzy bellowed and began to cry again. She placed her hand firmly on the glass as Joe positioned his to hers on the other side.

Joe felt the coolness of the glass beneath his fingers as he flexed them.

"Izzy," he stated, "move away from the window."

"Why?" she asked.

"Just do it," he commanded.

Izzy took steps back towards her bed and watched the window.

Izzy focused on the window as she watched Joe rear back with his arm and punch the window as hard as he could. Izzy saw the window recoil against his fist.

"Joe, you can't..." Izzy said as Joe punched again. The second punch left a small crack in the thick pane of glass.

Joe pulled his arm back and thrust with all his might, yelling as he did. His fist and forearm broke through, sending glass shattering inside and out of the room. Izzy screamed as it broke.

Joe used his left hand to pick away some of the glass from the window, so he had an ample enough space to climb through and collapse onto the floor. Izzy rushed to him, seeing his right arm covered in glass shards. She looked at his right hand and saw areas where the skin had utterly torn away on his fingers, exposing tendons.

Izzy rushed over to her dresser and grabbed a t-shirt to wrap his hand to try to stop some of the bleeding. Joe grimaced in apparent pain but took his left arm and pulled Izzy to him to hug her around his neck.

"Thank you, thank you," Izzy cried.

"That was the easy part," Joe said through gritted teeth. "Getting down will be tricky."

"I don't think you can do it," Izzy said. "You're hurt pretty badly."

"You go," Joe said, nodding toward the window. "You can get down and go and get help."

"I can't leave you like this," Izzy said with tears falling.

"Go!" Joe yelled.

Izzy started toward the window, wrapping her hands in a bath towel to remove pieces of glass before she could climb out. Just as she started out the window, she heard a rumble outside her bedroom door.

"Stay back!" a muffled voice yelled. Moments later, a chainsaw blade cut through the door around where the lock and doorknob were positioned. Shortly after, the door kicked open, and Arthur stood there with smoke coming from the saw in his hands.

Arthur placed the chainsaw down on the floor and ran over to where Joe sat on the floor.

"Oh, God," Arthur said. "We need to get you to the hospital before you lose fingers."

"Call me an ambulance and get her to the courthouse," Joe told Arthur.

"Are you sure?" Izzy said, frightened.

"The ambulance will get here fast enough," Joe said. He gripped the blood-soaked shirt on his hand. "Go put an end to this."

Arthur hung up his cell phone and squatted down next to Joe.

"They'll be here in a few minutes," Arthur said. "Just hold on, okay?"

"Arthur, please, just take her," Joe insisted.

Arthur glanced at Izzy, and she nodded in agreement.

Izzy bent down and kissed Joe deeper and more passionately than she had ever kissed anyone before.

"You're my hero," she whispered to him.

"Maybe now we can go out on a date," Joe said with a smile.

"We'll see," Izzy told him and kissed him quickly again before getting up.

Izzy ran from the room, with Arthur right behind her. They passed a couple of the landscapers on their way down the staircase.

"Your chainsaw is in the bedroom," Arthur told the one young man. "And sit with the guy in there until the ambulance and police get here."

Arthur ran towards the front door, but he saw Izzy move towards the study.

"Where are you going?" Arthur questioned.

"I have to get one thing first," Izzy yelled.

Chapter 21

The sun was shining brightly on the April morning when Wes, Kristin, and Wyatt arrived together at the Chandler courthouse about fifteen minutes before the hearing was scheduled to begin. They were greeted by Sybil Crawford, Wes's attorney, for the proceedings, just outside the front door. Sybil was smartly dressed in a gray business suit, and she shook hands with Wes, Kristin, and Wyatt.

"Are you ready for this?" Sybil asked Wes. "It's probably not too late to try to make a deal with them. I can pull her lawyers aside before the hearing starts."

"No," Wes said with resolve. "Let's just get it over with. I'm tired of fighting about it, and Rachel has dragged me through the mud enough over all of this."

Two reporters approached Wes for a comment about what was going on, surprising him that this would even be a news story. The problem was now that people were aware, rumors would begin to spread, and his reputation would be tarnished, whether the story was true or not.

"No comment," was all Sybil said when she stepped in front of Wes to face the reporters. She then ushered the family inside and hurried off to the courtroom so they could wait for the hearing to begin.

Rachel and her attorneys were already positioned at her table, and Rachel gave a smile to Wes and Kristin. She acted like nothing was wrong at all, and this was just another day for her.

"I'd like to go over there and smack that smile off her," Kristin whispered to Wes.

"Easy, Tiger," Wes said, taking hold of Kristin's hand. "We have to just let this go and play out. There's nothing more we can do at this point."

Wes and Sybil went to sit at the table to the left of Rachel and her lawyers.

"Remember, Wes," Sybil reminded, "keep your cool, answer questions directed at you, and be respectful. It will go a long way and maybe bring the time down on the permanent order."

Wes nodded in agreement as he straightened his blue tie.

The bailiff entered the courtroom and immediately announced: "All rise" to get everyone on their fit. Wyatt and Kristin sat in the first row behind Wes, and the only other attendees in the courtroom were the two reporters from outside.

"The Honorable Judge Anita Pena presiding," the bailiff stated.

Judge Pena entered the room wearing her black robe and strode directly to the bench before telling everyone they may be seated.

Wes overheard Rachel saying loudly and angrily to her lawyers, "Where's Judge Waner?"

"Good morning, everyone," Judge Pena stated. "Judge Waner, the judge assigned to this case, was called away unexpectedly at the last minute. I'll be filling in for him today."

Stirring and commotion occurred over at Rachel's table before one of her lawyers, an older gentleman with thinning white hair, rose.

"Your honor, I am Jack Garrett, lead attorney for Ms. Hebner," he stated in a gravelly voice. "I ask for a postponement of the case for a few days... so that we may gather more evidence."

"I object your honor," Sybil said, standing up and speaking loudly. "There is no reason why this cannot be completed today. My client has been through enough stress with this situation, and to drag it out further would mean extending the temporary order, and greater hardship for my client."

"I concur," Judge Pena added. "I see no reason for this to get postponed, Mr. Garrett. The hearing seems somewhat cut and dry to me. Objection sustained. We'll continue with the hearing."

Rachel's demeanor changed dramatically after the judge turned her down. She sat with a dour look on her face as the judge read through the briefs supplied by both attorneys. Jack Garrett and Sybil Crawford both made statements for their clients. Mr. Garrett referred to the police report of the night Wes was removed from Rachel's premises, along with a video that Wes did not know existed of the night in question, showing him yelling at Rachel and trying to get into her home. Once Wes saw that he felt defeated and slumped back into his chair.

"Everything appears clear regarding the issue with Ms. Hebner," Judge Pena stated as she flipped through the paperwork. "Now, what about Ms. Martin?"

"I'm not sure what you mean, your honor?" Mr. Garrett offered.

"Isabelle Martin, the second person named in the protection order you filed for, Mr. Garrett," Judge Pena replied. "Is she your client as well?"

"Yes, your honor, but she is not present in court today. We felt that her status as a minor might make it too upsetting..." Mr. Garrett began.

"The problem is Mr. Garrett, that Ms. Martin is not a minor in the eyes of the law. She turned eighteen on February 11th. This order was filed just a week ago. Since she is not a minor, she cannot be included in the same protection order. If she wants a PFA order, you will have to file a separate paperwork with the county. Judge Waner should never have approved this. I'll issue a PFA order for Mr. Martin to stay away from Ms. Hebner for a period of three years, the maximum the law allows, based on the evidence I have seen. There is clearly animosity between the two parties, but I can't rule on anything involving Ms. Martin. There is no protection order filed for her."

Judge Pena began to sign the paperwork in front of her. At the same time, Rachel, her face bright red, became more agitated and prodded her lawyer loudly.

"Your honor, if you can just..." Mr. Garrett stammered.

"If Ms. Martin has issues with Mr. Martin, she can take them up with the court immediately, and we will assign another temporary order and set up a hearing date, but she needs to do it, Mr. Garrett. She's legally an adult. You should have known that."

"Fool!" Rachel hissed. "We need to speak with Judge Waner," Rachel yelled, standing up. "He can straighten this out and get it right."

Judge Pena banged her gavel angrily.

"Ms. Hebner, you are in my courtroom right now. Judge Waner is not present; I am the one making the decisions. You have your PFA approved. Mr. Garrett, instruct your client to sit down and behave herself before I have her removed and cited for contempt."

Jack Garrett attempted twice to get Rachel to sit before she agreed. Wes watched on, not saying much of anything.

The courtroom door swung open wildly, and Izzy walked in, wearing her jeans and a t-shirt now partially covered in dried blood. Arthur trailed not far behind her.

The judge looked up as the bailiff rushed to the center aisle to stand in front of Izzy and stop her from moving towards Judge Pena.

"Izzy?" Wes yelled. "What happened?"

Rachel sat with her mouth partially open, stunned to see her daughter standing before her.

"Please, I need to be heard," Izzy said as she struggled to move past the bailiff. Judge Pena banged the gavel loudly as she stood up behind the bench.

"What is going on here?" Judge Pena barked.

"Your honor, I am Isabelle Martin," Izzy said, out of breath. "I did not consent to be part of this protection order..." she began.

"I just went through this, Ms. Martin," Judge Pena said as she tried to restore order. "You are a legal adult. If you want a PFA, you need to file one of your own."

"I don't want one," Izzy said. "I never did. This whole proceeding was manipulated by my mother," Izzy said as she pointed to her mother. "She tried to blackmail my father to get him to go along with everything. Once she knew I was aware, she held me against my will in her home until I was able to escape."

"I never did any such thing," Rachel yelled. "Isabelle, why would you make up a story like that? Has your father gotten to you?"

"No, no one has gotten to me," Izzy said as she glared at her mother. Izzy turned her attention back to Judge Pena.

"Your honor, I have proof," Izzy said, holding up the small video camera that Rachel had hidden in the study.

"This is all out of hand," Judge Pena said. "I want to see both parties in my chambers immediately with their attorneys. You come along too, Ms. Martin." The judge swept out of the room, and the bailiff guided Rachel, her lawyers, Sybil, Wes, and Izzy out of the courtroom and back to the judge's chambers.

"Izzy, are you okay? Are you hurt?" Wes asked with concern as he hugged his daughter.

"No, Dad, I'm fine... it's not my blood... it's a long story. Hopefully, this will straighten it all out," Izzy said, clutching the camera.

Everyone entered the judge's chamber as Judge Pena took off her robe and sat behind the desk. She took a deep breath as she sat and looked out over the people in the room.

"Now, what is it you have, Ms. Martin?" Judge Pena asked.

"Your honor, we have no way of knowing..." Mr. Garrett started before he was interrupted.

"I wasn't speaking to you, Mr. Garrett," Judge Pena told him. "You'll get your chance."

Izzy stepped forward and handed the camera to the judge.

"Your honor, this is a camera my mother had secretly operating in the study several nights ago when she invited my father over to talk. You can see and hear the conversation that took place between them."

"Several nights ago? You mean after the temporary order was already issued?" the judge inquired.

"Yes, your honor," Izzy spoke.

"Why would you do that, Ms. Hebner? If you feared for your safety, as you said when you filed the complaint, why would you invite Mr. Martin into your home?" Judge Pena asked.

Rachel was at a loss for words and stuttered some unintelligible sounds.

"If you watch the video, your honor," Izzy continued, "you will see a point where my mother attempts to blackmail my father. She threatens to ruin his reputation and destroy his life."

Judge Pena plugged the camera into the USB port on her laptop and accessed the video. Rachel whispered wildly to her lawyers while the Judge watched and listened to the brief clip. Kristin and Wes heard the conversation on the video as well, making it even more evident that Wes did nothing wrong and attempted to get away from Rachel.

Once the video was completed, Judge Pena removed the camera and looked over at Rachel.

"Do you have anything to say for yourself, Ms. Hebner?" Judge Pena asked.

Rachel moved forward in her chair as she prepared to say something to the judge, but Mr. Garrett stepped in.

"I think it is best if Ms. Hebner states nothing at this time, your honor," Mr. Garrett insisted.

"A wise decision, Mr. Garrett," Judge Pena replied. "However, I think it best that Ms. Hebner is held until the police can arrive to investigate this further. You're facing some potentially severe charges, Ms. Hebner, as I'm sure your attorneys will explain to you. Ms. Martin, do you need medical care?"

"It's just some minor cuts," Izzy said, looking at her hands and arms.

"Still, I am calling over to get an ambulance here so you can be examined. Bailiff, please place Ms. Hebner in the holding room until the police arrive," Judge Pena ordered as she picked up the phone.

The bailiff, a tall, burly gentleman, walked over to Rachel and ordered her out of her chair. Rachel was hustled from the room, but she made sure to sneer and glower at Izzy and Wes as she left. Her attorneys quickly followed her out.

***

Izzy was spent physically and emotionally. Once the police and EMTs arrived, chaos reigned in the courthouse. The police hustled Rachel and her lawyers outside and to the police station for what promised to be some interesting questioning regarding her behavior and actions.

The paramedics tended to Izzy's mostly superficial wounds. They did pull a few small shards of glass from the broken window out of her hands, and she shook her hair out several times to get bits of debris and glass out as well. She was interviewed by another officer regarding the imprisonment she experienced so they could have the full details to compare to the statements her mother provided.

Once that was completed, Wes and Kristin came right over to Izzy to be with her. They both gave wrapped around her tightly.

"Dad, you have to know that I never meant for any of this to happen. I didn't know what she was doing... what she was really like. I thought... I thought she just wanted me to be part of her life again. I'm so sorry."

"I'm sorry, too," Wes added. "I didn't treat you fairly, or like an adult, which clearly you are," Wes said as he stepped back to look at Izzy. Even though the paramedics had helped her clean up her face and arms, she still had nicks, scars, and smudges all over. "And I'm sorry that all this happened with your mother. I know you wanted a relationship with her."

Izzy turned her attention to Kristin.

"I apologize to you too, Kris," Izzy said sincerely. "You didn't deserve any of this. All you have ever done for me is support me, help me, and be my friend. You have been more like a mother to me in these last two years than my birth mother has been in my entire life. I hope you can forgive me."

Kristin and Izzy embraced and cried a bit on each other's shoulders before Wes walked over and put his arms around both.

"How did you get out of the house?" Wes asked.

"I had a lot of help," Izzy remarked. "We need to get over to the hospital," Izzy said as they started to leave the courtroom. Arthur stood up as Izzy approached the door.

"Do you need me to bring you, Miss Isabelle?" Arthur asked, his face still covered with exhaust particles from the chainsaw.

"No, Arthur, you have done way more than I ever could have asked anyone," Izzy said. She reached over and gave Arthur a kiss on the cheek. "Thank you."

"Dad, this is Arthur. He's Mom's driver and one of the people who helped me," Izzy said proudly.

"Arthur, I can't thank you enough for helping my daughter," Wes mentioned. He presented his hand and gave Arthur a firm handshake.

"You have a fine daughter," Arthur declared. "She is a lovely young woman... and a good friend," Arthur said with a smile. "As for being Ms. Hebner's driver, I have a feeling that will be ending shortly once she learns I assisted in your escape."

The four walked towards the outer doors to the courthouse.

"Arthur did more than help me, Dad," Izzy said as they walked towards Wes's vehicle. "He helped you, too."

Wes stopped at the car and looked at Izzy and Arthur.

"Helped me? How?"

"Tell him, Arthur," Izzy beamed. "It's pretty cool."

"It was nothing, really," Arthur said modestly. "I had overheard Ms. Hebner talking in the back of the car when I drove her to the Washington County courthouse to file paperwork. She mentioned how she needed to make sure that Judge Waner was there to sign papers, that he was an old family friend of her father's, and would make sure everything got pushed through. When Miss Isabelle explained to me what was going on this morning, I made a phone call to an old friend that owed me a favor. Judge Waner was unexpectedly unavailable for the proceedings this morning."

"Well, now I owe you a favor," Wes added. "Let me know what I can do for you anytime."

"He's like some cool, mysterious guy," Izzy said, bumping shoulders with Arthur.

"You need to go," Arthur reminded Izzy, hurrying them along.

"Are you coming?" Izzy asked.

"No, I think I need to go back to the house and deal with what's there, and then figure out what I am doing next. I will talk to you, though, Miss Isabelle."

Izzy hopped into the back seat of her father's truck and watched Arthur go to the Town Car, while Wes raced off toward the hospital.

***

Izzy explained what happened at Rachel's house and how Joe was able to save her. Wes, Kristin, and Izzy arrived at the hospital and rushed to the front desk to find out where Joe was. The guard directed the family to the surgical floor, where Joe was in emergency surgery for his fingers and hand.

The staff wouldn't provide much information to Wes since he was not family, so the three of them waited for Joe's family to arrive. Izzy paced the waiting room, unable to sit or relax, and afraid of what happened to Joe. Wes and Kristin attempted to comfort her as best they could and stayed by her to keep a vigil. Kristin even went down to the shop at the hospital and bought a clean t-shirt for Izzy to change into.

Izzy and Kristin had gone to ladies' room, so Izzy could change. She stripped out of the torn and blood-stained t-shirt and saw some blood had seeped through enough that she had it on, leaving traces of blood on her stomach, bra and chest. Izzy walked over to the sink to dampen some towels and wipe the dried blood away before she put the new shirt on. Kristin stood next to her and helped her reach a couple of spots that Izzy could not.

"What's this red here," Kristin noted, seeing the mark on Izzy's hip.

"Oh, that," Izzy said. "That's not blood... it's... it's my tattoo. A birthday present to myself."

Izzy tugged down the waistline of her jeans so Kristin could get a better look.

"I love it," she said. "it's adorable. Your father was okay with it?"

"I didn't actually tell him about it," Izzy said, getting her new shirt into place.

"Today may not be the best day for that," Kristin advised.

By the time Kristin and Izzy returned to the waiting room, Joe's parents had arrived. Wes had met Carol and Steve Johnson several times when he went over to speak with Joe about joining the Washington Wild Things. They were both in their early forties, and each had the same color hair and eyes as Joe. Izzy could see right away where Joe got his looks from.

"Carol, Steve, this is Kristin Arthur, my fiancée," Wes introduced. "And this is my daughter, Izzy."

Carol walked over to Izzy and smiled at her.

"So, you're Izzy," Carol said. "Joe talks about you all the time. It's nice to meet you."

"It's nice to meet you as well, Mrs. Johnson," Izzy said politely.

Moments later, a doctor walked into the waiting area and introduced himself as Dr. Theodore, a tall, gangly man with glasses.

"Mr. and Mrs. Johnson?" he asked as he entered the room. Steve Johnson raised his hand, and the doctor walked over to the couple.

"If you would like to step outside, I can tell you about how things went with your son," Dr. Theodore told them.

"You can tell us in here," Carol stated. "They are family to us."

Dr. Theodore nodded and began.

"Joe needed extensive patching up to deal with the cuts on his fingers and hand. We performed some surgery to clean out the glass and treat the wounds, but he is going to need skin grafts and cosmetic surgery. I can recommend a hand specialist to you that can help him out. It's going to be a long haul for him with healing. There will be scar tissue, physical therapy, and more, and I can't guarantee he'll get full use of his hand again. I wish I had better news."

"He's alive," Carol stated. "That's the most important news. We'll figure out how to deal with everything else. Can we go see him?"

"They are bringing him up to a room on the fifth floor in a few minutes. You can see him once he is there."

Steve let out a sigh of relief.

"Well, he survived it, that's what matters," Steve said as he sat. "it sounds like there are going to be plenty of doctor visits, surgery, and more," Steve worried.

Wes was well aware of the Johnsons' tenuous financial situation from the visits he had with them and concluded they likely did not have health insurance right now.

"Steve, Carol, I want to say something," Wes said as he looked at both. "I know how things are right now for you, and there are challenges ahead. I want you to know that I will take care of all of Joe's medical bills and needs. It's the least I can do for you and for Joe for getting my daughter back."

"Wes, I couldn't ask you to do that," Steve replied.

"You didn't ask me at all, Steve," Wes answered. "I offered, and I intend to do it. I don't want you to worry about it at all."

"Thank you so much," Carol said. She walked over and gave Wes and Kristin both big hugs.

"We should get up to the fifth floor, honey," Steve remarked to his wife.

Carol nodded in agreement as the two walked towards the waiting room doorway.

"Are you coming up with us?" Carol asked Wes, Kristin, and Izzy.

"You two should have time with him," Wes said. "But please call me and let me know how he is doing. We can swing by to visit him tomorrow when he might feel more up to the company."

"Dad," Izzy said softly. "Is it okay if I go up and see him? I just want to see him for a minute or two."

"Sure, if it's okay with the Johnsons," Wes replied.

Izzy looked over at Carol and Steve, and Carol extended her arm to Izzy.

"You don't even have to ask, honey," Carol said.

Izzy ran over and took Carol's hand.

"We'll meet you downstairs," Wes told Izzy.

Izzy nodded and walked off with the Johnsons, leaving Wes and Kristin alone.

"She's an amazing girl," Kristin told Wes, as she took his hand. "You have a fantastic daughter, Mr. Martin."

"I think WE have a fantastic daughter, soon-to-be Mrs. Martin," Wes said with a smile.

Wes and Kristin ambled down the hall to the elevator and pressed the button to go down.

"Do you think things might settle down for us for a while now?" Wes asked as the elevator arrived.

Kristin stepped in alongside Wes and pressed the button to go down to the lobby.

"We still have wedding plans to iron out," Kristin noted. "We have dress shopping this coming weekend."

"At least you will have Izzy to be part of that now," Wes said proudly.

"I know, it's wonderful," Kristin smiled.

"And I'll get to stay home and hang out with Molly," Wes added. "Maybe I'll take her up to the batting cage with me."

"You will not, Wes Martin," Kristin chided. "She's not even six months old. The bat is taller than her!"

"She has to learn how to recognize a curveball at some point," Wes said.

"Don't we all," Kristin added.

***

Izzy let Carol and Steve Johnson go into Joe's room alone while she waited out in the hallway. Izzy's nerves calmed down some, and for the first time in weeks, she had a sense of relief and accomplishment about her. Izzy sat in a nearby chair and could see her reflection in a door window across the hall. Her red hair was strewn about, and she had some small slits on her left cheek from some of the glass. She ran her hands quickly through her curly hair to try and get it looking better, and she patted her pockets to see if she had a hair tie that she could use to help make herself look more presentable.

Carol Johnson walked out of the room behind Izzy and smiled.

"You don't need to fuss with your hair," Carol said to her. "He's not going to care what it looks like. He just wants to know you are okay. Why don't you go on in and see him?"

"Are you sure? If you want more time with him, it's okay."

"He'd much rather see a pretty girl than his parents," she laughed. "Go on."

Izzy tentatively walked into the room and over to the far bed area where Joe was. Steve was just finishing propping up some pillows behind his son when Izzy came in.

"Hey there," Joe said in a raspy voice. Izzy gave a light wave to him and smiled. Steve arranged the blanket on Joe, so he was covered and warm.

"You need anything else right now?" Steve asked.

"I think I'm good now, Dad, thanks," Joe said, hinting with his eyes that maybe his father should leave the room now.

"Steven, come out here," Carol yelled into the room. "Let those kids be alone."

Steve embarrassedly left the room, and Izzy moved closer to Joe on the left side on the bed. She saw that his right hand was completely enveloped in bandages so that it looked more like Joe was holding a club.

"How are you?" Izzy said tenderly.

"Well, right now, okay, I guess," Joe said. "They have me on so much pain medication right now that I barely feel anything there, but the doctors say it is going to hurt like hell eventually. I guess I'm going to need a lot of work done."

"I'm so sorry," Izzy said compassionately.

"Don't be," Joe answered. He took Izzy's right hand in his left and caressed her fingers with his.

"What about baseball?" Izzy asked Joe.

"I have a feeling that's off my radar now," Joe sighed. "The doctor said there's probably nerve damage to my fingers. I might not be able to even hold a ball in my right hand, never mind pitch with it."

"Joe... your career..." Izzy lamented.

"Over before it started," Joe said. "And you know what? It doesn't bother me one bit, Izzy. I told your father when he recruited me that baseball was not the most essential thing in my life. It was fun, but it was never first. Taking care of my family and loved ones mean more to me than throwing a ball. There are other things I can do with my life. Now I'll have more time to spend with you this summer."

"Oh, you think so, huh?" Izzy laughed.

"You are going to be around, right?" Joe asked.

"You bet," Izzy said, bringing her face close to his. "Are you much of a dancer?"

"Dancing?" Joe said. "I can hold my own, I guess. Why?"

"I just think that I need someone to take me to the prom in a few weeks, and if you can dance..."

"Are you asking me out on a date, Miss Isabelle?" Joe said in mock surprise.

"Maybe I am," Izzy said as her lips got closer to Joe's. "One of us has to make the first move. I can't wait around forever, you know."

Joe moved forward and kissed Izzy, and his fingers curled around hers. Joe snuck a quick peek through one eye to look at Izzy while they kissed, while Izzy felt the strength of it all the way to her toes.

"Trust me, you don't have to wait anymore."

Epilogue

S pring and summer flew by like flashes of lightning for the Martin family. Izzy finished her time in high school the way she had intended. She took great pride in walking across the stage in her cap and gown with her father, Kristin, Molly, her grandparents, Melissa, and Joe, all in attendance to see it. The party that took place at the Martin house to celebrate might typically have been the party of the year if it were not for the wedding that was coming in the fall.

Izzy spent the whirlwind summer working on the farm, getting involved with the wedding plans, spending time with her sister, getting alone time with her father, and seeing Joe whenever she could. She tried to help Joe as much as she could with his rehab for his hand, going to therapy sessions with him when she could and being at the hospital for him when he had another surgery for more skin grafts. With the bandages off, Joe's hand was severely scarred, and his fingers unable to straighten correctly. Still, Joe took it all in stride and with better spirits than most patients would have done.

August came around, which meant just a month until the wedding. It also meant it was time for Izzy to head off to college. It was a heartbreaking time for everyone when Izzy was packing up her car with everything she would need to bring with her for her dorm. In the end, even though Izzy had gained admission to the NYU Drama School, Izzy thought it was best to pass on New York for a while. She told her father she hadn't earned that admission on her own merits, and the reminder of how she got there would have been too much for her. Izzy would go to the University of Pittsburgh, live there, and be part of the Drama School there. As much as she longed for independence earlier in the year, situations were different now, and she wanted to be closer to home.

Naturally, Wes was elated at the decision, though he did his best to hide it. He followed Izzy in his car with the rest of her belongings to Pittsburgh and helped her get settled. Joe had ridden to the school with Izzy and did what he could to assist, but also because he wanted some extra time with her. Once the unpacking was done, Izzy walked Joe and her father out to Wes's Jeep.

"I guess this is it," Izzy said to her Dad.

"I guess so," Wes said. He did his best to hold back any tears. "I am so proud of you, honey. I know you are going to do great things here."

Wes hugged Izzy and held her tightly.

"Thanks, Dad, for everything you have done and keep doing for me. I wouldn't be here without your help. Love you," Izzy said. She sniffled back tears of her own and smiled at her Dad, wiping the tears from his shoulder and his cheek.

"Call me if you need anything," Wes reminded her. He then walked to the driver's side of the car and got behind the wheel, leaving Izzy with Joe.

"I'll call you tonight," Izzy said. She draped her arms over Joe's shoulders.

"You don't have to," Joe told her. "You might meet some new people, get to know your roommates, you know, the whole college thing."

"I'll call you anyway," Izzy laughed. "And you're only an hour away. I can come home, you can come here, it will be fine, right?"

"Better than fine," Joe said. Joe's lips closed in on Izzy's, and they kissed, and both had waves of warmth wash over them.

"I love you," Joe whispered.

Izzy stared at Joe as the words escaped his lips.

"That's... that's the first time you've said that to me," Izzy said, her lips barely apart from his.

"I know," Joe smiled. "It'd be okay if you said something back."

"I love you, too."

Joe stepped back and walked toward Wes's truck to get in.

"Now, you better call me tonight," Izzy remarked.

"Count on it," Joe laughed as he hung out the window and watched as they pulled away from Izzy.

***

Kristin was busy readying herself. Her makeup and hair had long been done, and she had a beautiful, elegant braid in her hair. Melissa, Karen and Izzy, and Kristin's sister, Lucy, all assisted Kristin with whatever she needed on her big day. The bridesmaids were all decked out in lovely sage-colored dresses that gave a bit of a southern feel and style to the event and harkened back to Kristin's upbringing in the South. Molly was the one standout, wearing a cute white toddler dress that had a similar skirt look to what the bride was wearing.

Kristin looked at her reflection in the mirror and smiled widely, and her sister came up behind her and gave her a hug around the waist.

"Kris, you look stunning," Lucy raved. "This is going to be an amazing day."

"I am so glad you are here, Lucy," Kristin replied. "You have no idea what it means to me to have you and Mom and Dad come up for this. I know it wasn't easy getting them here."

"You know Dad, he hates to travel anyplace," Lucy said. "But he would never miss the chance to walk you down the aisle."

Kim came knocking on the door and peeked her head around the corner. She wore a headset that blended in nicely so that it could barely be seen.

"We're all ready for you, Kris. You gals ready to do this?"

"Yes!" they yelled out in unison, raising their hands, causing Molly to raise her hands and laugh.

The four bridesmaids and Molly all climbed into one horse-drawn buggy positioned just outside of Wyatt and Jenny's house. Kristin got into the carriage just behind that one, and the two were off slowly down the pathway past the barns and the stables and out towards the lake area, a special location for Kristin and Wes.

The buggies arrived in moments, and Kristin's father, wearing a black tuxedo, greeted her and helped her from the carriage.

"You look, beautiful honey," Lyle Arthur commented to his daughter in his southern drawl.

"Thank you, Daddy," Kristin said as she kissed her father on the cheek.

The two waited dutifully for the signal from Kim that it was their turn to walk down the aisle. Runners and flooring had been carefully placed so that the walk would be more comfortable in the grassy areas. Each row of seats was adorned with a mix of white roses, peonies, and eucalyptus so that they matched the bouquets that each of the women carried.

When Wes caught first sight of Kristin in her bridal gown, it took his breath away. He watched as she edged closer to him, wearing her strapless, floor-length dress. The tulle skirt gently rustled as Kristin walked, and the beaded embellishments on the bodice and bottom of the gown added the final touch as they glistened in the sunlight.

Kristin reached where Wes was standing and received a gentle kiss from her father, who then turned and shook Wes's hand to leave the couple at the altar.

"Wow," Wes said quietly as he looked at his bride. Kristin smiled and giggled lightly.

The couple then turned to face Judge Pena, who was presiding over the ceremony. The two and all the guests had a beautiful look at the lake in front of them, and two swans glided past on the lake just as Wes and Kristin were completing exchanging their vows and rings.

The glorious moment arrived where Judge Pena pronounced Wes and Kristin man and wife, and Kristin practically leaped into Wes's arms so they could kiss. Applause rang out from the crowd of friends and family as the two marched down the aisle together and back to one of the buggies that would take them up to one of the barns where the reception would be held. They held hands tightly and snuggled the whole ride back to the barn, where they snuck off to a comfort room set aside for them during the reception.

Wes followed Kristin in, and then quickly shut the door so he could take his new wife in his arms.

"Congratulations, Mrs. Martin," Wes said as he dipped Kristin, causing her to laugh loudly.

"Same to you, Mr. Martin," she replied.

A quick knock on the door interrupted their moment together.

"Sorry, guys," Kim told them. "The rest of the bridal party is here, and we want to get some more pictures before the reception. I told the photographer that after these, it's only candid shots. No more interrupting the fun."

Plenty of pictures followed with everyone until every conceivable combination of bride, groom, parents, children, wedding party, and more could be done outside with the sun setting behind them over the mountains.

The reception in the stable was set up with several long tables made to accommodate the small number of guests Wes and Kristin wanted. Both had decided to keep things simple, inviting immediate family and close friends, so that the entire guest list was not more than fifty people. It made for a cozy, welcoming atmosphere where everyone could talk, laugh, dance, and have a good time.

Wes and Kristin danced their first dance to True Companion, a tune that had become special to them and fit how they felt about each other perfectly. Once the first dance was done, and the obligatory champagne toasts took place from Wyatt, who was Wes's best man, and Karen, who was the matron of honor, the party got underway. Romantic strings of lights were set up along the paddocks for the horses, and the horses were roaming freely out in the pastures for all to see and admire. Buggy rides were available to anyone who chose, and the catered meal offered a little bit of everything so people could choose just the meal they wanted.

After dining, the dancing took off in full furor as the band played songs everyone loved. Wes and Kristin not only often danced with each other, but they made sure to get involved with as many others as they could. During one slow dance of "I Only Have Eyes for You," Wes interrupted Izzy and Joe on the dance floor.

"Is it okay if I cut in?" Wes asked politely.

"Of course," Joe said, blowing a kiss to Izzy as he let Wes step in to finish the dance.

"He's a nice guy," Wes said as he started dancing with his daughter.

"Yeah, I think so," Izzy laughed. "I can't believe you actually like someone I'm dating."

"I know, it surprised me too," Wes replied. "Take it while you can. It may not last."

The two danced quietly for a moment before Wes spoke again.

"I'm so happy you're here with us today to celebrate, Izzy," Wes said.

"Where else would I be?" Izzy questioned. "This is where I belong."

"I know, but with all that happened, there was a time where I wasn't too sure..."

"Let's not talk about that stuff, Dad," Izzy interrupted. "That's all in the past. What matters most is that I am here now, with both of you. I'm not going anywhere."

"So, I shouldn't empty out your room then?"

"Maybe wait on that for just a little while," Izzy smiled as she hugged Wes.

The reception carried on well into the night, and it was nearly eleven when the last of the guests packed up to leave.

The catering crew was busily breaking down everything from the party so the stable could be restored to its natural condition, all under Wyatt's watchful eyes.

"Kim, thank you so much for everything you did," Kristin said as she gave her new friend a hug.

"It was my pleasure," Kim replied. "This was probably the most fun I had planning a wedding."

"Well, we'll certainly let everyone know how great it was for us," Wes added as he hugged Kim as well.

Melissa walked over to Wes and Kristin, carrying a Molly who was sound asleep.

"I'm going to get her up to the house," Molly said quietly. "I can't believe she fell asleep with all the noise going on around her."

"She gets that from her mother," Wes joked. "Kris can fall asleep in a crowded room, no problem."

"Remember that when I fall asleep on you later," Kristin told him.

Wyatt ambled over as he supervised the final table getting broken down.

"Heck of a party," Wyatt said as he gave Kristin a hug and a kiss.

"Thank you, Wyatt, for everything," Kristin said.

"Yes, thanks, Dad," Wes added, giving his father a hug.

"Don't thank me yet," Wyatt remarked. "Wait until you see my facility rental bill. Will you be down here in the morning to help with the horses? Baseball is over now, you know. You can start doing some real work."

"Dad, I just got married. I'm not getting up at 5 AM to help with the horses. Kris and I are leaving for Bermuda tomorrow morning."

"Always with the excuses," Wyatt replied with a wink. "Have a good night, you two."

Kristin and Wes walked out of the barn and headed toward the pathway so they could walk back to their house on top of the hill. They spotted Izzy and Joe holding hands as they climbed into the bed of Joe's pickup truck.

"What are you two up to?" Wes said nosily.

"We're just looking up at the stars, Dad," Izzy answered. "It's beautiful tonight. The sky is full."

"We're headed up to the house," Wes said. "Don't stay out too late."

"Dad, I'm an adult now, remember? Say, Joe," Izzy said as she turned to face her boyfriend. "Let's walk down to the lake. We'll be able to see everything clearly down there."

"Sounds good to me," Joe said as he sat up carefully. He still had part of his hand covered from his last surgery.

"Down by the lake? This late at night? I don't think that's a good idea," Wes pointed out.

"Wes, leave them alone," Kristin said. "They'll be fine. I want to go home."

"But you know what happens down by the lake," Wes intimated.

"Yes, I do," Kristin replied. "But I trust Izzy and Joe. Besides, it's OUR wedding night."

"Have fun, kids," Wes remarked as he and Kristin hustled up towards the house.

Wes and Kristin were at the house in moments, and all was quiet. They moved into the bedroom, alone at last, since moving Molly upstairs to one of the bedrooms.

Wes walked behind Kristin and started kissing her neck while he steadily unzipped the back of her dress. Once the zipper was down, Kristin let the dress fall, revealing the lacy garter belt, stockings, and panties she wore. Wes took the vision in, picked Kristin up in his arms, and brought her over to the bed. He lay next to her, his left hand roaming up her leg until he came to her hip.

"What's this?" Wes asked, noting the tattoo on Kristin's hip.

"It's something all the girls got about a week ago," Kristin said. "Well, not all the girls. Melissa and Izzy already had it, so Karen, Lucy, and I decided to get matching ones too."

Wes took a closer look and saw the red heart with a lacy banner that read 'Sisters 4 Ever.'

"Izzy got this too?"

"Yes, Wes, but let's not talk about her right now, okay? Do you like the tattoo?" Kristin asked.

Wes traced the outline of the heart with his index finger.

"I love it," he said. "It's perfect for all of you."

"Thank you, Mr. Martin."

"You're welcome, Mrs. Martin. But what are you thanking me for?" Wes asked.

"For everything. For coming into my life, making me feel safe, happy, and loved. For giving me a family... our family together. For being you and letting me be me. It's perfect."

"I'm glad you think so because I believe it is too," Wes said.

Acknowledgments

This is just a brief note to say thank you to a few people that helped tremendously with this book and all three books in the series.

Thank you to Kim Lyons for assisting me with some of the research needed. What you brought to the table was invaluable to me.

To the Hudson Valley Romance Writers of America, thank you for all the support, guidance, and encouragement to write.

To the Washington Wild Things, whether they know it or not, for helping to inspire a lot of the series.

To my friends and family, for their undying support and inspiration to all that I do.

To Scarlet Lantern Publishing for taking a chance on me and allowing me to live a dream.

And to Michelle, my biggest supporter, fan, critic, and muse. Without you, none of this happens, ever. I can never say thank you enough to you.

Also By M. Geraghty

Standalone Romances

For What It's Worth
A Christmas, Rockstar Romance

www.ingramcontent.com/pod-product-compliance
Lightning Source LLC
Chambersburg PA
CBHW020843260626
47169CB00003B/1117